Small Mercies

Alex Walters has worked in the oil industry, broadcasting and banking and provided consultancy for the criminal justice sector. He is the author of thirteen previous novels including the DI Alec McKay series set around the Black Isle in the Scottish Highlands where Alex lives and runs the Solus Or Writing Retreat with his wife, occasional sons and frequent cats.

Also by Alex Walters

Detective Annie Delamere

Small Mercies
Lost Hours

Alex
WALTERS
SMALL
MERCIES

First published in the United Kingdom in 2020 by Canelo

Canelo Digital Publishing Limited
31 Helen Road
Oxford OX2 0DF
United Kingdom

A CIP catalogue record for this book is available from the British Library.

Print ISBN 978 1 80032 013 0
Ebook ISBN 978 1 78863 952 1

Look for more great books at www.canelo.co

Printed and bound in Great Britain by Clays Ltd, Elcograf S.p.A.

Chapter One

Annie Delamere could tell something was wrong.

They'd spotted the sign as they were walking from the car to the footpath. It was attached to what had once been a bus stop, though Annie had no idea if any buses now passed up this way. The sign itself was pitted with rust, and read simply: 'Buses no longer stop at Hell Bank'.

Gary, as usual, had treated it as a joke and embarked on one of his familiar routines, wondering if the service had been discontinued because too many demons had crowded the back seats, or because customers couldn't buy return tickets. He'd ended, inevitably, by questioning whether Hell Bank offered a savings account. Annie had had sufficient experience of Gary's sense of humour during her years of working with Zoe to tune it all out until he'd exhausted his ideas, which generally didn't take long.

Zoe normally seemed to do the same. Today, though, she turned away while Gary was still speaking and strode away up the footpath towards the moorland, clearly unhappy. Gary had finally stopped talking, aware something was wrong. 'Oh, God,' he said. 'Have I said the wrong thing again? It's like walking on eggshells with Zoe sometimes.'

'She's probably just tired,' Annie said. 'We've had a tough few weeks.' She was beginning to think it had been a mistake to come today. It had been her idea originally. Gary was supposed to be away this weekend on one of his football trips. Annie's partner Sheena was stuck in London attending some Labour Party event. As she and Zoe were both at a loose end, Annie had suggested a joint outing to enjoy what promised to be the first decent weekend weather of the year. Then Gary's trip had been cancelled at the last moment, and he'd decided to tag along as well. And, as always in the Peak District at the first sign of good weather, everyone else seemed to have had the same thought.

They'd already had one run-in while parking the car. Most of the available roadside spaces had been taken, but Annie had eventually managed to squeeze the car in beside a couple of badly parked motorbikes. The two heavily-built bikers had watched her manoeuvres with evident disapproval while making no effort to position their bikes more helpfully. As she'd climbed out of the car, one of them had muttered something about 'women drivers'.

On another day she might have pointed out to them that she was an expert driver, who'd succeeded in parking her car in a space considerably smaller than that occupied by their two bikes. But she was feeling relatively relaxed, looking forward to nothing more than a bracing walk and afterwards a bite to eat in Bakewell. She was content just to treat them to one of her icy looks and walk on by.

But Zoe's behaviour had made her uncomfortable. She didn't know if there was some issue brewing between Zoe and Gary, and she'd no desire to be an onlooker if anything should come to a head. But there wasn't much she could do about it now, other than leave Gary to chase after his wife while she followed more slowly behind. If they had something to discuss, she was happy to leave them to it.

Annie had been up here the previous summer with Sheena. It had been a fine clear day like today, but later in the year and several degrees warmer. The moors had seemed to bask in the heat, rich with heather, dramatic views opening up in every direction. The walk had been exhilarating, and she'd wanted to return.

But now she remembered other aspects of that walk. At the time, they'd only added to the fascination of the place, giving an eerie extra dimension to its beauty. The open moorland was dotted with prehistoric barrows, cairns and stone formations, an epitaph to those who had once lived and died in these high spaces. Their walk had culminated in a visit to Hob Hurst's House, an ancient barrow mound on Harland Edge. Sheena, who made a point of reading up on the places they visited, had told her it was thought to be of Bronze Age origin and that the rectangular shape of the barrow was unusual. She'd probably said much more, but Annie recalled no further details except that the name of the barrow referred to some kind of sprite or hobgoblin. Or perhaps to the devil.

As they emerged from the trees on to the open moorland, she stopped and looked around, already able to identify the undulations that marked the sites of barrows and burial mounds. From where she was standing, the land fell away across the moorland, opening up to the Derwent Valley and the Chatsworth estate to their left. It was a glorious spring day with only a few white clouds dotting the clear blue of the surrounding sky. But a sharp breeze was blowing from the east, and she found herself shivering.

Gary and Zoe were waiting for her at the end of the path. Zoe still looked tense, but there was no other sign of any disagreement between the couple. 'You okay, Zoe?' she asked.

'Just a bit cold suddenly.' Zoe was gazing around her. 'Funny old place this, isn't it? I'd forgotten.'

'Striking views,' Gary offered.

'Definitely that.' Annie looked back. On the path behind, she saw the two bikers, who had removed their leathers and were strolling along in sweatshirts, shorts and walking boots. She half-expected they might say something as they passed, but they were deep in conversation.

'But the burial mounds,' Zoe was saying. 'Don't you find them a bit – creepy?'

Gary stared out across the moor, as if evaluating what she had said. 'They're only bones.'

'You two just ignore me. I'm in one of my weird moods. Let's get a breath of air, then we can go and get some lunch.'

They continued along the path, occasionally encountering other walkers who invariably nodded an amicable greeting. It ought to be hard to be spooked on a day like this, Annie thought, with the sun shining and the whole Peak District thronged with visitors. If they'd come on a dank November day with a mist lying heavily across the moor, it might feel rather different.

They eventually reached Hob Hurst's House. As far as Annie could see, there was little left other than a broadly rectangular arrangements of stones, largely overgrown with bracken and heather. Gary stopped by the English Heritage sign. 'Probably built around 1000 BC, apparently,' he said. 'Though some people think it might be later— What is it?'

Annie was looking past him out to the open moorland. 'What's going on over there?'

Zoe and Gary turned to follow her gaze. 'Where?'

'There. It's those two bikers.'

'Bikers?'

'What are they up to?'

The bikers were a hundred or so yards away from them, standing among the heather, apparently engaged in a heated discussion. One of them was pulling the other's arm as if trying to force him to look at something. The second biker gave an odd cry and dragged himself away, turning his back on whatever his companion was showing him. A moment later, he was doubled over, vomiting into the undergrowth.

'I'm going to check everything's all right,' Annie said. She was already on her way, striding unstoppably across the moor. As she drew closer, she saw the first biker look up at her, his expression a mix of fear and disgust.

'Is everything okay?' she called.

The sun was high in the clear sky, throwing the grassland into sharp relief. She could see something on the ground beside the bikers, an object largely hidden by the undergrowth.

'I don't think you'd better—' the biker said. 'We need to get some help.' He gestured towards Gary, who had been following behind her with Zoe in his wake. 'Maybe your friend there can help us deal with it?'

Annie was almost tempted to laugh. From what Zoe had told her, Gary had many good qualities but providing practical support wasn't generally one of them. 'What is it?'

The second biker was still dry-heaving, having apparently emptied his stomach of that morning's breakfast.

It was only as she drew almost level with the two bikers that she finally saw it, half concealed among the heather.

The breeze was blowing towards her and there was no mistaking the stench, even in the open air.

It was a naked human body, a white male. The undergrowth around was stained thickly with blood, now dried almost to black. The throat had been cut almost to the point of decapitation, and the torso and limbs were savagely mutilated. There was a haze of flies above the body. Her guess was that it had been here for some days.

'I did try to warn you, love,' the first biker said, in a tone that sounded inappropriately triumphant. 'Now, perhaps you could ask your friend to help us call the police so we can get this properly dealt with.'

Her eyes had been fixed on the body, her brain collecting as much information as possible about what she was seeing. Now, finally, she looked back at the biker. 'He doesn't need to. We're already here.' She reached into her pocket for her warrant card. 'I'm DI Delamere and the woman over there is my colleague, DS Everett.'

Chapter Two

'Your mam was on TV again last night.'

'That right? Don't tell me they've finally caught up with her. Corruption? Fraud? Something like that, I'm guessing.'

DCI Stuart Jennings regarded her for a moment. 'You really don't like her, do you?'

'Funnily enough we get on okay when we're together. As long as we avoid discussing virtually any subject under the sun. But at a distance – no, I really don't like her.'

'She's always struck me as a game old bird.'

Game old bird. As always, Annie felt that Jennings' language was designed to rile her. But she'd decided to allow anything he said or did to wash right over her. He wasn't worth the grief. 'Mum's lively enough,' she conceded. 'If you like that sort of thing.' Quite what sort of thing this might be was left hanging in the air. 'What was she on this time?'

'*Newsnight*. The challenges of contemporary policing.'

'Of course. Let me guess what she said. The service is still bloated and inefficient, and the cuts to our funding haven't been anything like deep enough?'

'Not in quite so many words.'

'I'm guessing she said it in rather more words. But that's what it would have amounted to.'

Jennings looked uncomfortable, as if he'd strayed into a discussion he'd rather have avoided. 'Something like that, anyway. A lot of stuff about how it was better in her day.'

'She only retired five years ago. And nobody ever talks about why she retired.' Annie knew that Jennings wouldn't risk responding to that one. 'Anyway, I'm old enough to remember when right-wingers were in favour of the police. Even ones as rabid as my mother.'

They were sitting in Jennings' office. The whole place was supposed to be open-plan, but Jennings, typically, had already managed to commandeer a room of his own. That was fine by Annie if it helped keep Jennings out of her hair. He'd transferred over here a month or so back as part of what was being referred to as the 'regionalisation agenda'. Yet another initiative, she assumed, that would require them to do more with ever-reducing resources. Her mother would approve.

At first she'd been suspicious of Jennings' blunt manner, but she'd quickly realised it was at least partly an act. She hadn't yet worked out quite how much of an act, but she was willing to give him the benefit of the doubt. No doubt he was equally wary of her background. Perhaps that was why she'd been so keen to emphasise her dislike for her mother. Though it never took much to prompt that particular response.

For the moment, she and Jennings were warily circling round each other, each trying to work out the other's characteristics and motivations. She imagined they'd settle down soon enough, particularly once they were faced with some real work challenges. He was still finding his feet, and she was happy to help him do so.

She glanced around the office. So far he'd left it fairly unadorned, with nothing beyond a couple of family photographs – his wife, his two children – to add a personal touch. In her experience, managers who were keen to appropriate an office of their own generally went to some lengths to mark their territory – a few carefully chosen books, a quirky souvenir from some international conference, one or two certificates or commendations. Annie found this faintly risible. She didn't know whether Jennings agreed, or whether he just hadn't yet got around to importing whatever junk he might possess.

'Anyway,' he said, breaking into her chain of thought, 'I just wanted to check that everything's under control. Any support you need from me at this stage?'

That was a positive sign, she supposed. The new enquiry was one of the more intriguing to come their way in some months. Jennings, as Senior Investigating Officer, had seemed happy to delegate the day-to-day management of the case to her. It was perhaps intended as a test, an opportunity to see how well she could cope with the pressures of a relatively complex enquiry. She'd even wondered if she was being set up to fail. It wouldn't have been the first time. But so far Jennings had been both supportive and unobtrusive.

'It's all going in the right direction,' she said. 'We had a kick-off session this morning, so things are moving. I've had the usual problems drumming up the necessary resources, but we're getting there.'

'If you need me to turn the thumbscrews on anyone, just let me know. This is potentially a big one.'

'Tell me about it,' she said. 'But we're pretty much there. If anyone who's promised us doesn't come across, I'll let you know. The main difficulty is that everyone's running on empty for staff. Especially for experienced officers.'

'As long as you've got what you need.'

'I'll tell you if we run into any issues.'

'How's it going at the scene?'

'The CSIs have nearly done. Later today, they reckon. I was planning to have a drive over once we're done here. Get a feel for the place. Tim's been running a tight ship, but then he always does.' Tim Sturgeon was the designated crime scene manager who had been allocated to the case. He had a reputation for thoroughness bordering on the obsessive.

'Still can't quite believe it was you and Zoe who stumbled across the body,' Jennings said. 'Now that's what I call dedication. Generating business even at the weekend.'

'Pretty unpleasant business. Throat cut. Multiple incisions on the body. Some unpleasant mutilation. Almost ritualistic, the CSI thought.'

'Some of those CSIs have too much imagination.'

In Annie's experience, the opposite was generally true. Most of the CSIs she dealt with kept their imaginations firmly tamped down, focusing only on facts and evidence. That, and the blackest forms of gallows humour. 'Maybe. But a naked body spreadeagled on a prehistoric stone cairn in the middle of the Peak District makes a change from the usual knife crime.'

'As long as it keeps you happy.'

She gazed at him for a moment, trying to work out if this was another jibe. She'd spent her career dealing with snide comments, usually muttered within her earshot but too quietly to challenge. Sometimes she thought she'd become oversensitive. At other times, as now, she wondered if she wasn't anything like sensitive enough. 'I'm not likely to be bored, anyway.'

'I'll let you get on then. Keep me posted.' Jennings' demeanour indicated that the meeting was over. She pushed herself to her feet.

Jennings had already moved on to his next task, tapping fluently away on the keyboard at his workstation. From this angle, his raw-boned features and swept-back greying hair made him look older than his forty-odd years, she thought.

Without looking up from his computer screen, Jennings said, 'And if you should run into your mam any time soon, tell her from me she's talking bollocks.'

She hesitated, wanting to rise to the bait. Then she took a breath and allowed him a cool smile. 'Don't worry,' she said. 'I always do.'

Chapter Three

'Is that us then?' Clive Bamford looked around the table. His tone and facial expression suggested disapproval that the assembled group was not more populous.

His disapproval was mainly directed at Greg Wardle. Greg had been responsible for publicising the event. In fairness, he had argued for an evening meeting, but Clive had insisted they'd get more people at lunchtime. He'd had the idea they'd attract bored office workers looking to liven up their lunch hour. Now it looked more likely they'd attract anyone who wanted to get out of the rain.

'Maybe give it a few more minutes, Clive?' Greg said. 'See if anyone else turns up.'

Clive's annoyance was increasing. He was always intolerant of any kind of unpunctuality. If he'd said the meeting would start at twelve thirty, it would start at twelve thirty.

'I think we'd better start,' Clive said.

There were only four of them sitting round the table, including Clive and Greg. The other two were newcomers, thankfully, so at least there'd been some point in holding the meeting here. But Clive had expected at least a dozen new members today. The landlord had offered them free use of the function room on the assumption that he'd sell more booze downstairs. That wasn't a mistake he was likely to make twice.

The two newcomers were looking understandably nervous and bemused, clearly not knowing quite what to expect. Clive shared some of their anxiety. This had seemed like a good idea when he and Greg had first come up with it. But he still hadn't really decided how he was going to run the session.

'Ladies and gentlemen,' Clive began, recognising a moment too late that no females were present, 'welcome to the inaugural meeting of the Conspiracy Theory Discussion Group.'

They'd had extensive debates about that name, too. Greg hadn't liked it. 'It makes us sound like fruitcakes,' he'd said. 'People who'll believe in any old bollocks.'

Clive had been baffled by the objection. 'We're not saying we necessarily subscribe to the theories,' he'd argued. 'Just that we recognise their existence, and we believe they merit consideration. They're theories, to be proved or disproved. That's science.' He'd said the last word in a tone that implied no further dispute was possible.

'Tonight's meeting is by way of an introductory session,' Clive went on, 'so we'll cover a wide range of material. I'd like to hear your views on issues or topics you'd like to see discussed.' He spoke as though addressing a multitude. 'In future meetings, we'll focus on one or two pre-agreed specific topics in each session, so that we all have chance to carry out some prior reading or research. I'll begin each session with a brief introduction on the topic in question and we'll perhaps ask one of you to prepare a short presentation, and we can proceed from there.'

The newcomers looked as if they were already beginning to regret their decision to attend. Clive feared that the threat of what might sound suspiciously like homework might dissuade them from returning. But it was important to do these things properly.

'So,' Clive continued, 'perhaps we should begin with some introductions. As you've probably guessed, I'm Clive Bamford. Author, journalist, broadcaster. Expert on the paranormal.' Most of that was at least notionally true. A couple of self-published books, a few articles largely for amateur journals, and some appearances on local community radio. Clive was serious about his chosen obsessions. 'If you'd like to ask me any questions about my background or work, please feel free.' He paused expectantly, but there was no response. 'Or we can chat afterwards,' he added. 'Greg?'

'Greg Wardle.' Greg cleared his throat awkwardly. 'I'm just an amateur enthusiast, really. Long-time associate of Clive's but I don't claim anything like his level of knowledge. Just here to share ideas and thoughts…' He trailed off.

Clive nodded, as if Greg had more than done himself justice. 'Thanks, Greg. Now, gentlemen…?'

The two men looked uncomfortably at one another, each clearly hoping the other would speak first. Eventually, they both managed to introduce themselves and say a few words about their own particular interests. It was the usual stuff, Clive thought. 9/11. JFK. The moon landings. The Illuminati.

'All very interesting,' Clive said, though his expression suggested the opposite. 'All worthy areas of enquiry.' He had already decided he should steer them away from some of the more extreme stuff. He knew how easily conspiracy theories could shade into views that were far less palatable. He'd been at too many meetings or conventions where those around him were using coded language to promulgate opinions he found frankly abhorrent. Bloody lizard people, for God's sake.

'Thank you all for turning out,' Clive said. 'I'm sorry we're a slightly select group today. Obviously the rain has kept a few people indoors—'

At that moment, as if in illustration of Clive's words, the door of the function room burst open to reveal two rain-soaked individuals. Clive looked up, his irritation at the interruption immediately replaced by gratification at the appearance of two more attendees.

The two individuals were a man and a woman. The man was tall and gangling, a mass of greasy black hair falling chaotically across his face. The woman had long, strikingly red hair. She was, Clive noticed almost immediately, really very attractive. Both looked older than anyone already present. Late thirties, Clive thought, or even older.

The man blinked and looked around the room, his gaze eventually fixing on Clive. His whole appearance suggested disorganisation made flesh, but there was something in the steadiness of his gaze that Clive found oddly unnerving.

'Is this the right place?' the man asked. 'Conspiracy theories and all that?'

Clive looked pointedly at his watch. 'That's us. Would you like to come in and join us?'

'Sure, sure.' The man stumbled his way across to the table. 'Sorry we're a bit late. Cats and dogs out there.'

The woman had followed him into the room. She was carrying two pints of what Clive took to be some variety of stout or porter. She sat herself beside the man, and placed the full glasses on the table between them.

They'd left the door of the function room open, and Clive could hear the hubbub of chat from the bar below.

Without saying anything, he rose, crossed the room and closed the door. As he returned to the table, the man winked an acknowledgement. He was looking at Clive expectantly.

Clive gave a brief sigh that eloquently expressed his exasperation. 'We've just completed introductions. I'm Clive Bamford. I'm sure you can all get to know each other better when we have a break. You are...?'

To Clive's slight surprise, it was the woman who answered. 'I'm Rowan Wiseman. And this is Charlie.' It wasn't clear whether Charlie shared her surname, or whether he simply didn't have one. He looked like the kind of man who might have mislaid his surname somewhere along the way.

They were both dressed in leather jackets dotted with an array of unreadable badges, which they wore over the top of black T-shirts and jeans. Charlie's T-shirt was adorned with a logo but Clive had no idea of its significance.

'Welcome, Rowan and Charlie.' Clive had risen to the occasion with impressive pomposity. 'This is our inaugural meeting. Our mission is to discuss all kinds of non-mainstream thinking with open but critical minds—'

'Conspiracy theories.' It was the second time that Charlie had spoken the phrase. This time it was imbued with undoubted contempt.

'We've used that simply as a catch-all term—'

'But it's a crap term, isn't it?' Charlie had the air of someone thinking out loud. He leaned forward over the table and pointed his forefinger at Clive. 'The kind of language that those shitty TV channels use. "Did aliens walk this earth back in the mists of time?" That sort of bollocks.'

'I don't think—'

'It's exactly the language the mainstream media use to dismiss this kind of thing, isn't it? As if only nutters could believe this stuff. I mean, don't you want to take this seriously?'

'Of course we take it seriously. But we approach each issue with a critical mind. It's a theory unless and until we can prove otherwise.'

'But you've got to discriminate,' Charlie said. 'I mean, a lot of it's clearly garbage. You don't want to waste your time on that. Focus on the stuff that's worth finding out about.'

Clive leaned back in his chair, irritated that his authority was already being undermined. 'So, in your not so humble opinion, what should we be looking at?'

Charlie exchanged a glance with Rowan Wiseman. 'Well,' he said, 'just thinking about what was on your poster, I wouldn't bother with all that moon-landing crap.'

'With respect—' Greg began.

Charlie ignored him. 'Do you really think that, if there was anything in it, some NASA underling wouldn't have blown the whistle? It's been fifty bloody years. 9/11, likewise. You couldn't do something like that without involving a lot of people. People talk.'

'Okay, so you don't think we should waste our time on either of those—' Clive said.

'All the Area 51 stuff, that's the same. And the flat earth bollocks. What sort of conspiracy would that be? How many people would you need to involve? Why would you even bother?' Charlie stopped and took a large swallow of his beer. 'Give me a break.'

Clive tried again. 'You've been very persuasive in telling us what not to discuss. Do you mind enlightening us as to what *is* worth talking about?'

Charlie seemed oblivious to the sarcasm. 'You should be looking at the real conspiracies. The Illuminati, for example. The Freemasons. The Bilderberg Group. All those,' Charlie concluded. 'And there are countless others. Call them what you like, but it amounts to the same thing.'

Clive nodded, as if giving serious consideration to Charlie's ideas. Then he said, 'With respect, though, that stuff's an even greater load of bollocks, isn't it?'

Charlie looked up and stared unblinkingly at Clive. 'You reckon?' His tone suggested his next words might well be a suggestion to take this outside.

Clive was unintimidated. 'It's either bollocks or it's just a truism. We all know that the ultra-rich conspire to stay that way and big business conspires to maximise its profits. None of that's news. They do it openly. They don't need any secret groups to make it happen. It's naive to think otherwise.' This was an argument Clive could continue all night.

Charlie smiled. 'You're the naive one if you really think that's the limit of it. What they do in public is the tip of the iceberg. The global conspiracy goes far beyond that.'

Greg had clearly decided it was time to offer Clive some support. 'The trouble is that terms like "global conspiracy" often lead to some pretty nasty politics.'

Charlie turned to face him. 'What are you accusing me of, son?'

'I-I'm not accusing you of anything. I'm just saying that phrases like "global conspiracy" are sometimes coded language. It's why the far right go on about it all the time.'

'So we should ignore it because it's not politically correct?' Charlie said. 'Even if it turns out to be true.'

'I just think we need to be careful—'

'Careful.' Charlie almost spat out the word. 'That's exactly what they want, isn't it? Everyone to tiptoe round the subject in case they offend someone.'

Clive could feel the meeting slipping away from him. 'I don't think anyone's saying that. I'm more than happy for us to add it to our list of topics. But I should make it clear to everyone here that we don't tolerate any form of racism in the discussions. We need to discuss these topics objectively.'

'Then there are the religions,' Charlie continued as if Clive hadn't spoken. 'We should look at the religions.'

Clive blinked. His usual authority had deserted him. 'Religions?'

'The Catholic Church, for one.' Charlie smiled. 'That probably wasn't what you expected me to say, was it?'

'I don't—'

'The thing is,' Charlie went on, 'I take an equal opportunities approach to conspiracies. What's that term they all use nowadays? An evidence-based methodology. I'm not bigoted or racist. I just follow the facts.'

'As I say,' Clive responded, 'we're open to discussing any of these topics as long as we adhere to the basic standards of the group.'

'That's excellent.' Charlie's tone was that of someone praising a dog for completing a simple trick. 'Then there are the churches of the left-hand path.'

'Well, yes, that's an interesting area of enquiry—' Clive began.

'You mean satanists?' Greg intervened.

Charlie redirected his gaze back to Greg. 'If you want to call them that. Religion that's about challenging taboos. Societal norms. Some see it as another way of seeking enlightenment. If enlightenment is the right word.'

Clive took the opportunity to move the discussion back into more familiar territory. 'All very interesting,' he said. 'I'm sure we can find time to focus on that. Perhaps you'd like to put something together by way of an introduction, Charlie?'

'Sure.' Charlie looked at Rowan Wiseman. 'We'd be delighted, wouldn't we, Ro?'

'Oh, aye. Delighted.'

'Right, then,' Clive said. 'Well, is that a good moment for us to take a break? I'll jot all these ideas down and we can have a chat about what order to take them over the next few weeks.'

Charlie looked as if he was about to offer some alternative suggestion, but Rowan Wiseman took him by the arm and whispered something in his ear. She looked up at Clive. 'We'll go and get another pint. Can we get you one?'

Clive was genuinely surprised by the offer. 'That's very kind of you. Thanks. I'm on the IPA.'

She nodded, then held up what was left of her stout. 'We prefer it more on the dark side, as you've probably seen.' She smiled. 'But good to finally find some kindred spirits.'

Chapter Four

As they emerged on to the open moorland, Annie paused and looked back. 'Sure you're up to this, Zoe?'

She knew there was no way Zoe would say anything other than yes. But she felt she ought at least to ask. Annie had seen the expression on Zoe's face as they'd pulled in off the road, sensed the tension in her body language. She'd worked with the other woman long enough to know this wasn't straightforward squeamishness.

Zoe was looking around her as if seeing the landscape for the first time. 'I'm fine. Just a bit preoccupied, that's all. Nothing important.'

The rain had set in overnight and was still falling heavily, whipped by a strong wind from the west. Both women were clad in heavy waterproof jackets, but Annie could already feel the rain seeping into her clothing. 'Bloody miserable one. Difficult to believe you can see for miles on a clear day.'

Today, much of the landscape was lost in a haze of mist and rain. Annie could see how the land dropped away across the bleak moorland before them, but she could only imagine the resulting vista of fields and moors and the further dark hills beyond. Chatsworth House would be somewhere to their west, the land around them largely part of the Devonshire estate.

'To be honest, even on a clear day the place gives me the creeps,' Zoe said.

Annie had never thought of Zoe as the imaginative type. That was one of her strengths, certainly compared to Annie herself. She was pragmatic, down to earth, pretty much unfazed by anything life might throw at her, up to and including the discovery of a severely mutilated body.

It was true that, on a day like today, this was a desolate place – just miles of empty, rain-soaked, windswept grassland, potentially concealing God knew what kind of secrets. Then there were the cairns and stone workings that dotted their immediate surroundings. Annie supposed it wouldn't take much imagination to sense some kind of energy being channelled through this place.

The crime-scene tents were barely visible through the driving rain and thickening mist. 'You reckon Tim'll have a cup of coffee waiting for us?'

'From what I've seen of Tim,' Zoe said, 'he keeps his coffee flask jealously guarded. I sometimes wonder if it's just coffee he puts in there.'

'Tim could have any number of secrets. We'd never know.'

They trudged across the wet grassland towards the tents. Crime scene investigation seemed to grow more thorough and complex with each case, and an incident like this would have had the works thrown at it. They'd been here for the best part of thirty-six hours and weren't likely to be finished yet. As Annie proceeded past the police cordon, a uniformed officer who'd been sheltering in the lee of the tent jumped up as if to demonstrate he hadn't been dozing on the job. He slowed as he recognised the visitors.

'Afternoon, Robbie,' Annie said. 'Couldn't you have arranged a bit better weather for us?' She knew PC Robbie Normanton a little from previous jobs, and remembered him as young, bright and enthusiastic. The sort of copper who was likely to progress, assuming that was what he wanted.

'I put in a request for sunshine, but you know how it is,' Normanton said. 'You looking for Tim? He's inside in the dry.'

'Of course he is. That's why you need to make sergeant, Robbie. Then you could be inside in the dry too.'

'One day.'

Tim Sturgeon had obviously heard their voices, and his face appeared through the tent flap. 'Afternoon, ladies. Come to join the fun?'

'As long as you're having fun, Tim. That's what matters. Are we safe to come inside?'

'Feel free. The body's gone and they're done with all the forensic stuff. I'm still kitted up but only because I get a kick out of wearing a white suit.'

They followed him into the tent. As Tim had said, the body had been removed and the only sign of its former presence was a dark area of blood staining on the under-growth. A couple of white-suited CSIs were performing some aspect of their arcane procedures at the far end of the tent, but the main work had obviously now been completed. The senior CSI, a man called Danny Eccles, walked over to join them.

Annie knew Danny well. In her experience, CSIs tended to fall into two main types. Some were gloomy and lugubrious, their manner suggesting that their minds were haunted by too many dark experiences and thoughts. Others, like Danny, were cheerful and apparently light-hearted. Annie had no idea which was the saner reaction to the job, but she knew which type was easier to work with. 'How's it going?'

'We're more or less done. Just taking a few more photos now the body's out of the way.'

'You still think we're talking about something ritualistic?'

Danny looked uncomfortable, as if he'd been challenged about an unfashionable opinion. 'That's just the way it looks. I was trying to describe it...'

'It's our job to work out the why and the how,' Annie said. 'I want you to tell me the what.'

'The throat was cut. I mean, sliced open from ear to ear—' He stopped and looked at Zoe. 'I'm sorry. I don't mean to be too graphic.'

Zoe looked more troubled than Annie had ever seen her. 'You sure you're okay, Zoe? Must have been a shock. It's different when you know what you're being called out to. For us just to stumble across it like that—'

'I'm fine,' Zoe said.

Annie knew better than to push it further. She was already regretting having asked the question in public. Danny's intentions had been good, but Annie knew better than most that the last thing a female officer needs is anyone suggesting they might not be up to the job. 'Go on, Danny.'

'Like I say, the throat was cut. Then there were a series of incisions to the torso. It had been sliced with a sharp blade. Two vertical, two horizontal and four diagonal. Then a further cut around them. Like a target, I suppose.'

'A target? So maybe not necessarily ritualistic, but perhaps some kind of message.' She paused. 'Which do you reckon was done first? The incisions or the throat?'

'The doc will tell you for sure,' Danny said. 'But my guess would be that the incisions were first. There'd been a lot of bleeding from the wounds. I think the throat was cut afterwards.'

There was silence for a moment, disturbed only by the incessant drumming rain on the tent. 'So the victim would have still been alive while the incisions were being made,' Zoe said.

'I'd have said so,' Danny responded. 'Like I say, I'm sure the doc will be able to give you a more authoritative view.'

For all his reticence, Annie had little doubt Danny would be correct. He was more helpful than some CSIs, who were reluctant to volunteer anything beyond a factual description of the evidence. Danny was prepared to offer you his best guess, even if heavily loaded with caveats. But his best guess was usually pretty accurate. 'Do we think the victim would have been conscious at that point?'

'Again, the doc can give you the medical view. But from the way the undergrowth was trampled, I'd say there were signs of a struggle. As if the killer or killers had been holding down the victim. There are also marks on the wrists and ankles that look as if they've been made by some kind of restraints. It's likely he was conscious at least at the start of it.'

'Christ,' Zoe whispered. It sounded almost like the start of a prayer.

'So we're effectively talking torture.' Annie voiced what they were all thinking.

'Looks like it,' Danny agreed.

'Followed by a pretty savage throat-slitting.' Annie felt as if she was saying the words just to hear them out loud. So the ideas wouldn't be sitting, unspoken, in all their heads. 'Any clues as to the victim's identity?'

'He was naked, as you know, so he didn't have any convenient ID stashed about his person. But he's got a few interesting tattoos.'

'Interesting?'

'There are rather a lot of them, for a start. He was clearly no stranger to the needle.'

'Wonder how much that helped him when someone started carving into his chest,' Annie said. She understood that Zoe had a couple of discreetly positioned tattoos, but for her own part she'd never seen the attraction. She had enough scope for regret in her life, without adding ill-advised body decorations to the pile.

'Most of them were fairly conventional stuff,' Danny went on. 'But a couple rang alarm bells.'

'Go on.'

'A swastika was the most obvious. On his right arm.'

'Of course on his right arm.'

'Then the number eighty-eight on his left arm.'

'Eight eight. Heil Hitler. Anything else?'

'A couple of runic things I'm guessing have dodgy connotations.'

Annie nodded. In a way, the only surprise was that the tattoos included anything as blatant as a swastika. There was a whole range of coded phrases, numbers and symbols that carried meaning for those who understood their significance. She guessed part of the attraction, for those who chose to display them, was hiding your beliefs in plain sight. It no doubt fed their sense of conspiracy and victimhood.

'One of our far-right pals, then,' she said. 'Of some variety, anyway.' In practice, that might mean anything from a seriously nasty piece of work to some sad case looking for scapegoats to blame for his own failings. Or just some halfwit who thought these symbols were an appropriate fashion accessory. 'Should help us identify him, anyway. He might be on the system, with a bit of luck.' She turned to Tim. 'Assume you've checked the surrounding area?'

She asked the question partly in the hope of getting a rise out of the always impassive Tim. His only reaction was to raise his left eyebrow. 'I think we might have done, don't you? Nothing in the immediate vicinity. No sign of a murder weapon. No sign of any further ID. No sign of his clothes.'

'We'll have to decide whether it's worth expanding the search area. But I'm guessing we're not likely to find much.'

'Raises the question of how they got him up here,' Zoe said.

'Any idea how long he'd been here?' Annie asked Danny Eccles. 'Just roughly, I mean.'

'Three or four days, at least, I'd say.'

'They could have brought him up at night. Don't suppose you're likely to be disturbed up here. This is sufficiently far from the paths that the body might not have been spotted for some time.'

'We've got statements from the guys who stumbled across it,' Tim said. 'They'd wandered over here to have a look at some of the cairns. But most people stick to the footpaths.'

'On the other hand,' Zoe said, 'no effort was made to conceal the body. Somebody would have found it sooner or later. Which suggests whoever did this didn't care too much about it being found.'

'Okay,' Annie said, 'let's leave these two to finish up. Thanks for the update, Danny. And you've done your usual grand job, Tim.'

'I live to serve,' Tim said.

'You live for Friday nights,' Annie corrected him. 'Come on, Zo. Let's brave the rain again and get things moving back at the ranch.'

Chapter Five

The chanting had grown louder as the meeting had proceeded, probably in proportion to the amount of booze being consumed.

'God, they're noisy,' Sheena Pearson said. 'I mean, there's only about a dozen of them.'

'We could get the police to disperse them,' Graeme Carter said. 'They're causing an obstruction.'

Sheena shook her head. 'I'm really trying to avoid the "leftie MP clamps down on free speech" angle. You know exactly how they'll play that.'

'The same way they always play it, whatever we do,' Graeme pointed out. 'The oppressed middle-aged white guy. The real victims of discrimination.'

Nazia Rashid nodded. 'The thing is, they really believe it. And I suppose in a place like this, they do have at least a fraction of a point. A lot of them have no jobs, no money, no prospects.'

'Except that it's not only the middle-aged white guys in that position,' Graeme said. 'They just have a greater sense of entitlement.'

Sheena shrugged. 'I've some sympathy. Not with the racist thugs. But with some of those who swallow their nonsense. They've had decades of being ignored by successive governments – mine as much as the other lot. It's just a pity they can't see it's an issue of class and status rather than race. But then we've also had successive governments who've been very adept at divide and rule. There's a real danger we'll reap the whirlwind.' Much of this was the standard spiel she trotted out on the rare occasions she was invited on to *Question Time* or *Any Questions?* It wasn't that she didn't believe it – she believed every word – but she'd internalised the ideas and phrasing to the point where she hardly knew what she was saying.

Apart from the protests, the meeting had been pretty routine, one of her regular get-togethers with the leaders of the various local community groups. Since her election, Sheena had devoted much of her constituency time to trying to highlight and address various forms of exploitation in these disadvantaged communities – dodgy landlords, loan sharks, intimidation. It had proved to be a slow process – it was often difficult to persuade people even to talk about what they had experienced – but she was gradually building a substantial portfolio of data and case studies. It was people like Nazia Rashid who had helped her identify victims and gather much of the information.

She liked Nazia, a smart and energetic woman who was more interested in practical initiatives than in political gestures. Sheena was as ideological as the next woman, but it became tiresome when meetings focused largely on sloganising rather than actually making anything happen. 'Anyway,' she went on, 'I'm sorry about the disruption. You'll be able to get out the back way. I don't think they've been bright enough to discover the rear entrance yet. The police are on hand, though we've asked them not to intervene unless they need to.'

Nazia shrugged. 'They don't worry me. All mouth, most of them.'

Graeme Carter had risen from the table and was peering through the blind at the street below. 'There's still only about a dozen of them. Reckon they must have interrupted a sesh at the Hare and Hounds to come here.'

'Real dedication,' Sheena commented.

'They took care to bring a few cans with them,' Graeme commented. 'There are a couple of police officers across the street keeping an eye on them. Reckon if they get too rowdy, the police will break it up anyway.'

'As long as it's their decision rather than mine,' Sheena said. 'Though I'll get the blame anyway.'

The reason for the protest, as far as Sheena had been able to ascertain from the badly-spelled posters, was that she'd made a public statement criticising Mo Henley, a far-right non-entity recently sentenced to three months in prison as a result of recurrent public order and other offences. Henley – a thuggish figure, risibly known to his followers as Bulldog – rarely appeared in public without an entourage of equally thuggish companions. Predictably, he was now being hailed as a martyr and a prisoner of the state by various right-wing groups.

Sheena knew little about Henley and cared less. But he was a local man by birth and upbringing, and, as MP for the constituency, she was repeatedly asked for an opinion. She'd been only too happy to say exactly what she thought in interviews on local radio and the local television news programme.

'Do you get a lot of this?' Nazia Rashid asked, gesturing towards the window and the street beyond.

'Not much. We've had the odd, very civilised protest, usually about environmental issues. But I was pretty much on their side. They were really just looking for a few photo opportunities. Don't think we've ever had a bunch like this before. Not in my time, anyway.' The constituency had always been strongly Labour, and Pearson had succeeded the retiring previous MP – an old-school hard-left product of the surrounding coalfields – at the 2010 General Election. She'd retained the seat since then, though with a slightly reduced majority.

'It's sad that we've come to this,' Nazia said.

'That tendency's always been there,' Sheena said. 'National Front. BNP. Britain First. It just pops up in different guises. There's always been a small but resilient bunch of them around here.'

'In this neck of the woods,' Graeme said from his position by the window, 'the only time they encounter a BAME person is when they get an Indian takeaway. I wonder how they'd feel if they were living in a genuinely multicultural community.' He stopped, as if it had suddenly occurred to him that, in Nazia's presence, his words might be tactless. 'I'm sorry, I didn't mean...'

Nazia laughed. 'No, you're right. I represent a small community, proportionally. Though of course many of those serving in the takeaways you mention have faced serious racial abuse.'

'Ignore Graeme,' Sheena advised. 'He means well, but he's a white male middle-class southerner. He can't help it.'

'This is exactly the kind of prejudice I have to put up with,' Graeme said to Nazia. 'I hope you're taking note.' He looked back out of the window. 'Hang on, something's happening out there.'

The two women rose and joined him at the window. The apparent leader of the group below, a man who looked to be in his mid-forties with a shaven head and an impressive array of tattoos visible outside his union jack T-shirt, was involved in an altercation with one of the police officers. From up here they couldn't hear what was being said, but the man was repeatedly jabbing his forefinger towards the officer's chest. The man had a can of cheap lager in his hand and was behaving with the exaggerated precision of someone who'd drunk a little too much.

'He's going the right way to get himself arrested,' Graeme said.

It was clear the gathering below was growing more unruly. Several other men were clustered behind the ringleader, chanting abuse at the police officer. The officer had been joined by a colleague, and Sheena could see they were trying to persuade the crowd to disperse.

'I'm going to go down,' she said.

'Police won't thank you if it inflames things,' Graeme pointed out.

'It's me they're protesting about. Seems a bit cowardly just to sit up here and let the police deal with it.'

'I don't get the impression they're particularly interested in participating in a reasoned discussion.'

'I'm going to give it a shot anyway.' She turned to Nazia. 'Sorry you've had to be subjected to this.'

'Oddly enough, it's not the first time I've experienced something like this.'

'No, I suppose not. Anyway, thanks for coming. Graeme can show you out the back way. At least I can provide a distraction while you're leaving.' She smiled. 'Covering fire.'

–

Halfway down the stairs to the ground floor, Sheena paused, wondering whether she was doing the right thing.

33

As Graeme had pointed out, she'd get no thanks if she made matters worse. He was good at restraining her more impetuous behaviour. It was one of the reasons she employed him.

On the other hand, he tended to be overcautious. That was partly why, despite his treble first from Oxbridge or whatever it was, he was still working as a spad while she was in the shadow Cabinet. Swings and roundabouts.

In the downstairs area, receptionist Carla MacDonald was still happily tapping away at her keyboard, despite the mounting fracas outside. Sheena had asked Carla whether she wanted to move upstairs for the duration of the protest, but she'd seemed unfazed. 'Gah, they're just big kids,' she'd said. 'Try anything with me and they'll get short shrift.' In the end, Sheena had reluctantly agreed. The door was locked and the toughened glass was supposed to withstand anything likely to be thrown at it.

'Getting a bit tasty out there,' Sheena said.

'Wee gobshites,' Carla said, succinctly. 'Playing tough.'

'I'm going to go and have a word. See if I can calm things a bit.'

'You sure about that? That big fella's got a few pints inside him.'

'The police are there. I can only try.' She could hear the sound of sirens somewhere outside. It seemed as if the two officers had summoned reinforcements. 'Wish me luck.'

She unlocked the front door and stepped out into the street. The man in the union jack T-shirt was still remonstrating with the police officer. As she moved closer, she heard the officer say, 'I'll ask you one more time, sir. Please leave the area. You're causing a disturbance and if you continue I'll have no option but to take action.'

'Bloody typical.' The man was swaying slightly. 'We know our rights under common law. Rights of peaceful process. It's in the Magna Carta.'

'Peaceful protest, yes, sir. We've been tolerant so far—'

'Tolerant? It's not your job to be fucking tolerant. It's your job to uphold the law. To uphold our common law rights.' The man had finally noticed Sheena approaching. 'There she is. There's the bitch.'

'Sir—'

'She's a fucking traitor, that's what she is. Selling the country down the river into the hands of immigrants and—'

'Sir, I must warn you—'

Sheena really wasn't sure her presence was helping the situation, but there wasn't much she could do about that now. She spoke as calmly as she was able. 'I understand you're protesting about my comments on Mo Henley. I'm very happy to discuss them with you if you'd like to do so.'

The man started jabbing his finger in her direction. 'You libelled fucking Bulldog. That's what you did. You said he was a fascist. Like bloody Hitler. We fought two bloody wars against Hitler. We shouldn't have fucking bothered. The country's full of bloody—'

'I'm very happy to discuss these issues with you. I'm sure we won't see eye to eye but we can at least debate it in a civilised way. We can do it now, if you like. Just you and me.'

The man seemed taken aback by the offer. 'You'd just try to bamboozle me with facts. I know smartarses like you with your public school educations. Treat the likes of me like dirt.'

'For what it's worth,' she said, 'I grew up in a council house and went to a comp in Ilkeston.'

She could tell he didn't believe her, though every word was true. He spat at her feet and took another swig of his beer. 'You're just a fucking traitor, that's what you are.'

She could see, from the corner of her eye, another police car drawing up on the far side of the street. It was clear the man had seen it too, and was considering how best to beat a semi-dignified retreat. He turned back to the police officer. 'See you've bought in the fucking cavalry. Can't deal with the likes of us on your own. Too tough for you.'

'If you and your associates would kindly just disperse and leave the area, we'll need to take no further action.' the officer said. 'Otherwise, we will arrest you all.'

The man glanced back at the others standing behind him. 'Know when we're not wanted, don't we, lads? Okay, we'll go for the moment. But we know our rights. You mark my words, soon the people will rise up.' He stared at Sheena, the veins in his reddened forehead standing out. 'And traitors like you will be the first to be strung up.'

Two more police officers had emerged from the police car and were crossing the street to join them. The man turned and said, 'Come on, lads. We'll leave it for now but we'll be back.'

They began to move away, still chanting 'Traitor, traitor', some of them pointing at Sheena.

'I'm sorry,' she said quietly to the police officer, 'I don't think I helped that. But I felt I couldn't just ignore them.'

'You're in a difficult position, ma'am,' the officer said, in the same tone he might have used in response to a polite question from the Queen. 'But we'll try our best to—'

Sheena never discovered what it was that the officer would try his best to do. The sound of the gunfire was sudden and shocking, the harsh noise echoing around the empty high street.

It took her a moment to realise what she'd heard, and another moment to realise that there was warm blood running down her face.

Chapter Six

Annie knew as soon as she walked into HQ that something had happened. It was like that sometimes. You could sense it. A change in the atmosphere, sometimes positive, sometimes negative. Sometimes, like today, unreadable but still undeniable.

Generally, the 'something' was a major incident, most commonly a large-scale road traffic collision, occasionally a high-profile crime. Sometimes it was good news – a significant breakthrough in an ongoing enquiry. Annie had heard nothing on the radio as they'd driven back, though she'd been mainly focused on apologising for her tactless comment about Zoe's well-being at the crime scene. Zoe had taken the apology with apparent good grace, but she'd remained unusually taciturn for the rest of the journey. Something was wrong, but Annie felt unsure how to probe further.

Back at her desk, she found a Post-it note from Stuart Jennings asking her to pop in to see him when she returned. That was untypical, she thought. Her usual experience was that when Jennings wanted to talk to her he just phoned, regardless of her location or circumstances. Still, best not keep him waiting.

He was on the phone when she poked her head round the door of his office, but he waved her in, ending the call with a curt 'Got to go now. Speak later.' It was reassuring to see that she wasn't the only recipient of his distinctive telephone manner.

Jennings gestured for her to take a seat. 'I'm afraid I've got some bad news. Assuming you've not heard already.'

She looked steadily back at him, wondering what the hell this was all about. 'I've heard nothing. Just got back.'

'There's been an incident. At Sheena Pearson's constituency office.'

'Sheena—?' She stopped, her mind suddenly filled with more thoughts than she could begin to articulate. 'What sort of incident?'

'A shooting.' He held up his hands. 'Look, as far as I'm aware, she's okay. She was wounded—'

'Wounded?' Shit. Shit. She and Sheena had talked about the possibility of violence directed at her since her election, but neither of them had really believed it could happen.

'She's been taken to the Royal Derby. I've just been on to the hospital. They weren't prepared to say too much, but my understanding is that it's only superficial. They say she's stable.'

'They always say that. I don't know what the hell it means. Look, I'd better get over there.'

'Of course. I hope everything's okay. Take as much time out as you need. Not the best time, but I can hold the fort here.'

She was momentarily tempted to snap back some sharp retort, but she knew she was being unfair. Jennings had his faults, but he seemed a decent man.

'Thanks, Stuart. I'll keep you posted once I know anything.'

As she hurried out of the building, she'd felt as if everyone else already knew what had happened. She could feel their sympathetic or simply curious eyes following her through the office, and she wanted to turn and tell them all that it was none of their business.

The truth was, though, that it was their business, or it soon would be. Sheena was a public figure, and some of these people would be her constituents. Whatever had happened would probably be the lead story on tonight's television news. This was a big deal.

She only realised quite how big a deal when she reached the hospital. The traffic in the city centre had been nightmarish, and she'd been aware of her anxiety mounting with every tailback. There'd been nowhere to park and in the end she'd just abandoned her car on the roadside, where she'd at least been confident she wouldn't cause an obstruction.

Outside the hospital, she'd rushed past an outside broadcast van from the regional TV station. Two uniformed officers were standing immediately inside the entrance, presumably stationed there in case any further incidents should occur. Annie was still unsure exactly what had happened. She'd listened to the radio news during the drive over. The story had topped the news as she'd expected, but the detail had been limited, referring only to a 'suspected shooting' at the constituency office. Sheena wasn't mentioned as the victim, and for the first time it had occurred to Annie to wonder if there might be others.

She approached the reception desk, deciding it was likely to be quicker to play this by the book. 'I'm here to visit Sheena Pearson. I'm her partner.'

The receptionist glanced over at the two officers. 'I'm afraid we've been told to refer any visitors to the two police officers over there.'

Annie nodded her thanks and hurried out to the two officers, this time already brandishing her warrant card. 'I'm here to visit Sheena Pearson. It's a personal visit, not official. I'm her partner.'

She tried to contain her impatience as the first officer squinted sceptically at her warrant card. He seemed finally to acknowledge it was genuine. 'She's in a private room. I'd better take you up there.' He glanced at his colleague. 'You okay for a few minutes, Josh?'

'Reckon so. Not much sign of anything kicking off here, is there?'

The first officer led her through to the lifts. 'Dave Reynolds,' he said, offering his hand. 'Bit of a shocker, this, isn't it?'

'Certainly is for me. Any word on how she is?' Other than Stuart Jennings' brief words of reassurance, she still had no idea of Sheena's condition.

'No one's said anything to me, I'm afraid. We've just been told to keep an eye out for any trouble.'

'You expecting any?'

'I doubt it. It was apparently some far-right protest where it kicked off. There was a worry they might decide to take advantage of the publicity. I reckon they'll just disappear into the woodwork. That sort always do. Biggest problem's probably going to be keeping the media out.'

Annie imagined the nationals were already on their way, looking to extract some juicy comment from anyone even peripherally connected to the case. No doubt her own position would be of interest, particularly given her mother's profile.

None of that mattered much at the moment, though. She wanted only to know what had happened to Sheena.

By the time they reached the third floor she could feel her composure crumbling. She'd managed to hold it together all the way over here, but the anxiety had been gnawing away at her. She just wanted to know.

Reynolds led her on to the ward and gestured to a door at the far end, where a further uniformed officer was sitting. 'That's the place.'

One of the nursing staff was already striding over to greet them. 'Can I help you?'

'I'm here to see Sheena Pearson. I'm her partner. How is she?'

'There's nothing to worry about,' the nurse said. Annie noted that this didn't entirely answer her question. 'She's asleep at the moment.'

'Can I see her?'

The nurse looked at Reynolds. 'I don't know. The police told us...'

'I'm also a police officer,' Annie said. 'So unless there's a medical reason for me not to enter the room, I'm sure it'll be fine.'

The nurse looked at Reynolds, who nodded his confirmation. 'No, there's no medical reason. I'll take you in.'

Annie turned to Reynolds. 'Thanks for your help. Appreciated.'

'No worries. All the best for her.'

The small room felt overheated and claustrophobic, cluttered with equipment. Sheena was lying on her back, apparently asleep, her face untypically ashen. There was a bandage around her temples, but otherwise she appeared unharmed.

'She was very lucky,' the nurse said. 'The bullet just grazed her head. The wound's very superficial. Not much more than a graze, fortunately.'

Annie took a breath, absorbing the implications of this. 'Why are you keeping her in?'

'Just for tests and observation,' the nurse said. 'As it's a head wound. There's always a risk that the damage is greater than it appears.'

Annie felt another clutch of fear in her stomach. 'You think that's possible?'

The nurse shook her head. 'It's just a precaution.'

'When do you think you'll be able to release her?'

'That's up to the consultant. He wants to keep her in overnight, but I think it's likely she'll be released tomorrow.'

'Is it okay if I sit with her for a while?'

'Yes, of course. We gave her a mild sedative to help her relax, but she may well wake soon.'

Annie lowered herself on to the bedside chair and gazed at her partner. Jesus, Sheena, she thought, that was bloody close. It struck her now how frail Sheena looked. She was one of the toughest, most resilient people Annie had ever met, someone who'd clawed her way up from a challenging background to achieve her current status. But physically, she was a relatively slight woman, her pale skin almost translucent in the glaring hospital lights. She looked dwarfed by the surrounding equipment, her body festooned with cables leading to the various monitors. Annie desperately wanted to reach out and take Sheena in her arms, but knew that, for the moment, it was impossible.

'You didn't even bring any fruit.' Sheena's eyes were still apparently closed, and for a moment Annie thought she was talking in her sleep.

'You don't like fruit.'

'That's not the point. It's what you bring hospital patients. That or chocolates. I don't see any chocolates.'

'You've got your eyes closed.'

'If I open them, will I see chocolates?'

'Not really. Not at all, in fact.' Annie finally reached out and took Sheena's hand in hers, taking care not to dislodge the monitors. 'Christ, Sheena. You nearly got yourself killed.'

Sheena opened her eyes and smiled. 'I didn't get myself anything. Some fascist fuckwit nearly killed me.'

'Fair. But it's the "nearly killed" bit that concerns me.'

Sheena was silent for a moment. 'I know. I'm trying not to think about too hard about that. It's really going to hit me at some point. At the moment I just feel numb. As if it happened to someone else.'

Annie nodded. She'd felt something similar herself on the few occasions she'd faced real danger as a police officer. It was a coping mechanism, she supposed, a way of dealing with emotions that were too painful to process.

'By the way,' Sheena added, 'that's really quite painful.'

Annie looked down and realised that, without knowing it, she'd been gripping Sheena's hand too tightly, as if still afraid she would be snatched away. She gave Sheena's hand a more gentle squeeze. 'Can you remember anything about what happened?'

'It's pretty clear up to the point I heard the gunshot,' Sheena said 'But then all I remember is that, as the protestors were starting to disperse, there was what sounded like an explosion. Then – well, this.' She gestured towards her head.

'You don't think it was the ringleader guy who shot you?'

'I'm pretty sure not. He was all bluster. He was walking away and he didn't do anything unexpected. It must have been someone else. Someone in the crowd.'

'We'll get him, Sheena.'

'You reckon? It was all a bit of a melee.'

'There'll be CCTV, and there'll probably be witnesses prepared to come forward. Either people who weren't directly involved or some of those who were. I'm guessing that some of them might shop one of their mates if we put a bit of pressure on them.'

'If you can identify them.'

'Some will be the usual suspects. We'll get them.'

'I'm not sure I care just at the moment. At least I'm still alive.'

'I care about some brain-dead arsehole walking about with a loaded firearm, even if he was too dumb to actually hit you.'

'Expressed with your characteristic sensitivity. And you're obviously right. The whole thing's terrifying. If I'd been giving my usual patronising nod to a constituent, he'd have got me squarely in the brain.' She closed her eyes again. 'I'm really not sure I want to think about it.'

'Neither do I,' Annie said. 'How are you feeling, anyway?'

'Oh, fine now. Weirdly exhausted, which I'm guessing is an after-effect of the shock plus the sedatives, and a bit of a sore head, but otherwise okay.'

'They're just keeping you in for tests and observations. Nurse reckoned you should be out tomorrow.'

'I had a chat with the consultant when he appeared on his rounds. Seemed pretty switched on, even though he was a Tory.'

'He told you that, did he? The Tory bit, I mean.'

'He did, actually. One of those "I don't share your politics and wouldn't vote for you in a million years, but I do respect your integrity and achievements" conversations. I get those a lot.'

'Mainly from my mother.'

'I don't recall the integrity and achievement bit coming up much from your mother. More the "dyke who stole my daughter", if I recall.'

'She's warmed to you,' Annie said. 'More than she's ever warmed to me, anyway.'

'If you say so.'

'So what happens to you now? In terms of work, I mean.'

'Nothing. I go back to it, as soon as I'm able. Which looks like it should be tomorrow.'

'I didn't mean that. I meant in terms of security, protection. Stopping you getting shot in the head again. That kind of thing.'

'The short answer is I don't know yet. There's a lot been done to try to protect MPs over the last year or two, but in the end you've still got to do the job. I'll speak to the Party and to the Speaker's Office and see if there's more we can do. Locally, we can look at security in the office, but that's fairly tight already and it doesn't stop anyone taking potshots at me in the street. I maybe need to think a bit about how I put myself out there. I don't want to overreact to what's probably just some one-off fuckwit, but I maybe need to be a bit more aware of the security implications of what I'm doing. It's not something I've ever really considered before. Not seriously, anyway. You just don't think it'll happen to you.'

'We may have people who can give you some advice on local stuff. I'm not keen to see you in the firing line again.'

'Me neither, oddly enough.'

'We're living in scary times,' Annie said. 'Who were this bunch of protestors, anyway?'

'As far as I know, a ragbag of random numpties who'd jumped onto the extreme-right bandwagon. Just your average racists and fascists, I'm guessing. They claimed to be supporters of this Bulldog character, but he doesn't represent any organised party these days. He's fallen out with most of the other nationalist groups because he thought they were a bit too establishment.'

'Sounds a nice guy.'

'A real charmer. He's mainly just a grifter, to be honest. Primarily interested in boosting his own profile and bank account.'

'Aren't they all?' Annie said. 'Even my mother. Though she's more interested in power and influence these days. It's people like her who enable and encourage these people.'

'It worries me. Those guys today – and it was mostly guys, though it isn't always – are just being taken for a ride. It's playing with fire.'

'You escaped this time.'

'Yes, thank Christ. But it's getting worse, and we're not taking it seriously enough.' She stopped. 'I'll shut up, though. I don't feel terribly rational about it at the moment, and that's never a good time for a politician to start pontificating.'

'That's why you'll never get to be Prime Minister. Most MPs love pontificating irrationally.'

'Tell me about it. You don't know how much bollocks I've had to listen to in the House.' She closed her eyes. 'Actually, it's quite nice to be out of the firing line for the evening.'

'Maybe not the most apposite metaphor.'

'Probably not. But you know what I mean. I can't remember the last time I was able just to do nothing with a clear conscience.'

That was true enough, Annie thought. When Parliament was sitting, Sheena spent the bulk of the week in the flat she rented in London. The weekends were mostly spent doing constituency business – meetings, surgeries, correspondence – before she headed back south on Sunday evenings. It was a much more demanding life than many people realised.

'Is there anything I can get for you? Apart from fruit and chocolates, I mean.'

Sheena hadn't reopened her eyes and Annie suspected she was on the point of falling asleep again. 'Fruit and chocolates are fine,' Sheena finally responded. 'And maybe something to read. Something really undemanding.'

'I'll see what I can do.' Annie rose from her seat and landed a kiss on Sheena's pale cheek, taking care to avoid the tangle of wires. 'I'll leave you to sleep. See you later on.'

There was a murmured response that Annie couldn't quite decipher. It seemed as if the sedatives, or perhaps simply the mental exhaustion, were kicking back in. She reached out to squeeze Sheena's hand one more time, then straightened and left the room.

Chapter Seven

Clive Bamford laboriously tapped out a few more words on his keyboard, then sat back to appraise the quality of what he'd written. He was never sure whether he loved or hated writing. A bit of both, he supposed, with the love usually just about winning out. At times like this, though, it felt as if hate might be gaining the upper hand.

Although he generally felt satisfied with the outcome, the process of writing didn't come naturally to him. For a start, he lacked the education. He'd always been the cocky one at school, ready to shoot his mouth off at the teachers, playing for the attention and approval of his classmates. When he wasn't suspended, he was studiously ignored by teachers who had better things to do with their time than waste it on him.

He'd left at sixteen, having failed virtually all his GCSEs, and eventually found himself work in the kitchen of an upmarket country house hotel near Buxton. He'd hated every second of it. The pay had been piss-poor, the conditions awful, and the head chef had fancied himself as the next Gordon Ramsay. He'd been more than a match for Ramsay in generating expletives, but his culinary skills were less impressive. The hotel went bust within a year of Clive joining.

In retrospect, that had proved to be a blessing in a very light disguise. He spent a few weeks on the dole, until the jobcentre found him a temporary job in a junior administrative role with the local authority. And Clive had quickly realised he was much less stupid than he'd always assumed.

By the time he'd lost his job at the hotel, he'd begun to wise up a little, finally realising he wasn't in much of a position to make a go of life. The administrative job, although not much in itself, had felt like a second chance and for the first time he'd actually found himself looking forward to going to work each morning. He'd applied himself diligently, demonstrated to his manager that he was more capable than his background suggested. The temporary job became permanent, and within six months he secured a promotion to a more responsible and demanding position.

Now in his late twenties, he was a junior manager in the same local authority. He earned a decent living, had a small but comfortable house on the outskirts of Buxton, and was reasonably content with life. The day-to-day work ticked over, satisfying enough if not exactly stimulating, giving him time to pursue his other interests.

He couldn't remember when he'd first developed his fascination with the arcane material that now dominated his life outside work. Even as that unruly teenager he'd had a mild obsession with the paranormal, always reading supposedly true accounts of ghosts, UFOs and strange phenomena. As he'd grown older his interest had widened and deepened, taking in a wide range of unexplained happenings, and, increasingly, the mechanisms used to conceal what he increasingly saw as the truth.

He'd pitched a few ideas for articles to online specialist magazines and, after several rejections, had finally received a positive response. His first published article had been something about the supposed recurrent UFO sightings in the Longdendale Valley in the north of the county. His own view was that the frequency of sightings could be at least partly explained by the proximity of the flight path into Manchester Airport, but he'd written a balanced piece recounting some of the more interesting experiences and potential theories. The piece now seemed clumsy and amateurish to him, but it had gone down well, and he'd been commissioned to write more.

His reputation was a very niche one, but it was slowly growing. He'd managed to persuade the *Fortean Times* to take one of his pieces, and he was hopeful they'd take more in due course, including possibly the piece he was currently writing. He'd pulled together a number of his pieces into a book, which he'd self-published online. He hadn't sold many, but his name was beginning to be recognised in the right places. He'd been invited to speak at a couple of small-scale conventions, and had begun to receive correspondence from readers interested by his work. Best of all, he'd made a couple of contacts in the national tabloids who had used, with credit, some of his material. He hadn't been entirely pleased with the way the tabloids had sensationalised the content, but it had helped to raise his profile. He felt as if he was finally beginning to atone for his wasted education, slowly gaining respect for his specialist knowledge and expertise.

He was hoping his current work might push him a further rung or two up the reputational ladder. He'd been intrigued that Charlie had mentioned the so-called 'left-hand path' religions during his diatribe at the meeting. As it happened, Clive had for a while been interested in the history of various satanist and occult groups in the UK, some of which designated themselves as 'churches of the left-hand path', and had been considering the possibility of a series of articles on the topic.

Although there were a number of existing books and articles in the area, Clive hoped that his focus on the more recent history would enable him to uncover some new information and insights. He'd also floated the idea with his tabloid contacts, who'd expressed some initial interest.

In his attempt to get the work started, he'd contacted a number of individuals who claimed either to have been involved in such occult groups or to have been affected by their activities. So far, though, he'd found it hard going. These organisations were notoriously secretive, fearful that their aims and activities would be misrepresented. It wasn't surprising that current or past members should be reticent about talking to him. Even so, he'd been disappointed that even those who'd initially agreed to his request for an interview had either changed their minds at the last minute or been reluctant to offer anything more than basic facts. At the moment, the expected new information and insights were proving depressingly elusive.

Partly prompted by Charlie's mention of the subject, he'd decided to have a first shot at drafting an opening to his article. He'd often found that producing those first few paragraphs helped him clarify his thinking and focus his subsequent research and interviews more effectively. He'd booked a day off work and had sat down at his keyboard to write.

So far nothing much was coming. He'd written his first sentence and then deleted it perhaps twenty times so far. He hadn't yet attempted a second sentence. He usually told himself just to write, not to worry about whether it was any good or not. Just get something down. Today even that approach wasn't working. He couldn't manage to make his thoughts cohere into anything even half-sensible.

Eventually, he decided to take a break. Go for a walk to clear his head. Perhaps get himself a coffee. The weather had improved since the previous day, and a weak sun was struggling to force its way through the clouds. His house was on the edge of town, and a walk into the centre might be just what he needed to allow him to mull over the ideas drifting around in his head.

He wondered about calling Greg Wardle to see if he was free to meet. He'd couldn't afford to waste one of his precious days away from work, but Greg was one of the few people he could bounce his thoughts and ideas off. They didn't always agree and Greg couldn't begin to match his own knowledge and erudition, but at least they were broadly on the same wavelength.

As it turned out, Greg's phone went straight to voice-mail. He was presumably tied up in some meeting or other. After a moment's hesitation, Clive pulled on his coat and stepped out into the grey morning. He'd walk down into town, grab himself a coffee in one of the cafes and see if he could remove the fog from his brain.

He was halfway down the street when his mobile rang in his pocket. He pulled it out and glanced at the screen, expecting it to be Greg responding to the message he'd left. But it was a number he didn't recognise.

'Hello?'

'Hi, there.'

The voice sounded familiar but he couldn't immediately place it. 'Yes?'

'It's Rowan. Rowan Wiseman.'

It took him another moment to recognise the name. 'Oh, yes, Rowan. You were at the meeting the other day.

What can I do for you?' He'd given them all his mobile number at the conclusion of the meeting in case any of them wanted to discuss any issues with him. He hadn't seriously expected any of them to take him up on this offer, least of all Rowan.

'I was just wondering if we might meet up sometime. Before the next meeting, I mean. I've got a couple of things I'd like to discuss with you,' she said.

Greg had commented after the meeting that he'd found Rowan Wiseman extremely attractive. Clive had offered some non-committal and vaguely disapproving response, because he felt it was patronising to judge women in those terms. Even so, he had to acknowledge that Greg was right. She was a striking-looking woman. 'When did you have in mind?'

'As soon as possible, really. I'm completely flexible.'

Clive hesitated 'I suppose today's not possible? I've got a day off work. Otherwise, one evening—'

'Today's fine for me. Do you live in town?'

'Pretty much. I'm walking into the centre now, as it happens. Was planning to go for a coffee. Been working on an article but hit a bit of writer's block.'

'That's one of the things I wanted to talk to you about, actually. Your writing. I've read a few of your pieces. They're excellent.'

'Really?' It was rare for Clive to meet anyone who'd actually read his work. 'I'm just starting out really. But it's good to feel I'm making some sort of contribution.'

'That was partly why Charlie and I came to the meeting. We recognised your name and were keen to come along and meet you. Sorry about Charlie, by the way. His heart's in the right place, but he can be a bit opinionated. He enjoys the debate.'

'No worries. So do I. That's the point of doing this kind of thing, isn't it?' He'd almost forgotten the obnoxious Charlie. As far as Clive was concerned, opinionated hadn't been the word. Clive had no idea whether or not Charlie's heart was in the right place, but his brain seemed to have gone AWOL.

'If you're heading into town anyway,' Rowan said, 'we could have a coffee together. It's only a five-minute walk for me.'

'Why not?'

'Well then, that was easy. Fortune must be smiling on us.'

She spoke the last words as if they were more than a familiar platitude. There was something in her manner Clive found mildly disconcerting, but he decided it wasn't exactly unpleasant. 'Looks like it,' he said.

Chapter Eight

'You okay, Zoe? You look a bit tired.' Annie had noticed her colleague stifling recurrent yawns in the morning meeting, though she'd obviously been doing her best to conceal it.

'Just had a bit of a disturbed night.'

'Tell me about it.' Annie had phoned the hospital first thing to check on Sheena. She'd woken in the small hours with a sense that something was wrong, that something further had happened. It had probably been nothing more than the lingering shreds of a bad dream, but the anxiety had felt frighteningly real.

But when she'd called the ward first thing, they'd confirmed that Sheena's condition hadn't changed and she'd had a decent night's sleep. They were still waiting on some of the test results but, all being well, they were likely to release Sheena later in the day. Annie was planning to visit after lunch, in the hope she'd then be able to take Sheena back home.

In the meantime, she was trying to focus on their current major enquiry – the Beeley Moor body, as Stuart Jennings had taken to calling it after the location where it was found. The case troubled her. This wasn't some spontaneous or accidental killing, but something cold-bloodedly planned. The nature of the killing implied there might be more than one killer and that those responsible might repeat the act. And then there was the whole question of those incisions. Was this some ritualistic killing, as Danny Eccles had suggested, or some more mundane form of brutality?

If the killing did have a ritualistic element, that led inescapably to the conclusion that the death might have been some form of human sacrifice. Was it possible that the pattern of cuts carried some religious or similar significance? She had done a cursory online search for images that might relate to the design, but had been unable to find anything relevant. She'd asked her team to follow up in more detail.

It might also be that Danny was wrong. There was no question that the incisions were hard to explain, but perhaps their meaning was more straightforward. Maybe they were intended simply as some kind of message. A warning to others. She knew of gangland murders where the perpetrators had taken photographs of the victim to forward to their rivals. Perhaps the message was merely that this man, whoever he might be, had been selected as a target.

Until they'd identified the victim, there was little point in speculating. Once they could attach a name to that mutilated face, they were likely to have a much better idea of the potential circumstances of his death. Annie was exasperated that so far they lacked even this basic information.

Even so, the morning's briefing had gone well. They'd finally got the full team in place and she and Jennings had managed to pull together a well-balanced and effective group of officers to work on the enquiry. Most were people she'd worked with and respected. There were one or two new faces – new to Annie, at least – and a couple she had less time for. But that was always the way, and the team was as strong as she could have hoped.

She and Jennings had agreed that for the moment much of the investigation was simply the application of standard procedure; the activities that should help determine the victim's identity and identify potential witnesses. Jennings had provided an introduction to the team, giving some background on the nature of the crime, and then handed over to Annie to allocate duties as appropriate. She felt relieved that, for once, Jennings' ego hadn't meant he'd felt the need to run the show.

She'd been pleased by the response from the team. There'd been good questions and some intelligent discussion of the approach and potential options. Everyone seemed engaged and focused. The trick would be to sustain that, particularly if they found themselves struggling to make progress.

Afterwards, she'd sat with Zoe Everett working through the details to ensure nothing had been overlooked, and had noted again that her DS seemed untypically distracted. Annie decided that, for the moment, it was better to stick to business, but couldn't help feeling a nagging concern.

'The key priority is to identify the victim,' she said. 'Until we do that, we're floundering in the dark.'

Zoe nodded. 'I'm hoping he's on the system somewhere. If we've had previous dealings with him, that might tell us a lot.'

'Fingers crossed. And some of those tattoos ought to be distinctive.' They allocated one officer to talk to some of the local tattoo parlours. If the designs were other than off-the-shelf, someone might recall who'd requested them. It was a long shot – they didn't even know if the victim was local – but worth trying. If that failed, and the victim wasn't on the police system, the next step would probably be to release the victim's description, including a description of the tattoos, to the media.

'If those tattoos do indicate he was some kind of far-right activist, should we be talking to some of those people?' Zoe said.

'That's next on my list,' Annie said. 'We may need to be talking to them anyway. I would prefer if we could find some other way of identifying our man first, so we'd have a better idea where to focus our attention. But it's another potential route.' She gave a mock shudder. 'Mind you, those people give me the creeps. And after what happened to Sheena yesterday…'

'Who's taking on that one?' Zoe said.

'I was talking to Stuart about it before the meeting. Obviously, it's not something I can be involved in. I don't care, as long as they give it to someone with a few brain cells. I want to see whoever fired that gun behind bars before he really does kill someone.' She sighed. 'I'm beginning to sound like my mother. Although these days she'd probably find some way of defending the bastard.'

Zoe offered no response, clearly recognising that this was territory best avoided.

'Sorry, Zoe. Shouldn't be venting my frustrations at you. It's not been the easiest twenty-four hours.'

'I can imagine. Poor Sheena – and poor you. Must be a nightmare for you both. Even the thought of it – of what might have happened – scares the hell out of me. It's like our job. You tell yourself nothing can happen to you, but there's always the tiniest possibility that one day it might.'

'Sometimes it feels as if the odds are getting shorter by the day.' Annie leaned back in her chair, momentarily closing her eyes. 'Okay, let's get started. Let's do our bit to apprehend at least one murderous bastard.'

Chapter Nine

Clive Bamford stopped inside the doorway and peered around. His glasses had steamed up as he'd entered the cafe and for a moment he could see nothing at all. Then he realised someone was waving to him from the far corner of the room.

The place was busy, and he had to push his way between the tables to where she was sitting. 'Rowan. Good to see you again.' She looked even more attractive than he remembered, her long bright-red hair set against her black leather jacket. He lowered himself into the seat opposite her, trying to look more relaxed than he was feeling. 'Not been in here before. Good suggestion of yours.'

'I sometimes come in for a coffee first thing,' she said. 'They're happy to let me sit and read, but it gets a bit busy at this time. They do decent food, as well.' She gestured towards the espresso in front of her. 'And excellent coffee.' There was a book spreadeagled on the table next to the coffee cup. A paperback with a pentagram on the front cover, and the title *Another Path to Enlightenment*.

'I might get a sandwich.' Clive picked up the menu, mainly as an alternative to staring at Rowan Wiseman. He hadn't previously registered the extraordinary emerald green of her eyes. 'Are you having something?'

'They do a hummus thing that's very good. I'm a vegan,' she added, as if some justification was required for her choice. 'This is one of the few places round here that does a decent vegan selection.'

'Sounds good,' he said. He'd been considering a salt beef sandwich, but that suddenly seemed inappropriate. 'I'll give it a try.'

He was about to ask about the paperback, but was interrupted by the waitress coming to take their order. He'd been intending to order a cappuccino with the hummus wrap but again found himself echoing her order of a large espresso. 'Anyway,' he said, once the waitress had departed, 'what can I do for you?'

'It might be more a question of what I can do for you.'

There was no edge of innuendo in her voice, but he realised he was blushing anyway. 'How do you mean?'

'I told you that Charlie and I are both big fans of your work?'

Her words did nothing to lessen his embarrassment. 'That's very kind of you. I'm just a beginner, really.'

'No, you're very good. We read an awful lot of stuff about the subjects you cover, and you're really one of the best.'

'I don't know—'

'No, seriously. I mean, you're very knowledgeable and you do your research. Your interest in the material shines through, but you're objective and balanced in the way you write about it.'

He was saved further embarrassment by the waitress arriving with their coffee. He took an immediate sip of the coffee to buy himself some time before he had to respond. 'That's very kind of you,' he offered finally.

'Like I said, it's one of the reasons we came along to the group. I was going to say something at the time, but thought it might be a bit awkward with the others there.'

Clive really wasn't sure where this was going, although he felt content enough for it to continue. 'I hope the meeting wasn't a disappointment. We were all just getting to know each other, really.'

'Things like that always need a bit of time to bed down. I'm sure you can make it work.' She paused. 'Anyway, Charlie and I heard on the grapevine that you were doing some work on the "left-hand path" religions. Is that right?'

Clive looked up at her, slightly startled. 'Yes. Well, sort of. Where did you hear that?'

'I'm not sure, to be honest. Just something someone said to me when I was enthusing about one of your articles, I think.'

Clive knew he'd been phoning around fairly indiscriminately trying to find contacts prepared to assist him with his research. That was the difficulty of researching an area like this. The organisations involved tended to be highly secretive and to lack any kind of conventional management structure. It was difficult to identify the key players, so all you could do was keep throwing out feelers in the hope they'd eventually reach the right people. On reflection, he supposed it wasn't surprising that word of his interest might have spread more widely, though It left him feeling slightly uneasy.

'I'm looking at doing something along those lines,' he said. 'I thought I could maybe add something new, especially on more recent developments. But it's not proving easy to research.'

'I'm not surprised. That's where we may be able to help you.'

'Any help gratefully received. I'm just hitting dead ends.'

'It's an area where Charlie and I have developed our own interests,' she said. She smiled and tapped the paperback book. 'Part of our continuing search for spiritual enlightenment.'

For the first time, it occurred to Clive that Rowan and Charlie might be an item. He hadn't really thought about it at the meeting, and they somehow hadn't seemed like a couple. But there seemed to be something between them that was more intense than mere friendship.

'I thought what they offered was the opposite of enlightenment.' He'd intended the words as a joke. As Clive understood it, one of the characteristics of the so-called 'left-hand path' religions was a willingness to embrace the darker, less positive aspects of humanity in their quest for salvation. Almost at once, though, he regretted his flippancy.

She gazed at him for a moment, and he found himself struggling to meet those emerald eyes. He felt like a schoolboy caught out by the teacher in a very basic error. 'You know better than that,' she said. 'It's much more complex and nuanced.'

'I was just playing, well, I suppose devil's advocate might not be exactly the most appropriate phrase here. I realise that we're not just talking about satanism.'

She laughed and he felt himself forgiven for his previous words. 'There are certainly satanists among the left-path followers, though not all of us are satanists. And the meaning of satanism is much more subtle than most people appreciate. Most so-called satanists don't believe in a literal Satan, but more in recognising the realities of the world we inhabit.'

Some of this sounded like part of a standard speech. Clive wondered how often she might have delivered these words, or something like them, and to what audience. 'That's exactly what I want to understand better. I've read plenty about Aleister Crowley and those historical occultist types, but I get the sense those are just the tip of the iceberg, and that there are many more recent developments.'

'That's very much the case. That's what attracted Charlie and me to the field, really. There are some genuinely innovative and creative spiritual ideas emerging.'

'It sounds fascinating.' Clive was never really sure what the word 'spiritual' meant, and he suspected many of those who used the word would have struggled to define it for him. But he was quite happy to go along with whatever Rowan Wiseman might have to tell him. 'I'd love to be able to talk to a few people, get a better understanding of what it's all about. That would help me to focus my research more effectively. At the moment, I feel as if I'm just blundering about trying to get someone to talk to me.'

'People tend to be wary of talking because they think their words will be misconstrued or misrepresented. People think we're all devil-worshippers prancing about naked in covens, but of course it's nothing like that. That's why Charlie and I thought it would be worth talking to you. We know your work and we trust you.'

'I should warn you, if I were to write something, it wouldn't just be a whitewash. I don't do PR. I try to be objective and to tell it as I see it.' Clive had a sudden unease that he was being set up, that they might be trying to exploit what little reputation he had for their own ends.

But that sounded absurd. He was a nobody. He had no reputation to exploit, other than among a tiny band of followers.

'That's the point,' she said. 'We don't want someone to do a PR piece. All we want is for someone to understand what we do, what we're about, and to represent it accurately. If you have doubts or reservations about what you hear, then we'd want you to express those. But equally if you see some value in our ideas, we'd hope you'd say so.'

The waitress interrupted them briefly to deliver their wraps, giving Clive a few moments to collect his thoughts. He'd finished his espresso and was wishing he'd ordered a longer drink. 'That's how I try to work. I aim to be as objective as possible. I think it's important to express an opinion where appropriate, but only on the basis of the evidence.' He was conscious he was drifting into pomposity, but Rowan seemed enthused by what he was saying.

She took a bite of her wrap. She did so very elegantly, he thought, by contrast with his own undignified struggles with the sloppy filling. She chewed for a moment before responding. 'That's exactly what we're looking for. Somebody who's prepared to listen properly to what we have to say, and to think about its meaning and its implications.'

'There are too many so-called commentators who allow their own prejudices and preconceptions to influence their thinking.' This was something of a hobby horse for Clive, one of the topics he and Greg Wardle debated endlessly. 'We need to be critical, but keep an open mind. Not simply dismiss approaches or concepts because they don't fit with our predetermined ideas.'

'That comes across in your writing. That's why we thought you were the right person to talk to.' She was smiling now, and he realised he'd been actively seeking her approval, wanting her to be impressed by his intelligence and expertise. He wondered again whether she might be playing with him, but he couldn't help feeling gratified. 'That's much appreciated.'

'You're exactly what we need.' She smiled at him, and once more he felt the force of those emerald eyes.

'What would be the next step?'

'I think the next step is for us to effect some introductions for you. Arrange for you to meet some of the right people.'

'You could do that? That would be enormously helpful.'

'Charlie and I are just small fry, you know, so I can't make any promises. But I think we can open a few doors. Obviously, it'll be up to you how you handle it from there.'

'That's very good of you.'

She smiled at him in a manner that made him wonder once more about the nature of her relationship with Charlie. He told himself it was really none of his business. He was probably ten years her junior and well out of her league anyway, though in fairness he might have thought the same about Charlie. 'I'd better run, actually. Got some things to do this afternoon. But really glad I was able to catch up with you, Clive. I'm sure you're exactly the man we need.'

As far as he could recall, it was the first time she'd called him by his name. It felt as if he'd been inducted into her inner circle. 'I hope we can make this work.'

'I'll be in touch in the next few days. See you soon.'

Almost instantaneously, even before he could offer a response, she was gone, striding towards the door of the cafe. Clive blinked, slightly taken aback. Her hummus wrap still sat, uneaten beyond that first bite, on the table in front of him. Her coffee looked almost untouched.

For a moment, he sat wondering quite what had just happened. After a minute or two, it occurred to him that, whatever else Rowan Wiseman might have done, she'd been smart enough to leave him with the bill.

Chapter Ten

'I can walk, you know.'

'You heard the nurse,' the hospital porter said. 'More than my job's worth.'

'We're only going to the back entrance,' Sheena Pearson said. 'I don't need a wheelchair.'

'Anyway,' the porter went on, 'I thought you were supposed to be a socialist. You wouldn't want to put me out of a job.'

'I am a socialist. That's why I don't want to exploit my fellow worker.'

'Fair day's work for a fair day's pay, and all that. And if I'm just pushing you along a corridor, I'm not being asked to do something more difficult, am I?'

'Okay, you win. I'll let you push me.'

Annie Delamere watched the exchange with relieved amusement. She'd been anxious to see Sheena all day. The nagging fear that had woken Annie in the early hours was soothed now by the sight of her partner's bright smile. Aside from the bandage, Annie thought Sheena looked pretty much herself. It would be good to get her home.

A gaggle of TV and newspaper reporters had been stationed outside the main entrance for most of the morning, and the police had decided to take Sheena to a rear entrance where Annie had left her car ready. Annie knew that Sheena's preference would have been to chat to the reporters, but she'd been persuaded by the powers-that-be that it was better to avoid what might turn into a media circus. There'd be plenty of time to talk to the media later.

Annie still wondered whether Sheena should have been provided with more public protection. Everyone from the Prime Minister downwards had publicly expressed their shock at what had happened and there was a substantial police presence here at the hospital, but Annie still felt concerned that the risks were being underplayed. The tacit assumption seemed to be that yesterday's incident had been a one-off, just the action of some trigger-happy halfwit. That might well be true, Annie thought, but it did little to relieve her own fears.

As it was, the plan was simply to slip quietly out of the back door. A single uniformed officer had been stationed there, but to Annie that felt like little more than a token gesture. Still, Sheena would be left exposed only for a few seconds, with Annie's car waiting in the pick-up bay just ahead of them. As the porter pushed Sheena out, Annie opened the rear door, ready to usher her into the car. 'Come on, missie. Let's get you home.'

'This must be what it's like to be a minister. Getting transported and chauffeured everywhere.' Sheena eased herself up from the wheelchair, giving the porter a friendly glare that clearly dared him even to think about offering to help.

'Only a matter of time before you find out, I imagine,' Annie said. She nodded to the porter and the waiting police officer. 'Thanks, both. I can take care of her from here—'

Even as she spoke the words, she felt as if she was tempting fate, but she hadn't expected her claim to be tested so immediately. The blast of the gunshot was deafening, echoing between the surrounding hospital wings. It was followed almost at once by the sound of shattering glass, and the shrill wailing of an alarm.

Almost before the echoes had died away, Annie was already beyond conscious thought, acting on instinct and training alone. As far as she could see, no one out here had been struck by the shot, but there was no way of knowing what might have happened once the bullet had passed through the shattered hospital window. Not pausing to reflect, she bundled Sheena into the rear of the car. 'Lie down. As low as you can.' For once her partner put up no argument.

The uniformed officer and the porter were both standing frozen, both clearly at a loss how to respond to what had happened. Annie gestured for them to get back into the hospital. 'Get hold of whoever's supposed to be in charge of this show,' she shouted. 'Tell them to organise backup. And to have the area sealed off. No one to come in or out. Go quickly!' She crouched down behind the car, trying to calculate where the shot had come from. The smashed window was behind to her right, which suggested that the shot had been fired from somewhere in the car park ahead. She peered over the roof of the car, squinting for any sign of movement.

A fine rain was still falling and visibility was limited, but she was confident that there was nothing there, other than an occasional passing car. Somewhere behind the hospital building, she could hear the rising wail of police sirens. At least the cavalry was on its way. She remained crouching by the car for another minute, her eyes fixed on the car park ahead of her, but could still see nothing. She took several deep breaths to calm her nerves, scrambled round to the driver's door and threw herself into the car, keeping her head low.

'You okay?'

Sheena was half-lying on the rear seat, her face ashen. 'I've been shot at twice in as many days. What do you think?'

'I know. Look, we're too vulnerable here if there is still anyone out there. I'm going to pull up on the pavement, get us as close to the door as I can, then we can both get inside and find out what the hell's happening.'

'You think anyone's likely to know what's happening?' Sheena was looking more shocked than Annie had ever seen her, her usual bravado for once absent.

'They might have more of a clue than we do. Though I wouldn't bet on it.' Annie peered through the rear window of the car, still alert for any sign of movement. She felt absurdly exposed, conscious that the gunman could be anywhere out there, that the gunsights could still be trained on them. She started the car and manoeuvred it into a spot immediately adjacent to the rear entrance. 'Okay, Shee. I'll go first. When I open your door, don't hesitate. Just keep your head down and get your backside into the hospital.'

She scrambled out of the car and pulled open the rear door, using it to shield Sheena as, head down, she clambered on to the pavement and into the hospital entrance. Annie paused briefly for another scan of the car park – there was still no sign of movement – then she followed, leaving her car abandoned on the pavement outside.

'Serve you right if you get a ticket. I believe they're very strict.' Sheena was waiting inside. The flippancy of her words was belied by the still-horrified expression on her face.

'Come on. Let's see what's going on.' Annie led them down the hospital corridor past a waiting area for one of the outpatient departments. This was where the bullet had ended up. The room was deserted, the cold wind and rain blowing in through the broken window.

It took them another few minutes to find their way through the maze of corridors to the main foyer. A cluster of uniformed officers was gathered inside the entrance, in the middle of a briefing from the officer in command. As they approached, one of the officers moved to intercept them. 'I'm sorry, madam. Can I ask you either to return to your ward or department or, if you're a visitor, to join the group in the cafe down there? There's been an incident outside, and we're keeping everyone in here as a precaution until we've resolved the situation.'

Annie took a breath, trying to contain her anger and frustration. 'Yes, I'm only too aware of that, funnily enough.' She brandished her warrant card. 'DI Annie Delamere. This is Sheena Pearson MP.'

The officer looked as if he'd been caught out in some moderately serious misdemeanour. 'I'm sorry, I didn't realise...'

Annie was tempted to vent her fury on the man in front of her, but managed to control her temper. 'No reason why you should have. Can I speak to whoever's in command here? I might be able to offer some information.'

She waited impatiently while the officer spoke to the figure who had been addressing the group. She knew him slightly. Chief Inspector Alan Cowley, she recalled. She'd had a few dealings with him, and found him efficient if a little brusque. She watched as he concluded his briefing and made his way across to her.

'Annie Delamere, isn't it?'

'Well remembered, Alan,' she said curtly. 'This is Sheena Pearson. Can I ask you what the hell's going on?'

Cowley blinked at the repressed anger in her tone. 'I wish I knew. I've only just arrived myself—'

'There should have been a senior presence from the start,' Annie said. 'After what happened yesterday.'

'With the benefit of hindsight...' Cowley stopped, clearly recognising that his usual PR emollience wasn't going to work here. 'No, you're right. We underestimated the risk. I'm sorry.' He nodded to Sheena. 'Delighted to meet you, Ms Pearson. I wish it could have been in other circumstances.'

'So do we,' Annie said. Her anger had lessened a little, and she at least felt gracious enough to acknowledge Cowley's honesty. From everything she'd heard, he was a sound enough copper, and no doubt struggling with scant resources as they all were. He wasn't a smooth operator like Stuart Jennings and had probably progressed as far as he was likely to in the force, but he'd always do a decent job. Whatever mistakes had been made, he looked in his element now, confidently marshalling a team to deal with an undoubted crisis.

'The shot was fired at the rear of the hospital, I understand?' Cowley said. 'We should have had more people stationed out there.'

Annie had noticed a large map of the hospital estate set on the wall of the reception for the benefit of visitors. She led Cowley and Sheena over to it. 'We were planning to leave through this entrance.' She pointed a finger at the map. 'I'd left my car in the pick-up bay so we could get Sheena out quickly. The bullet hit the window here. So it looked to me as if it was fired from somewhere in the car park out here.' She gestured towards the relevant area on the map.

'We've got the site sealed off,' Cowley said. 'If there's anyone still out there, we'll get them. One way or another,' he added, ominously.

'My guess is that they're long gone,' Annie said. 'After the first shot, there was no sign of any movement. There were only a few minutes before you began to arrive, but I'm guessing it was probably enough.'

Cowley nodded. 'We'll get the CCTV cameras checked urgently. There must be decent coverage of the car parks outside.' He paused. 'I hope this doesn't sound too insensitive, Ms Pearson, but the main question at the moment is whether this person has a personal grudge against you, or whether they're a more general danger.'

'They're a danger either way,' Annie pointed out. 'Even if Sheena was the target, other people could easily have been hit both today and yesterday.'

'Definitely,' Cowley said, morosely. 'So I think we have to assume there's a significant public risk. Okay, I'll relay that up the line.' He allowed them a faint smile. 'Let the senior ranks earn their money for once, eh? I'd better get back to the operation here but you'll both need to give a statement. We're taking one from the porter who was with you too. For now we're mostly concerned with securing the premises. There's still a chance our shooter might be outside.'

'Good luck,' Annie said.

'Thanks,' Cowley said. 'I have a feeling we're going to need it with this one.'

Chapter Eleven

'Jesus,' Jennings said. 'Do you people always attract trouble like this?'

'It's a knack.' Zoe Everett was clearly focused on navigating the single-track road in the thickening mist. 'Some people collect stamps.'

Jennings had just taken a call from Annie Delamere, updating him on events at the hospital. His first response had been, 'So I guess you're not going to be in for a while, then?' Even he'd realised his words had sounded graceless in the circumstances. But that was what happened when he was extracted from the warmth of his office and forced to attend a crime scene in the back end of nowhere on a day like this.

Annie had responded, quite reasonably, that she'd be back in as soon as she'd been allowed to leave the hospital site and had managed to get Sheena Pearson home and under appropriate protection.

'Yes, of course,' Jennings had agreed, wearily. 'In other news, it looks like we have a second one.'

'Another one?'

'Another naked body with its throat slashed.'

'You're joking.'

'Wouldn't be that much of a laugh, would it? Zoe and I are heading out there now. Christ knows where we are.'

'Somewhere between Buxton and Ashbourne,' Zoe added. 'Beyond that, I'm just following the satnav.'

Jennings had finished the call with Annie and sat watching what was visible of the passing landscape. Mostly it was just hedgerows and trees looming briefly out of the rain, with the occasional glimpse of the open moorland beyond. Even on a fine day, this would be a remote area. On a day like this, with the weather closing in, it felt a thousand miles from anywhere.

He hadn't exactly expected a quiet life when he'd moved over here – a posting in Major Crimes was never likely to result in that – but he hadn't expected things to be quite so eventful. Mutilated naked corpses. MPs under fire. For a while now, he'd had the sense the whole country had gone off the rails, that the calm and measured society he'd grown up in had been replaced by something much less stable. Passing through this bleak landscape, it felt as if some of that might be coming even closer to home.

Ahead of them, through the thickening drizzle, he could see the steady pulse of blue lights. 'Looks like we're in the right place, then,' Jennings observed.

Zoe slowed the car. Ahead, the road forked, with the main road curving over to the left and a rougher track diverging off to the right. A faded sign read 'Higher Wenlow Farm' with an arrow pointing along the track. 'That's the address,' she said. 'Should have brought a four-by-four.'

Jennings nodded. 'And, as ever, they've picked the right bloody day for it. Some of our killers have no consideration. Let's go and see what's going on.'

They bounced their way down the track into a cluttered farmyard. There was a large open barn to their right, housing an array of farm machinery. Ahead of them was a large if shabby-looking farmhouse, with two patrol cars parked outside, lights still flashing. Jennings climbed out into the cold afternoon. He pulled up the hood of his heavy waterproof, but he could already tell it would offer limited protection against the persistent rain.

A uniformed officer was hurrying towards them, slowing as he recognised the identity of the new arrivals. Jennings nodded to him. 'Afternoon, Dick. You drew the short straw, did you?'

PC Dick Kenwright grinned and nodded. 'Story of my life.' He was a large red-faced man with a strong Derbyshire accent, very much the copper you'd want beside you in any difficult situation.

'What's the story?'

'Farmer here found the body. Or at least his dog did. Out on the moorland out back.'

'What you're telling me is that I've got further to walk?'

'Aye, there is that. And nothing pleasant to see when you get there, by all accounts.'

'So I understand. Where's our farmer?'

'Back in the house. He knows you'll be wanting to talk to him.'

'We'll take a look at the scene and have a chat with him on the way back.' Jennings turned to Zoe. 'Shall we go for a stroll?'

'Perfect weather for it,' she said.

They left Kenwright and made their way along the side of the farmhouse. Jennings noted that, although they were presumably on private land, the route they were taking was a designated footpath. That might prove significant when it came to investigating quite how and why the body had come to be up here.

After a few minutes, they arrived at a line of fencing that marked the edge of the farmyard itself, with a gate set across the path ahead of them. Jennings peered into the drizzle. 'Wonder how much further it is?' he said, morosely.

'Too far,' Zoe said.

The path ahead looked uninviting, overgrown and muddy from the rain. Jennings trudged forward, trying to keep to the drier edges of the path. As they walked, the ground descended and then rose again. Somewhere in the distance they could hear the bleating of sheep, but everything was lost in the blur of rain and mist. Then, as they trudged upwards, a thicket of trees loomed unexpectedly out of the rain. As they drew closer, Jennings saw that the woodland was partly obscured by the white bulk of a crime-scene tent. Tim Sturgeon, the crime scene manager, was standing inside the entrance, talking earnestly on a mobile phone. They climbed towards him, and he waved a greeting and gestured for them to enter, mouthing 'Be with you in a second.'

'Are we okay to go in?' Jennings said. 'Where's the body?'

Sturgeon finished his call and then turned to them. 'Sorry about that. Trying to drum up more resources. Not the easiest place to work in. Yes, you're fine to go in. The body's up the hill in the trees. We couldn't get the tent in there, so we're just using one of the small portable ones. We've set up this mainly just to help keep dry.'

'Must be fun for the CSIs.'

Sturgeon shrugged. 'Laugh a minute. But it's Danny Eccles leading it. He always keeps cheerful.'

'We'll go and have a chat in a sec. I take it this is similar to our other body?'

'Almost identical, from what I understand. Naked white male, probably twenties. Same kind of mutilations.'

Jennings turned to Zoe. 'Shall we go and talk to Danny?'

To his surprise, she appeared to hesitate. 'Do you mind if I stay here for the moment?' She looked as if she were about to say something more, then stopped.

Jennings' first instinct was to tell her not to be so bloody daft, but he had the sense her reluctance was motivated by something more than the weather or the prospect of viewing a body. He'd seen enough of her to know that she wasn't normally squeamish or uncooperative. Now wasn't the moment to enquire. He'd have to have a word with Annie Delamere when she returned. Jennings had always prided himself on his people management skills, and there were times when that seemed the most demanding part of the job. 'See you in a minute, then.'

He made his way round the side of the tent into the woodland. The trees were clustered thickly on the summit, standing out starkly in the otherwise largely empty moorland. It was an odd, slightly unnatural location, Jennings thought.

The smaller protective tent was in a narrow clearing ahead of him, a pale ghostlike presence in the verdant gloom. Danny Eccles, clad in some waterproof variant of his usual white suit, was emerging from the interior.

'Having fun in there?' Jennings said.

'Not so's you'd notice. Bit claustrophobic. Not much space to share with a badly mutilated corpse.'

'I'll take your word for it. I hear we've another one.'

'Take a look, if you like. Long as you don't actually go inside. But, yeah, pretty much the same. Throat cut in the same way. Same, or at least very similar, cuts to the chest. Again, my guess is that there were made before death.'

'And the killing took place here?'

'Looks like it, from the amount of blood.'

'Any idea how they might have got him here?'

'Not sure. There's a road runs across the moorland in that direction.' He pointed off into the trees. 'My guess is they either approached from there, or they brought him down the footpath past the farmhouse. But that would carry a greater risk of being spotted.'

'I'll get the roads checked out. I'm guessing the chances of any witnesses or CCTV are limited. How long do you reckon the body's been here?'

'I'd guess since last night. Yesterday at most.'

'That gives us a relatively tight window to work with. What about ID?'

'No sign of anything around. But this one's also obligingly tattooed. A couple of distinctive-looking ones.'

'We'll get them checked out. But that would fit with the last one. Interesting, if so.'

'Starts to suggest a pattern, doesn't it?'

'Definitely. Though God knows what sort of pattern. And it might just be coincidence. Or gang-on-gang stuff, maybe.'

'Neither of them looked the tough-guy type, physically at least.'

'Maybe that's why they ended up dead.' Jennings looked up at the rain-heavy sky. 'Don't know whether you're worse off inside the tent, or out here in the rain.'

'Trust me,' Eccles said. 'It's worse in the tent.'

–

'Really does feel like the back of beyond, doesn't it?'

'We're not that far from Buxton,' Zoe said. 'But you'd never know it. Don't imagine this landscape has changed much in centuries, other than repairs to the dry-stone walling.'

She and Jennings were making their way back along the path to the farmhouse. The rain had grown heavier and they both had their heads down under their heavy waterproof hoods. Jennings couldn't see Zoe's expression, and there was no clue from her voice how she was feeling.

As they reached the front of the house, Jennings waved to Dick Kenwright, still stationed by the rear gate. Kenwright returned a cheerful thumbs-up, not obviously fazed by his long period in the pouring rain. Jennings pressed the doorbell.

After a moment, they heard the sound of bolts being drawn back. The door opened and a gaunt face peered out at them. Jennings showed his warrant card. 'DCI Jennings and DS Everett. Can we have a word?'

The man nodded and opened the door fully. He was taller and younger than Jennings had initially assumed, his thinning hair cut short. He looked anxious, his face pale in the gloomy daylight. 'Sorry about all the security. To be honest, I'm a bit freaked out by what's happened.'

'It's always wise to be cautious,' Jennings said. 'Though I think you're unlikely to be in any personal danger, Mr...?'

'Miller. Tom Miller. I'm sure you're right. But it's not a nice thing to find on your land.'

'That's your land out there, is it? Beyond the fence, I mean.'

'Aye, all mine. Sheep-farming.' He gestured for the two police officers to follow him into a comfortable-looking sitting room. The furnishings and decor were more modern than Jennings had expected from the exterior of the building. 'Can I get you a tea or coffee?' He waved them to take a seat.

'No, that's fine. We'll not keep you long. We'll need to take a formal statement from you in due course, but I wanted to have a chat while things were fresh in your mind.'

'Not sure how much I can help you.' Miller lowered himself into one of the armchairs opposite. 'But fire away.'

'You found this body earlier this morning?'

'About half ten, eleven, something like that. I'd just let Beth – that's the dog – out for a bit of exercise. She went racing off, like she does sometimes. But then she didn't come back, which isn't like her. So I went to find her and – well, there it was.'

'I assume you're up and about early. The dog, Beth, didn't show any signs of interest in that area earlier? I'm just trying to get a sense of how long the body might have been there.'

'We hadn't been out that way earlier. I've got another stretch of land off the other side of the road, and we were there first thing. So that was the first time today Beth had been at the back.'

'What about yesterday?'

'Oh, aye. We were out there yesterday afternoon.'

'Beth showed no signs of any abnormal behaviour then?'

'She's a daft dog most of the time, but, no, nothing out of the ordinary.'

Jennings exchanged a glance with Zoe. From Miller's account, it seemed almost certain the killing had occurred over the previous night, which aligned with Danny Eccles' judgement. That gave them a relatively precise timing for checking out any sightings of suspicious activity in the area. It wasn't a lot, but it was something.

'Do you see or hear anything unusual yourself last night, Mr Miller?'

'Nothing, I'm afraid. I'm always in bed by nine, and not much disturbs me till the morning.'

'So someone could have come down the footpath and you wouldn't have heard.'

'Probably, to be honest. I mean, my bedroom's on that side of the house so it's possible I'd have heard if someone had come past. But, like I say, I do usually sleep very soundly.'

'We understand there's a road passes by the far side of your land. Is it possible they could have come from that direction?'

'More than possible, I'd say. If you were going to take someone to that spot without being seen, it's more accessible from that side than this. There's woodland by the road where you could hide a vehicle, and the ground's relatively flat.'

Jennings nodded. 'That's been very helpful, Mr Miller. As I say, I'll get one of the team to take a formal statement from you, just for the record, but I hope we won't need to disturb you too much from here. You're happy for us to continue our investigations out there? We'll try not to cause too much disruption.'

'Yes, of course. If you need anything, just knock on the door.'

Miller led them to the front door. As he opened it, they caught the chill blast of the wind and rain. The weather seemed worse than ever. 'Don't envy your lads out there. It's the devil's own place at the best of times.' Miller made it sound as if the description was more than just a figure of speech.

Jennings was already heading for the car, waving his farewells as he pulled his hood over his head. 'One of those days,' he shouted back, 'when I'm only too glad to have reached the exalted rank of DCI.'

Chapter Twelve

'Didn't expect you in yet.'

Annie looked up to see Jennings poking his head around the door of the large office. 'They decided it was safe to release us from the hospital. Looks like whoever shot at Sheena legged it pretty much immediately. Typical, though. Busy weekday afternoon, but so far no witnesses. They're checking all the CCTV footage but no luck yet. They don't even know if the shooter left by car or on foot.'

'It won't stay like that for long.' Jennings sat himself opposite her. 'They'll get something.'

'Who's been allocated to the investigation?' Annie asked.

'I've put Andy Dwyer in charge. He'll do a decent job.'

DI Andy Dwyer was a little younger than Annie, but already seemed destined for higher things. She knew him a little but she'd never warmed to him, although he had a decent reputation. The word was that he was ambitious and that he had the political skills to support his ambition, and she'd seen a few instances of that in her dealings with him. But in this case, it might work in Sheena's favour. This would be a high-profile case and Dwyer would be keen not to mess it up. 'Sounds a good choice.'

'How is she?'

'She's fine physically. They completed all the tests and found no cause for concern. Emotionally – well, let's say she's a bit shaken.'

'I can imagine. Yesterday was one thing, but today...'

'Yesterday looked like some numpty waving a gun around. Today we know she's being targeted.'

'We'll throw everything at it. You know that, don't you?' For once, Jennings sounded entirely sincere.

'Of course. I mean, we would anyway. But targeting an MP is taking us into scary territory.'

'Not the first instance.'

'No, but that makes it even worse.'

'What's she going to do?'

'She won't let it stop it doing her job. But that's Sheena. I need to persuade her to be suitably cautious. She's been talking to the Party and to the Speaker's Office about what can be done. But if there's a sniper out there, there's only so much you can do. She can't do constituency surgeries wearing a Kevlar vest.'

'What about at home? To be honest, I was a bit surprised you came in. I thought you'd have wanted to stay with her. Not that I'm not pleased to see you back,' he added, perhaps a moment too late.

'If it had been left to me, I'd have stayed with her. But Sheena was insistent I should come in. We've got decent security at the house and there's a police presence there for the moment. She said there was nothing I could do there. She was right, I suppose, but I'm still not sure I did the right thing.'

'It scares the hell out of me,' Jennings said. 'And not just because it's currently happening on my watch.'

'If it helps, I do come bearing one bit of good news.'

He looked up. 'Really? We could do with some of that.'

'Our first victim,' she said. 'The Beeley Moor body. Looks like we might have an ID.'

'Go on.'

'Turns out he was on the system. Fingerprints and DNA. Couple of fairly petty misdemeanours as a teenager. A drunk and disorderly that cost him a night in the cells. Then a shoplifting offence. Nothing serious, but enough to put him on our radar.'

'So who is he?'

'Name of Darren Parkin. Last address we have is in Loscoe. From the files it looks like it's probably the family home. I've checked the electoral roll and the occupants are still a Mr and Mrs Parkin, so even if Darren had moved out, they're presumably his next of kin.'

'Good work.'

'I didn't do much,' Annie said. 'But, yes, it's potentially a big step forward. At least gives us some insights into Parkin's private life.'

'And how he came to be naked on Beeley Moor with his throat cut? That must be a hell of a private life.'

'Though quite possibly one his parents knew nothing about, of course. But I hope they'll at least be able to give us some leads. I was just waiting for you to get back before heading over there.'

'You planning to take Zoe with you?'

'We're going to have to break the news to the Parkins. Zoe would be useful. She's good at that kind of thing.'

'How does Zoe seem to you?'

'Not quite her usual self, if that's what you mean.'

'That's exactly what I mean. She was behaving a bit strangely when we were out together earlier. Nearly lost my rag with her, to be honest, but thought there might be something I wasn't aware of.'

'I don't know exactly. I thought she seemed tired. Tired and anxious. Disturbed by something.'

'Maybe something at home?'

'Not that I'm aware of. Not that she'd necessarily tell me. She's a fairly private individual. I'll have a go at talking to her about it.'

'We all have off-days,' Jennings said. 'But I need everyone fully focused at the moment. The Chief will be breathing down my neck on this case and on Sheena's. If Zoe can't hack it, for whatever reason, I need to know.'

'I get the message. I'm sure it's something and nothing but I'll talk to her.' Annie was keen to move the conversation on. 'Anything I should know about the second body before I go and see the Parkins?'

'Zoe can fill you in on the detail. But it looks like the same MO. Similar-looking victim – young, white male. If he turns out to be on the system too, we might have something to work with. As with the first, looks like he was killed on the spot. The spot being even more remote than the first. Which means it'll be even harder to find potential witnesses or CCTV.'

'Our killer seems to like getting away from it all.'

'Killer or killers. I'm struggling to see how this can be the work of one person.'

'That's what worries me. The whole thing's disturbing,' Annie said. 'Whatever the motives. Right, I'll go and grab Zoe, and we'll see what the Parkins can tell us.'

'I'll leave you to it,' Jennings said, pushing himself to his feet. 'And good luck.'

'Thanks,' she said. 'At the moment I'll take any luck that's going.'

Chapter Thirteen

'Must be the one at the end,' Zoe Everett said.

'Numbering always seems cock-eyed on estates like this,' Annie said.

'Probably because they keep squeezing in more and more houses. It's a bit of a jumble, isn't it?'

Loscoe was a former mining village in the heart of the county, north of Derby. Like many of the towns and villages in the area, it had undergone a transformation in recent decades. The pits that had once sustained the area were long gone, along with the slag heaps and pit buildings that had once dominated places like this. The land around had been landscaped and, as far as possible, returned to its former rural state. Only the occasional glimpse of a remaining set of headstocks, retained for heritage purposes, gave any sense of what this region had once been.

The result was a sometimes disconcerting mix of country and city. Through the houses, it was possible to see green open fields and gentle hills, but the houses were often rows of narrow terraces of a type more commonly found in urban locations. Many of the people living in these villages commuted to work in and around Derby or Nottingham. The area wasn't exactly poor, but Annie knew there were significant pockets of deprivation.

The Parkins' address was in an estate on the edge of the village. Most of the houses looked as if they dated back to the 1970s, although some parts of the estate appeared much newer. The house was at the far end of what had been the original central road in the estate, now criss-crossed with numerous side avenues. It was a pleasant-looking bungalow, set a little back from the road, with a neatly tended front garden. It looked like the residence of an older, probably retired couple. Not the kind of place she could imagine a young man like Darren Parkin living. But then they knew almost nothing about Darren Parkin, which was why they were here.

As they climbed out of the car, Zoe gestured almost imperceptibly towards the neighbouring house, another similar bungalow. 'Literal twitching curtains.'

Annie gave a surreptitious glance back and saw that she was right. Someone in the neighbouring house had pulled back the net curtain and was peering out at them. 'Must be a quiet day in Loscoe.'

'Judging from the pristine state of these gardens, every day's a quiet day. Wish mine was as tidy as this.'

The rain had stopped and a faint late-afternoon sun was struggling through the clouds. Annie led the way to the Parkins' front door. The whole house looked well-maintained, Annie thought. The exterior had been repainted in the last year or two, and the windows were spotlessly clean. It wasn't a luxurious or imposing house, but she guessed the owners were well enough off. She pressed the doorbell.

The door was opened so promptly that their arrival must have been observed here too. Clearly, this wasn't an area that received many unexpected visitors. The door was held on a chain, and a face peered out at them.

'Mr Parkin?'

'Yes?'

Annie held her warrant card close to the opening. 'DI Delamere and DS Everett. I wondered if we might have a word with you?'

'Police?' The door closed and then reopened, this time with the chain removed. 'Is this about Darren?'

'I'm afraid it is. May we come in?'

'Yes, of course.' He gestured for them to pass him into the hallway. The interior of the house was as Annie had envisaged – neat, slightly fussy, well-maintained. 'Come through. Meg, it's the police, I'm sorry to say.' The last statement was addressed to an elderly, white-haired lady who was in the process of switching off the television, apparently struggling with the complexities of the remote control.

'The police?' She finally managed to deal with the television, and rose unsteadily from the armchair. 'Is this about Darren?'

Annie was already intrigued that the couple seemed unsurprised by their arrival. 'I'd ask you both to sit down. I'm afraid I've some bad news.'

This time, Parkin did look surprised, as if the tone of Annie's voice hadn't been what he'd expected. 'About Darren?'

'There's no easy way for me to say this. I'm afraid Darren has been found dead. I'm sorry.' There ought to be a softer way to break this kind of news, but she knew it was important to leave no room for ambiguity.

'Dead?' Whatever Parkin had been expecting her to say, it clearly wasn't this. 'My God. How?'

'I'm not able to go into too much detail at this stage, Mr Parkin. But we think he was the victim of an unlawful killing.'

'You mean he was murdered?'

'I'm afraid so. Your son—'

'You mean grandson,' Meg Parkin interrupted.

Annie exchanged a glance with Zoe, knowing she should have confirmed this at the start. In retrospect, it should have been obvious the couple were likely to be too old to be the parents of a son in his early twenties, and it was standard policy to establish the relationship before informing a relative of a death. 'I'm sorry…'

Meg Parkin shook her head. 'No, don't be. Ron and I looked after Darren like a son.'

'I'm very sorry. This must be distressing for you.'

Ron Parkin looked up. 'In a way it is. But I can't say I'm entirely surprised.'

'Ron…' his wife interjected.

'Oh, I know. Don't speak ill of the dead. But you know it's true.'

'You didn't seem surprised when I told you we were police officers.' Annie decided she might as well take advantage of Ron Parkin's unexpected honesty. She'd pull back if Meg Parkin began to seem distressed, but both grandparents appeared so far to have accepted the news calmly.

Ron nodded. 'I wasn't. It wasn't the first time we'd received a visit. Though the previous times were less shocking than this.'

'We know that Darren had a criminal record. That was how we were able to confirm his identity. But they were relatively minor offences, and some years ago.'

'I don't like to say it, but he was just a bad 'un,' Ron Parkin said. 'He was up to his ears in stuff. We used to get visits here…'

'Ron's right,' Meg said. 'I don't want to be too hard on poor Darren. We did our best for him, but he was just out of control. Mixing with the wrong people.'

'You said you received visits?' Zoe prompted.

'A couple of times. People looking for him,' Meg Parkin said. 'Thugs. He owed them money. They were trying to track him down.'

'They threatened you?'

'I wouldn't say threatened. They were intimidating. But when it became obvious we didn't know Darren's whereabouts, they didn't push it, I'm glad to say.'

'He wasn't living here then?' Zoe asked.

'Moved out when we was eighteen. Just didn't want to be here. I can't say I blamed him. To be honest, by that point we didn't really want him here either. We were getting too old for that kind of thing. The kind of friends he had, the people he associated with. In fairness, he kept in touch, let us know he was all right. But he never came back.'

'Do you know where he was living?'

'Somewhere in Derby, I believe. He never gave us his address, and we never asked for it. When we got those visits, I was glad I hadn't.'

'Did you inform the police about the visits?' Zoe asked.

Ron Parkin nodded. 'I did the second time it happened. They were sympathetic but couldn't do much. Said to call them immediately if they returned. But it was just those two times. Couple of years ago now.'

'Do you have any idea what Darren was doing? Work? Friends?' Annie would normally have been reluctant to take the interview as far as this in the circumstances, but she sensed the Parkins were keen to talk. As if this was an opportunity to offload all the anxieties they'd felt about their grandson. She guessed that, for all Ron Parkin's harsh words, they'd felt more for Darren than they might be prepared to admit.

'Not really. He had no real qualifications. He was trouble at school as well. From the little he said to us, I got the impression he was mainly doing bar work. Last time he was in contact, a few months back, he was saying he'd got some big opportunity.'

'He didn't tell you what?'

'No. I thought it was all just nonsense. He was always exaggerating. He reckoned he had a load of friends, but he never told us who any of them were. I don't imagine the names would have meant anything to us anyway.'

'Did he have any friends locally? From before he moved out, I mean.' Despite the Parkins' honesty, this was proving less informative than Annie had hoped. It was clear the grandparents knew almost nothing about Darren's recent circumstances.

'There were one or two,' Meg Parkin said. 'From when he was at school. Gang of tearaways. I can give you a couple of names and tell you the streets where they lived, I think. But I don't know if any of them will still be living there.'

'Anything would be helpful,' Annie said, sincerely. 'If we can track them down, they might have kept in touch with Darren.'

'It's possible,' Meg Parkin said, though her expression suggested doubt. She thought for a moment. 'There was a Carl. Carl Francis, I think. They lived somewhere over in the council estate.' After a moment, she came up with a street name. 'I've pretty sure that's where he lived. I don't know the number, I'm afraid.'

'That's fine,' Annie said. 'It gives us somewhere to start. Is there anyone else?'

'Who was that other one?' Ron Parkin said. 'Arrogant little toerag.'

'Jonny,' his wife said, after a moment. 'Jonny Garfield. Lived with his dad, didn't he?' Again, she was able to come up with an approximate address. 'I'm pretty sure his dad's still there. I've seen him once or twice in the supermarket, so he's still living somewhere nearby, anyway.'

'That's very helpful,' Annie said. 'Look, I'm sorry. I shouldn't really have been asking you these questions. Not now. Are you both okay? This must have been a shock for you.'

Meg Parkin exchanged a look with her husband. 'It's a shock, of course it is. But we both felt we lost Darren a good while ago. We've both been expecting – well, not this, but some sort of bad news. It was only a matter of time.'

'Would you like us to arrange for someone to be with you? A friend or relative?'

Ron Parkin shook his head. 'I don't think we need anything like that. We'll be fine.' He paused, thinking. 'What about the funeral? That kind of thing.'

'We won't be able to release Darren's remains for a while,' Annie said. 'In the circumstances. But when we do… I assume you're his next of kin.'

There was a hesitation before Meg Parkin responded. 'I suppose we must be.' She looked to her husband to help.

'The reason we ended up looking after Darren,' Ron Parkin said, 'was that his mother, our daughter, left him with us.'

'I don't understand,' Annie said. 'Left him?'

'She was a single mother,' Ron Parkin said. He stopped for a moment, as if unsure how much more to say. 'It's a long story. She wouldn't tell us who the father was. She claimed it was someone she'd met at a party and she couldn't track him down anyway. I don't know if that's true, but there wasn't much we could do.'

'But you helped her look after the child?'

'She was our daughter. What else were we supposed to do? We're not exactly rich but I've a decent pension – I was a pit deputy – so we could afford to help her.'

'What happened to your daughter?'

'I wish we knew,' Meg Parkin said. 'It wasn't the easiest relationship, especially after Darren was born. But we loved her, and we thought she still loved us. We supported her as best we could, and we looked after Darren so she could get out to work. But I think she resented how much her life was constrained, and, to be honest, I think she resented having to be dependent on us. Eventually she walked out.'

'Walked out?'

'Just like that. We realised afterwards she must have been planning it for some time. Had been saving money, had moved some of our stuff out. One day she just went off, supposedly to work, and never came back.'

'She left Darren?'

'She left Darren,' Meg Parkin said.

'You tried to find her?'

'Of course. But she'd walked out on her job as well, also without warning. She'd said nothing to anyone there about what she was planning. We contacted her friends – or at least those we knew about – but no one admitted knowing anything. I don't know whether or not they were telling the truth, but I suspect she had other friends that neither of us knew about.'

'Did you report her missing?'

'Eventually.' Meg Parkin allowed Annie a smile. 'No offence, but the police have never seemed to be able to help us very much. They were very sympathetic. But what it came down to was that she was an adult, she wasn't vulnerable, and we had no evidence she hadn't simply left of her own free will. I don't know what the police did, if anything, but I guess they didn't pursue it too far.'

Annie imagined that was probably true. If there was no evidence of foul play, and no obvious reasons for concern, there would be no strong reason for the police to devote resources to this kind of case. It was unusual for a mother to leave her child behind but not unprecedented, especially when the child had been left in apparently safe hands. 'And you've still no idea where she is?'

'We've heard nothing since she walked out. We expected that at some stage she'd have been in contact if only just to let us know she was safe. But we heard nothing.'

'I'm sorry.'

'It was a long time ago,' Meg Parkin said. 'We spent years agonising about what had happened, hoping one day we'd get that phone call or letter. But it didn't happen, and by then we were more focused on dealing with Darren. Eventually we were made his legal guardians.'

'How old was he when his mother left?'

Meg Parkin looked at her husband. 'He must have been… what, seven or eight?'

'He was seven,' Ron Parkin said with certainty. 'I remember how much we spent on his eighth birthday, as if that was going to compensate for his mother walking out.'

There was an edge of bitterness in his voice, Annie thought. 'I'm sorry. I really shouldn't be dredging up this stuff for you at a time like this. You're sure you'll both be okay?'

'I think so, don't you?' Ron Parkin said. 'If we've lost something, it didn't happen today.'

Annie could think of no immediate response. 'We'd better not take up any more of your time. We'll keep you informed about Darren and what's happening on the case generally.'

'Case?' Meg Parkin said. 'Oh, I suppose you need to investigate.'

Her words confirmed Annie's suspicion that the couple hadn't fully taken on board what she'd told them. It was often the way. People heard the parts they wanted to hear, and didn't necessarily process the rest. In this case, she felt the Parkins hadn't registered much more than that their grandson was dead. 'We're looking into the circumstances of his death, yes. I'm afraid the story may gain some media coverage, but we'll give you advance warning if that's likely to happen and we can provide support if it causes any problems.'

'Media coverage?' For the first time, Meg Parkin looked genuinely alarmed. 'You mean the newspapers and TV?'

'It may happen. We try to manage these things as carefully as we can, but there may be a need to release details of the case to the media, yes.'

'Including our identities?' Ron Parkin said.

'Not necessarily, no. We'll be as discreet as possible, but in a murder case we do need to be transparent. And the media have a habit sometimes of digging further than we'd like. If it comes to it, we'll give you all the support we can.' She almost wished now that she hadn't raised the topic, but she knew that, with two apparently linked killings, they wouldn't be able to keep a lid on this for long.

'We won't keep you any longer.' Annie pulled one of her business cards out of her pocket and handed it over to Meg Parkin. 'We'll keep you informed as much as we can, and we may need to talk to you again as the enquiry proceeds. But if you need anything, or if you think there's anything you can tell us about your grandson that might be useful to us, please do contact me on that number.'

Meg Parkin scrutinised the card for a moment, as if suspicious of its provenance. 'Thank you for coming,' she said after a moment. 'It might not have sounded like it, but we loved Darren. We really did. What's happened is awful.'

'You have our deepest sympathy, Mrs Parkin. And we'll do everything in our power to find out what's behind his death.' Annie spoke the last words sincerely, but she knew that in reality they were little more than a platitude.

The expression on the Parkins' faces suggested that they had received her words almost as a kind of threat. For some people, Annie thought, the truth was perhaps better left buried.

Chapter Fourteen

'That was interesting,' Zoe said, once they were back in the car.

'You thought so too, did you? Tell me how it struck you.'

'It was their reaction. They didn't seem surprised when we turned up on their doorstep. They didn't even seem too surprised when we told them their grandson was dead.'

'That was what struck me first,' Annie agreed. 'Darren Parkin had a record, but only for minor stuff, and he hadn't done anything for several years.'

'Nothing we caught him doing anyway,' Zoe pointed out. 'But maybe any kind of law-breaking would be a shock to a couple like that. They seemed fairly conservative types.'

'Maybe,' Annie said. 'Maybe these visits from debt collectors added to that. Even so, it's a big jump to not being surprised that he'd been murdered. It felt as if they knew more about Darren than they were saying. The stuff about the mother was interesting, too. The unknown father. Just walking out and leaving her child behind. Wished we could have probed a bit further. As it was, I pushed it further than I should have done.'

'Maybe,' Zoe said. 'They didn't exactly seem distraught at Darren's death, though.'

'I couldn't fathom what their feelings were.' They were still sitting outside the Parkins' house, and Annie was conscious that they were probably still being watched by the neighbour, if not by the Parkins themselves. 'While we're here, shall we try to track down these old friends of Darren's. Might be a wild goose chase, but we may as well give it a go. Don't know how far we'll get without the house numbers, but we can see.'

She started the car and pulled back out into the street. From the corner of her eye, she caught a movement at the neighbour's window as the curtain was dropped back into place. She turned back out on to the main street and then followed the directions given by Zoe, who was checking out the addresses on her mobile. 'I've found a Francis on that street from one of the directory enquiry websites,' she said. 'Number six.'

'Let's try that first, then.'

A few more turns brought them into another estate of houses. The houses themselves had unmistakeably been built as council housing, probably in the 1950s or 1960s. The area seemed less salubrious than where the Parkins lived, although most of the houses and gardens were tidy and well-maintained.

It took them a few moments to find their destination. The house looked neat enough, but there were fewer of the personal touches that distinguished many of the surrounding residences. The front garden had been given over largely to concrete to create a driveway, which held an unmarked white van. By contrast with the two neighbouring houses, there were no pot plants or hanging baskets around the door.

The front door opened before Annie could press the doorbell. A woman peered suspiciously out at them. 'Yes?'

Annie showed her warrant card. 'Police. We're trying to contact a Carl Francis.'

The woman frowned. 'Carl? What do you want with Carl?'

'Does Carl live here, Mrs…?'

'Francis,' the woman confirmed. 'Kelly Francis. Carl doesn't live here any more.'

'Do you have contact details for him?'

'Of course I do. Whether I'm prepared to give them to you is another matter. What do you want with him?'

Annie paused. Her first instinct had been to withhold Darren Parkin's name until she was able to speak to Carl himself, but Carl's mother might conceivably be able to offer them some insights. 'We understand he was a friend of your son's some years ago. You may know him yourself. Darren Parkin.'

Kelly Francis frowned. 'Darren Parkin. Yes, I knew him.' She seemed to hesitate. 'He was trouble.'

'You didn't approve of him?'

'That's one way of putting it. Another is that I wouldn't trust the little toerag further than I could throw him.'

'I wonder if we should continue this conversation inside?'

Kelly Francis took the hint. 'Aye, you're right. Folks round here have their tab-holes open for any word of gossip. You'll have to take us as you find us, though.'

As it turned out, the house was pleasant enough. It was much less tidy than the Parkins', but had a comfortable, lived-in air. A pile of children's toys sat in the corner of the sitting room. 'My granddaughter's stuff,' Kelly Francis said. 'Carl's sister's kid. I look after her a couple of days a week while her mam goes to work. Grab a seat.'

'We won't take up too much of your time. But if there's anything you can tell us about Darren Parkin, that would be helpful.'

'What's he been up to, then? Not that anything would surprise me.'

'I'm not at liberty to discuss any details of the investigation at this stage, I'm afraid. We're really just gathering some background information. How well do you know Darren Parkin?'

'He and Carl were mates at school and for a bit after. There were a few of them used to hang around together. Causing trouble, mainly.'

'You didn't like Darren?'

'He was a bad influence. Him and another one in particular. Garfield. Jonny Garfield. Nasty pieces of work, both of them.'

It was the same name Darren's grandparents had mentioned along with Carl Francis.

'Bad influences in what way?' asked Annie.

'You name it. Look, I'm not saying Carl was an angel. He's not the brightest kid, but he's willing and good-natured. They took advantage of him. They got into trouble in all kinds of ways – petty crime, booze, drug-taking. Garfield was excluded from school a couple of times, and both of them ended up in trouble with the law. But they used to get others to do stuff on their behalf, including Carl. Carl almost got into serious trouble a couple of times because of stuff they'd put him up to.'

'Do you think he might still be in contact with Darren?' Zoe asked.

There was another hesitation. 'Not as far as I'm aware. Carl's living in Derby. Got himself a job in one of the supermarkets, and he's renting a flat with a couple of mates. He phones a couple of times a week, and pops over every couple of weeks or so. He's doing all right.'

'When did you last see Darren?'

'Me? Not sure. He walked out on his nan and grandad, didn't he? But I probably hadn't seen him for a while before that. I don't know if Carl saw anything much of him after they left school.'

'And what about the other boy? Jonny Garfield?' Annie said.

'To be honest, he was worse than Darren. He was probably the brains behind anything they got up to, if that's the right word. He really was an unpleasant little so-and-so. The others were – well, not the brightest, including Carl. And including Darren, too. He was the big I-am, but I think it was Garfield who was the real bad influence. He was smart enough to get others to do his dirty work. I've no idea what happened to him, but I'm willing to bet it was nothing good.'

'Carl's no longer in contact with Jonny Garfield, presumably?'

'I bloody well hope not. He was the one I really tried to keep Carl away from. If Garfield's not inside himself – and he's probably been smart enough to avoid it – he's probably been responsible for one or two other people ending up there.'

'That's very useful. Mrs Francis. Thank you. Are you able to let us have contact details for Carl?'

'Are you sure Carl's not in any trouble?'

'This isn't about Carl. We're just looking to find out more about Darren Parkin. Anything Carl might be able to tell us could be useful.'

'I'll get you his details,' Kelly Francis said. Annie noticed she'd been glancing at the clock on the mantelpiece and suddenly seemed keener to draw the discussion to an end.

'Thank you. That's very helpful. I hope we don't need to disturb you again.'

Francis retrieved the details from her mobile phone, and Zoe dutifully scribbled them down in her notebook. When they rose to leave, Annie could almost feel Francis willing them out of the door. As Kelly Francis opened the front door, Annie stopped and said, 'Is the van yours?'

'My husband's,' Francis said. 'He's a painter and decorator.'

'He's not using it today?'

'He's doing a couple of small local jobs this afternoon. Didn't need a lot of equipment, so he's just taken the car. Easier to park.'

'Thanks again for your time, Mrs Francis. We'll be in touch if we need anything else, but I hope we won't need to trouble you.'

'No problem. Glad to have been of assistance.' Annie could see that Francis was looking past her, scanning the length of the street for any sign of an approaching vehicle. She waved another farewell, then turned to join Zoe by the car.

Chapter Fifteen

'There's clearly a pattern emerging, anyway,' Zoe said, as they headed back towards the main road.

'That everyone thinks Parkin was an unpleasant bastard? Certainly doesn't seem to have much of a fan club.'

'Though it sounds as if this guy Garfield was the brains behind whatever they got up to.'

'Brains may be a bit strong, but he seems to have been the ringleader. Shall we try him next?'

'We may as well see the sights.'

Zoe had managed to track down an address for a Garfield living in the street Meg Parkin had mentioned, so it appeared that Garfield's family at least were still living there. The house was just a few hundred metres away, in a narrow street of terraces running parallel to the main road.

These were houses that had presumably been built originally as miners' cottages during the heyday of the industry in the area. It wasn't quite back-to-back housing, but from the layout of the streets they could have only tiny backyards running between the rows. Some had clearly been divided into flats, with multiple doorbells, but the house they were seeking seemed still to be a single residence.

Annie pressed the bell, and heard an answering barrage of dog-barking from within the house. After a moment, the door opened and a male face peered out at them. The barking of the dog grew louder behind him. 'Yes?'

'Police.' Annie could barely make herself heard above the barking. 'We're looking for a Jonny Garfield.'

'He don't live here.'

'Do you know where he is living, Mr...?'

'I'm his dad. Pete Garfield. But if I did know, I wouldn't tell you.'

'Why's that, Mr Garfield?'

'If he's in trouble, he can look after himself. But I'm not going to make it harder for him by doing your job for you.'

'Why do you think he might be in trouble?'

The man turned away, and for a moment Annie thought he might be about to close the door. 'Shut it, Rex! Bloody mutt. Why do I think Jonny might be in trouble? Because the fucking police have turned up on my doorstep. Why do you think?'

'He's not in any trouble, Mr Garfield. At least not as far as we're aware. But we think he might be able to help us with an enquiry.'

'Grass, you mean.'

'That's not what I mean.' Annie took a breath and decided to try a different tack. She had the sense she might make more progress with Garfield by telling him the truth, or at least part of the truth. 'We're trying to gather some background about the victim of a crime, who we think might have been an acquaintance of your son.'

'Who are we talking about?'

'Darren Parkin.'

'Darren?' Garfield finally opened the door fully. 'What's happened to him?'

'May we come in, Mr Garfield? It'll be easier to talk inside than on the doorstep.'

'Okay. But wait till I shut Rex up. He won't do you any harm, but he'll slobber all over you.' He gestured to the large German Shepherd sitting behind him.

He disappeared briefly and they heard him muttering as he dragged the dog back into the kitchen. He returned, rubbing his hands together. 'Bloody dog. Don't know why I keep him. Come in. It's a mess, but I don't doubt you've seen worse.'

Annie wasn't sure she had, at least not in a residence where the householder was still living. The living room was cluttered with all manner of debris, scattered randomly across the floor and sofa. There were copies of magazines, most apparently devoted to motorcycles, as well as numerous books, and what seemed to be piles of cardboard packaging. At the far side of the sofa, there was a pile of empty beer cans and a stack of used takeaway containers. The pervading smell in the room was a mix of ripe Indian food, dog and human body odour. Annie wrinkled her nose and tried her hardest not to gag.

Garfield was clearly oblivious to the smell, but he'd noted the reaction of the two women. 'I'll open a window,' he said. 'Sorry. I'm a bloke living on his own. We don't tend to register these things.' He crossed the room, making his way between the detritus with no obvious effort, and unbolted the patio doors into the rear yard. The damp spring air swept cleansingly into the room, while Garfield busied himself throwing magazines and books off the sofa on to the floor, gesturing for the two women to take a seat.

Annie did so, conscious she was sitting on the edge of the sofa in the manner of a prim maiden aunt. Zoe took a seat beside her. Garfield threw himself into an armchair opposite. Annie guessed he was in his mid-forties. He moved slightly awkwardly, and had the physique of someone who'd once worked out but was gaining weight. 'So what's happened to Darren?'

'I'm afraid he's dead, Mr Garfield.'

'Dead? How?'

'We believe he was murdered.'

'Jesus. I wasn't expecting that.' He was shaking his head, his eyes staring blankly into space.

'I'm sorry.'

'I mean, I knew Darren as a mate of Jonny's but that's all, really. It's always a shock when something happens to someone that young, isn't it? Only just out of his teens.'

She had the sense, as she had with all the afternoon's interviews, that there was something being left unsaid. 'Was he still in contact with your son, Mr Garfield?'

'With Jonny?' She could see he was hesitating now, as if unsure how much to say. 'You'd have to ask Jonny. I think they were in contact fairly recently. Just from things Jonny said. But I don't know how recently.'

'Do you have contact details for Jonny?' Zoe said. 'It's probably best if we speak to him directly.'

'Hang on.' Garfield fumbled a mobile phone out of his pocket and thumbed through the contacts. 'He's in Derby.' He read out the address and number, and Zoe scribbled it down in her notebook.

'When did you last see Darren?' Annie said.

The question seemed to take Garfield by surprise. 'Me? Jesus, I don't know. I think I saw him with Jonny a while back. A few months ago, maybe.'

'So they were in contact as recently as that?'

'I suppose so. It might be longer ago than I think. You know how it is.'

'Of course. What does your son do? Work-wise, I mean.'

'Jonny? Various things. Can turn his hand to anything. He seems to get by well enough.'

'Not easy for young people, these days,' Annie said.

'Tell me about it. Lost my own job a couple of years back. Company had been there for forty or fifty years, then got into difficulties and was bought up by some bunch of bloody asset strippers. They weren't interested in the workforce. They weren't interested in anything but making a quick buck.'

'I'm sorry.'

'It's not like I'm the only one, is it? There's still plenty of poor buggers round here lost their jobs when the pits closed. Some of them went to their graves without ever working again. And nothing's really replaced them. Zero-hours fucking contracts. Temporary jobs. All the usual crap.'

'What are you doing now?'

'Me? I drive a minicab. Enough to make ends meet, just about.'

Annie felt that any response she could offer would simply sound patronising. 'Thanks for your help, anyway, Mr Garfield. We're very grateful.' She pushed herself to her feet. 'We've taken up enough of your time.'

'You'll be talking to Jonny, then?'

'We'd like to have a word with him. We're just trying to gather more background information on Darren.'

'I don't imagine his grandparents were able to tell you much.'

'You know his grandparents?' Zoe asked.

'Never met them. But I got the impression Darren didn't exactly get on with them.'

'What about Darren's mother? Did you ever meet her?' Annie said.

She had the impression of another hesitation. 'His mother? She left years ago.'

'So I understand. Did your son know Darren then?'

'I suppose so. They were at primary school together. But they didn't really become friends till they were teenagers at the comp. You know how it is.'

Annie nodded. 'Well, we won't take up any more of your time, Mr Garfield. Many thanks for your assistance.'

Outside the weather was slowly improving, the clouds scudding across a gradually clearing sky. Garfield said, 'I can't say I'm the greatest fan of you lot, for one reason or another, but I wish you well with this one. I hope you catch whoever's responsible.'

'We'll do our best, Mr Garfield. The more help we get from people like yourself, the easier it'll be.'

'I hope Jonny can tell you more than I've been able to.' Garfield closed the door. From inside the house, they heard the sound of Rex's barking resume as the dog was released from the kitchen.

'Christ,' Zoe said, as they made their way back to the car. 'What a dump. I'm not sure I could have stayed in there if he hadn't opened the window.'

'Amazing how people live, isn't it?'

'And another one who wasn't telling us everything.'

'You thought that, too, did you? There seem to be plenty of people harbouring secrets round here.' Annie smiled. It was good to know that Zoe's instincts were as sound as ever, whatever else might be troubling her. 'I wonder if they're all sharing the same secrets or if they all have secrets of their own. And whether any of them are relevant to what we want to know.'

Chapter Sixteen

'You think they were all hiding something?' Jennings said.

Jennings was sitting with Annie and Zoe in a corner of the Major Incident Room. Annie and Jennings had just finished their latest briefing with the team. On the surface, Jennings had seemed his usual polished self, but Annie could tell he was under increasing pressure. Intense activity continued around them – officers collating information, making call after call to potential witnesses or sources of information, preparing schedules of interviews. Other staff, here and elsewhere, would be examining and analysing CCTV footage and ANPR camera data. It was the usual endless routine that was essential in progressing an enquiry like this, but Annie was conscious of how little substantive information they had so far.

'It felt like a community with more than its share of secrets,' Zoe said. 'Though I suspect most of them have more to do with preserving social niceties than covering up for murder. It felt like that with the grandparents, anyway.'

'I'm not sure that guy Garfield would recognise a social nicety if it popped up in one of his rancid takeaway containers,' Annie said. 'But I know what you mean. I suppose you've also got to recognise that, for a lot of people in those communities, we're still the enemy.'

'Not any more, surely?' Jennings was flicking impatiently through his papers as though already wondering how to draw the meeting to a close.

'Some of those memories die hard,' Annie said. 'Still a lot of bad blood in these parts from the eighties. In these parts, there were families split apart by the miners' strike. Both sides viewed the police with suspicion in those days.'

'No doubt your mother's given you her perspective,' Jennings said, with an edge of irony in his tone.

'I don't think anyone had much doubt which side she'd have been on. But she's never really said much about it.'

'I'm sure she's got her stories,' Jennings said. 'All the old coppers seem to. And most of them are only too keen to tell you.'

'My mother only tells you about her past when she wants to let you know how much better it is than the present.'

'I think Annie's right, though,' Zoe said. 'There's stuff that someone like Garfield won't ever say to us. Not because it's necessarily incriminating, but just because he wouldn't trust how we'd use it. He's the sort who's always ducking and diving, and that probably means keeping on the good side of some bad people.'

'If so, we need to start winkling it out.' Jennings said. 'People up the line are getting twitchy. Two similar cases. The nature of the killing. We've kept a reasonable lid on it with the media so far. I don't think we'll be able to do that with the second case. Which means we'll have the media crawling all over us, national and local. And they've already got a major presence here because of what happened with Sheena Pearson.' He gestured towards Annie, as if to imply that she carried some responsibility for that particular situation.

Annie said, 'That's going to explode still further after what happened this morning.'

'Exactly. We've got an MP being targeted by a gunman, plus a potential multiple killer, all in a few days and all in our own little rural patch. So nobody says a word to the media or allows anything to leak out of here. I mean nobody. Make that bloody clear to your team. If anybody even gets approached, I want to know about it PDQ. Anything that's said goes through Comms.'

'They can be a devious bunch, though,' Zoe pointed out. 'The danger isn't someone approaching you directly. It's the sly phone call to some junior member of the team where they pretend to be someone in a position of authority, or they fish for information by sharing what little they already know so you confirm it without realising it. I've been there more than once. You're two minutes into the discussion, trying to be helpful and polite, before it occurs to you to wonder who it is you're talking to.'

'Then tell your team exactly that. Tell them to be on their guard at all times. Don't say anything unless you're absolutely certain who you're talking to. And no gossiping to their partners or friends or some guy in the pub.'

'Careless talk costs lives,' Annie said. 'Or at least careers. We get it, Stuart. I'll spread the word.'

He sat back with his eyes closed for second. 'Sorry,' he said. 'Teaching you to suck eggs.'

'I'm not your granny,' Annie pointed out.

'It's just that I had the Assistant Chief bending my ear for the best part of an hour this morning about this. He basically had two messages. Don't say a bloody word to anyone, and get these two enquiries sorted as quickly as you bloody can.'

'Helpful contribution as ever.' Annie was gathering up her papers. 'I assume he realises we're not just all sitting around on our backsides down here.'

'He knows full well what we do,' Jennings said. 'And he probably does his best to shield us from the worst of the crap. I can live with him letting off steam from time to time. So what's the next move? Tracking down this Jonny Garfield?'

'I'd have said so. He's our best bet for learning more about Darren Parkin. I want to know who visited his grandparents. It sounds like he was wanted by someone. That may be key.'

'He's clearly got some history, anyway. Okay, I'll leave you to get on with it. Let me know if there's anything else you need.'

'More resources would always be good.'

'I'll bear that in mind,' Jennings said, 'and I'll procure you a couple of spare unicorns while I'm about it. How's Sheena, by the way?'

'She seems fine. I called her when we got back. She's a bit shaken still, but she's focusing on getting the security sorted. She's been talking to the Speaker's Office, who look after all this, and she can claim for some extra stuff at home and in the office, apparently. Mind you, Sheena's always very sensitive about what she claims, so that may be another battle I have to fight with her. My big worry is that she'll want to jump straight back into the fray. I take it we've not succeeded in identifying our gunman yet?'

'I was just talking to Andy Dwyer,' Jennings said. 'Whoever fired that shot today seems to have just disappeared into the woodwork. Not on any of the hospital CCTV, and no sightings on any of the surrounding roads. Andy's got people checking out vehicles entering or leaving the hospital site and in the area generally, but that's a long slog.'

'Sounds like whoever it was knew what they were doing.'

'Or just had a lot of dumb luck. But something will turn up,' Jennings said, confidently. 'Andy reckons they've got some leads on the protestors yesterday. If they can get hold of some of those and start turning the screws, I reckon they'll shop whoever fired that shot quickly enough.'

'Assuming the two shots were fired by the same person,' Zoe said. 'We can't necessarily assume that.'

'You always know how to cheer a person up, Zoe, you know that?' Jennings emitted a theatrical sigh. 'But, yes, anything's possible. We don't even know if it was the same type of gun. They've found the bullet from this morning neatly lodged in an interior wall of the hospital, but yesterday's hasn't been found so far.'

Annie gave a weary sigh. 'Meanwhile I have to persuade Sheena to keep her head down. Which isn't a position that comes naturally to her.'

'I can imagine,' Jennings said. 'By the way, I assume Dwyer will want to talk to Sheena and you formally. Assume you're happy with that?'

'I just want to get this bastard behind bars before he does any real damage to Sheena or anyone else. And Sheena's a tough cookie. She'll be ready to talk to him now.'

'I'll let Andy know, then.' Jennings nodded his usual perfunctory farewell, then turned and headed out back to his office.

'You should get off home,' Zoe said. 'Before Sheena slips out of the window and heads back to Parliament.'

'Given half a chance she'd do exactly that.' Annie looked at her watch. 'How do you feel about trying to track down Jonny Garfield first, though? If he's working, this might be just the time to catch him in.'

'Why not? I was planning to stay on for a while anyway. Gary's playing football this evening so I've nothing to rush back for.'

'Everything okay, Zoe? At home, I mean.' She hadn't been able to think of a better way of raising her concerns, and tried to ask the question casually.

'Same as usual, pretty much. Why do you ask?' Zoe was regarding her with suspicion. 'Has Jennings said something?'

'Jennings?'

'I suppose I was a bit – I don't know, distracted when we were over at the crime scene.'

'Distracted by what?'

Zoe had risen to her feet, but now sat down again. 'Not sure, really. I just felt a bit overwhelmed. I couldn't bring myself to go and look at the body.'

'You're not usually the squeamish sort.'

'That's the thing. It wasn't about being squeamish. I've seen plenty of dead bodies. Admittedly most of them not quite as extreme as this one, but I've seen plenty of blood and gore. It wasn't that.'

'So what was it?'

'I don't know exactly. I'm just finding the whole thing a bit unnerving. The nature of the killings, I mean.'

'I think we're all feeling that. I've never encountered anything quite like this. Do you think you're okay with it?'

'I'm sure I will be. Like I told you, I've not been sleeping well lately. I'm just a bit tired.'

'If you want to get off home and rest tonight, that's fine by me.'

'I'm fine, really. I just had a slight wobble. I'm only sorry Jennings was there to witness it.'

Annie knew what she meant. This was still an environment where some would see any sign of metal or psychological fragility as a sign you weren't up to the job, especially if you were a woman. 'He probably didn't even notice. Not always the most sensitive of souls, our Stuart.'

'You might be right.' Zoe sounded unconvinced.

'You sure you're okay, though? If you need to take a bit of time out, just say.'

'In the middle of a case like this? Are you kidding? No, come on, let's go and track down Jonny Garfield's flat.'

Annie nodded, recognising that Zoe had no desire to talk further. 'Fair enough. Let's just hope his flat's a bit more salubrious than his father's place.'

Chapter Seventeen

'Tonight?'

'I realise it's short notice. I mean, if you can't make it…'

'It's not that. I'm sure I can juggle things if I need to. It's just, well – tonight?'

Clive Bamford sighed. 'Look. Greg, if I could have given you more notice, I would have. But that's not how they work.'

'So how do they work?' Greg Wardle said. 'They just say "jump" and we ask "how high?"'

'It's not like that, Greg. At the moment, they don't know they can trust us. They're playing everything very close to their chest.'

'They're not bloody MI5. They're just a bunch of religious nuts.'

Clive could feel his patience ebbing away. 'Greg, if you don't want to be involved—'

Greg shook his head. 'Sorry, I shouldn't have said that. It's just that I don't like being bounced into things.'

'I'm sure that's not the intention. But you know they've been repeatedly misrepresented in the media. We've been recommended to them by Rowan Wiseman, but other than that they don't know us. They don't know if they're being set up. My guess is they want to test us out. Do we know our stuff? Are we really prepared to listen to what they have to say?'

'And do we know our stuff?' Greg said. 'I'm not sure I do.'

Clive shrugged. 'Just keep your mouth shut and follow my lead, then.'

They were sitting in a corner of the same pub where they'd held the first meeting of their Conspiracy Theory Discussion Group. Clive was still wondering what to do about the group. He'd felt the initial meeting had been hijacked by Charlie and Rowan Wiseman, though that now seemed to have paid dividends of its own. He suspected that the other two attendees had mostly come along out of curiosity. He'd phoned them both after the meeting, and they'd been non-committal about whether they'd be returning. Greg thought it was worth giving it one more go and putting a bit more effort into the promotion, but Clive thought they should maybe cut their losses and move on. After all, if tonight was successful, he might have plenty of other work to be getting on with.

'So where are we supposed to be going?'

'Not sure exactly. Rowan said she'd meet up here and drive us over. Assuming you want to go.'

Greg nodded. 'Okay, you've talked me into it. Do we have to wear blindfolds or what?'

'What?'

'When she drives us over to this secret location.'

'It's not a secret location. She just thought it would be better for her to be there to introduce us.'

'I'm just pulling your leg.' Greg pulled out his phone. 'Hang on a sec. I just need to cancel a couple of things.' He rose and wandered off towards the pub entrance.

Like Clive, Greg was single, but he tended to have a much more active social life. He played various sports and was a member of clubs and societies that largely remained a mystery to Clive. No doubt he was having to unscramble some commitment to a game of five-a-side football or badminton, or whatever it was he was supposed to be doing tonight.

'Clive?'

He'd been watching Greg and had missed Rowan Wiseman entering the pub through the rear entrance from the car park. He found himself slightly disappointed to see that Charlie was also present. Clive pushed himself awkwardly to his feet. 'Rowan. Good to see you. Charlie.'

'We got time for a drink, Ro?' Charlie asked. 'I could murder a pint.'

Rowan looked at her watch. 'Yes, why not? They're not expecting us till six thirty.'

'I'll get these,' Clive said. 'It's the least I can do.'

'You owe us one from last time anyway,' Charlie pointed out. 'But thanks. I'll have a pint of that stout.'

'Just a tonic for me,' Rowan said. 'As I'm driving.'

By the time Clive returned from the bar with the tray of drinks, Greg had already rejoined the group. 'All sorted,' he said. 'I'm yours for the evening. Assuming I'm welcome.'

Rowan nodded. 'Of course. Clive had told us you might be coming. You work as his assistant, he tells us.'

Clive hadn't quite expressed it like that, or at least he didn't think he had. But he'd felt flustered when Rowan had called him, so he might have said almost anything. He could see Greg wasn't pleased by the description.

'I think of him more as the Watson to my Holmes,' Clive said, though he wasn't sure that was any better.

'The Tom to his Jerry,' Greg said, acidly. 'I'm really there mainly to take notes.'

'So where is it we're going?' Clive said, in an effort to move the conversation on.

'They have a place near Bakewell,' Wiseman said. 'It's a former farmhouse. They've converted it mostly them-selves, and done an impressive job. They use it now as a kind of retreat and spiritual centre, if that's the right phrase.'

'They?' Clive was beginning to think that this sounded suspiciously cultish.

'The main guy you'll be meeting is Robin Kennedy. They don't have a hierarchy as such. It's more a collection of largely autonomous groupings.'

'Nexions?' It was a term that Clive had picked up during his research, and he was keen to demonstrate his knowledge.

'Exactly.' Rowan spoke with the slightly exaggerated enthusiasm of a teacher praising a normally slow pupil. 'That's why I wanted you involved in this. Because you understand the background. Anyway, Robin is – well, I suppose I'd describe him as first among equals there. It's a little hard to describe. He wouldn't describe himself as the leader, but he gives spiritual direction to the group.'

'How many are based there?' Greg asked.

'It's very fluid,' Rowan said. 'There's a small group living in the house, including Robin. And there are various people who come and go. Charlie and I stayed there for a while.' She glanced across at Charlie. 'It helped us out at a difficult time, didn't it?'

Charlie nodded, clearly prepared to offer no other comment. Clive wondered again what exactly the nature of their relationship was.

'On top of that,' Rowan went on, 'there are people who stay there on retreats. Some come for a weekend, some for a little longer. That's partly how they fund the upkeep.'

'I'm looking forward to hearing more about it,' Clive said. 'I want to understand the realities of it all, rather than just the stuff I've read.'

'Robin's definitely your man,' Rowan said. 'I should warn you that he'd likely to treat tonight as something of a test.'

Clive exchanged a glance with Greg. 'A test?'

'That's partly why he invited you at such short notice. I should have said he sent his apologies for that.'

'No, that's fine. We entirely understand. Don't we, Greg?'

Greg nodded. 'My five-a-side team were very understanding. Remarkably few expletives, in the circumstances.'

Wiseman smiled. 'Robin wanted to see you cold, as it were. He didn't want you to be able to prepare for the meeting. He's had that before. Tabloid-type reporters who've genned up on the most salacious stories about satanism, in the hope that Robin or one of the others will say something provocative or outrageous. Completely missing the point, obviously.'

'Obviously,' Clive agreed. 'But you know that's not how I work.'

'I've told Robin that. He's had a look at some of your work, and he likes what he's seen.'

'He doesn't need to be worried,' Clive said. 'I'll be mainly there to listen. I mean, I'll want to question if I'm not following something or if I'm not convinced by what I'm being told. But my first objective will be to absorb information, to understand what this is all about.'

'That sounds perfect,' Rowan said. 'I don't want to give you the wrong impression. Robin isn't an intimidating man—'

'He scares the hell out of me,' Charlie said over the top of his pint.

Wiseman glared at him. 'Ignore Charlie. He and Robin have a bit of a fractious relationship, but they go way back.'

'We go way back right enough,' Charlie said. 'That's why I don't take any bullshit from him. And neither should you. But Ro's right. He talks a bit of bollocks sometimes, but he knows what he's about and he's nobody's fool. Don't underestimate him.'

'I don't intend to,' Clive said. He was keen to ensure that Rowan didn't have misgivings about the introduction.

Rowan had finished her drink, and rose to leave the table. 'I think everyone can potentially benefit from this. But we'd better get moving. We don't want to start off on the wrong foot by being late, do we?'

Chapter Eighteen

The journey took place almost in silence. Clive had hoped that Rowan would provide them with more background information as they were travelling over, but she said little, clearly focused on driving. Charlie sat in the front seat beside her, apparently lost in his own thoughts.

Clive himself sat in the cramped rear seat of Wiseman's small Fiat, Greg squashed up against him. Greg had muttered a few sarcastic comments as they'd made their way out to the car park, but had since remained silent.

'Not far now,' Rowan said, as they entered the outskirts of Bakewell. 'It's just the other side of the town. The place itself feels fairly remote, but it's really only a mile or two out.'

After another mile, Wiseman took a left turn and then, shortly afterwards, a further turn to the right, taking them on to a single-track road. Clive had been trying to keep track of their location. He knew the route well until they'd turned off the main road, but now was in countryside he'd never visited before.

After a few minutes, Charlie gestured through the windscreen. 'That's the place ahead. Kennedy Towers.'

Clive finally spotted a small cluster of lights ahead. As they approached, he saw an illuminated sign that read 'Kennedy Farm'.

'You thought I was joking, didn't you?' Charlie said. 'Okay, not Towers, but close enough. He's not exactly devoid of ego, old Robin.'

Rowan shot Charlie a look that was clearly intended to shut him up. It seemed to have the desired effect. She turned past the sign on to a rough uphill track. 'Sorry it's a bit bumpy. They've been talking about sorting this drive for years, but I reckon Robin likes it the way it is. Deters unwelcome visitors.'

As they reached the summit of the hill, the house suddenly appeared before them. It was an older building than Clive had expected; he guessed that the original cottage, or perhaps cottages, that formed the core of the building probably dated back to the eighteenth century. At some point in the subsequent decades, the house had been sympathetically extended to form a sizeable farmhouse. It looked welcoming enough. There were a couple of brass carriage lamps set each side of the front door, casting a warm orange glow across the gravelled parking area. The overall effect was of an upmarket country bed and breakfast.

'It looks lovely,' Clive said. 'Not entirely what I was expecting.'

Rowan had parked close to the front door, and now looked back over her shoulder at him. 'What were you expecting?'

'I'm not sure exactly. Maybe somewhere a little more austere. This looks positively cosy.'

'Whatever else he does, Robin will always make sure he gets his creature comforts,' Charlie said, earning himself another icy look from Rowan.

Outside, the earlier rain had passed and the sky was clear and rich with stars. As they emerged from the car, the front door of the house opened, a figure silhouetted in the entrance. Rowan hurried towards the doorway. 'Hi, Eric. Hope we've not kept you waiting?'

Clive heard the man say, 'Perfectly timed, Rowan, as always. You always knew how to keep Robin happy.'

Then he went on, more loudly: 'Gentlemen, welcome. Welcome to Kennedy Farm.'

Clive stepped forward. 'We're delighted to be here, Mr...?'

'Eric Nolan. But call me Eric.' The man shook Clive and Greg vigorously by the hand. There was a trace of an American or Canadian accent, Clive thought, though overlaid with something more local. 'I'm Robin's... number two, I suppose you'd say. His right-hand man.'

'Monkey to his organ grinder,' Charlie offered from behind them.

'And a good evening to you, Charlie,' Nolan said. 'I see you're in your usual fine spirits.'

'I'm never not, Eric.' Charlie shivered exaggeratedly. 'Don't hang about. Bloody cold out here.'

'Of course, of course.' Nolan ushered them in through the front door. 'Robin's waiting for you in the lounge.'

'Of course he is,' Charlie said. 'Not one to answer the door himself when he's a lackey to do it for him.'

Nolan led them down a broad hallway into a large living room. Clive's first response was to feel slightly overawed by what greeted them. It wasn't that there was anything particularly distinctive about the room or its furnishings, but the whole effect spoke of a good taste and opulence beyond anything Clive was accustomed to. The furniture and decor had clearly been chosen with an expert eye, and much of it looked as if it had been hand-crafted to suit the age and character of the building. The wall opposite the door comprised one enormous picture window. The curtains were still drawn back and through the glass Clive could see a panorama of scattered lights across the adjacent valley. He guessed that in daylight the view would be spectacular.

The man he took to be Robin Kennedy had been sitting on a large sofa at one side of the room, and now rose to greet them as they entered. 'Good evening, gentlemen. And Rowan, of course.' He gave a slight nod in Rowan's direction, and then came forward to shake their hands.

Kennedy was a tall, fairly heavily-built man. He was older than Clive had expected, perhaps in his early sixties, although that impression was partly contradicted by his thick mane of slightly overlong hair. The hair was slightly greying at the temples, but had otherwise retained its colour. Likewise, Kennedy's dense beard showed no signs of grey. He was dressed casually, although to Clive's inexpert eye the open-necked shirt looked expensive and well-tailored.

If you'd glanced at Kennedy superficially, you might have assumed he was in his forties, Clive thought. It was only as you looked closer that the lines in his face became apparent.

Kennedy grasped Clive by the hand, then gave him the kind of two-handed handshake normally favoured by overenthusiastic politicians. There was an intensity to his manner that Clive found both compelling and oddly disturbing.

'You must be Clive Bamford,' Kennedy said. 'Rowan's told us so much about you. And I've read some of your work, of course. I'm delighted you've managed to find the time to come and see us here tonight. You sound like exactly the man we need.'

Clive nodded warily, taken aback by Kennedy's manner. 'It's a privilege for us, Mr Kennedy. I'm looking forward to hearing more about the...' He hesitated. 'About the movement, if that's the right word.'

'I'm hoping that's something you'll be able to help us with, Clive – I can call you Clive? And please do call me Robin.'

'Of course,' Clive said. 'How do you mean? About helping you?'

'One of the questions we wrestle with is how we should describe ourselves. I'm personally not keen on terms like "religion" or "faith". They're accurate enough as far as they go, I suppose, but they don't really convey the right impression. And we don't want to use any terminology that would suggest we were some kind of cult. We tend to talk about the "movement" for want of any better term, but for me it slightly smacks of something political. That's not quite what we want to convey either.' He turned to face Greg Wardle. 'You must be Clive's assistant?'

'We work together, yes,' Greg said. 'Greg Wardle.'

Kennedy treated Greg to a much more perfunctory handshake. 'Good to meet you, Greg. I hope you have an interesting evening.'

'I'm sure I will, Robin.'

'Now, can I get you something to drink?' Kennedy said. 'Tea, coffee or perhaps something stronger? I'm on this fine single malt.' He held up his glass.

'I wouldn't say no to a Scotch.' Greg had clearly decided to extract maximum value from the evening, one way or another.

'Just a coffee for the moment, please,' Clive said. 'Best if I keep a clear head.'

'A wise man,' Kennedy said. 'Perhaps we can tempt you once we've got business out of the way.'

'Whisky for me,' Charlie said. 'Can always trust your taste in single malts, Robin.'

'Of course, Charlie, I'll make it a double in your case. What about you, Rowan?'

'Just a coffee,' she said. 'Driving.'

'Of course.' Kennedy nodded to Nolan. 'Can you do the honours, Eric?'

'Charlie and I will give you a hand, Eric,' Rowan said. 'Give Robin a few minutes to get to know Clive and Greg.'

Kennedy gestured for Clive and Greg to take a seat. Greg lowered himself into one of the large armchairs, allowing Clive to sit alongside Kennedy on the sofa.

'Do you mind if Greg takes notes for us?' Clive gestured towards Greg, who was pulling out a laptop from the bag he'd brought in with him.

'It's one of my duties,' Greg said. 'As Clive's assistant. I'll just tap away quietly, if that's okay.'

'Of course. Whatever you feel is most useful.' Kennedy's attention immediately returned to Clive. 'I suppose the first question is how much you know about our movement.'

Clive paused, conscious that a misstep now could destroy his credibility in Kennedy's eyes. 'As Rowan probably told you, I've really only recently begun researching in this specific area. Obviously, I've done considerable research into other areas of what I suppose you might call esoterica.'

'Esoterica,' Kennedy echoed, and for a moment Clive thought he might be about to mock the choice of word. 'Yes, that's a good, non-judgemental description.'

'I'm not sure if it's quite the right word,' Clive acknowledged. 'But I'm really just using it to describe a wide range of – well, less conventional belief structures. I've researched widely in that area, and that's really what led me to look at the so-called "left-hand path" religions.' He hesitated. 'I don't know whether that's terminology you approve of?'

Kennedy shrugged. 'It's better than some terminology that's sometimes applied to us. We're not satanists, for example. Not in any clichéd sense, at least.' He offered them a smile, presumably intended to indicate he was joking. 'I suppose my problem with the term "left-hand path" is that it associates us with a largely indiscriminate group of belief structures, to use your words. I'm not sure that's always helpful.'

'How would you characterise your movement, Robin?' Greg had been apparently focused on his note-taking, and asked the question without looking up from the laptop. 'How would you describe it?'

Kennedy looked at Greg with apparent surprise, as if he hadn't been expecting him to contribute to the discussion. 'Since you ask, Greg, I'd say we were realists. Materialists. Perhaps even humanists.' He turned his attention back to Clive. 'Does that surprise you, Clive?'

'I'm not sure. I suppose it does slightly in that I'd assumed your beliefs were primarily spiritual. But perhaps that's not a contradiction?' He hoped the question sounded incisive. The discussion wasn't quite going in the direction he'd anticipated. He already felt quite confused and wasn't sure what they were discussing, but didn't want to appear dense.

'That's an excellent point, Clive. You've pinpointed very precisely the tension that's intrinsic to our thinking.

Of course you're right. There's a very substantial spiritual component to our beliefs. The whole purpose of this is to seek enlightenment, to move beyond the earthly into something much more transcendent. But whereas conventional religion seeks to achieve that by denying life, by denying humanity, we believe that true enlightenment can be achieved only by embracing the material and the mundane.'

Clive had no real idea what Kennedy was talking about. 'Of course. And how exactly do you do that?' He glanced at Greg, hoping that some help might be forthcoming from that direction, but Greg continued to tap away on the laptop, with only a slight shrug that eloquently conveyed the message: *You're on your own, mate.*

'Another excellent question, Clive. I can see that Rowan's judgement was as sound as ever. This isn't perhaps the moment to get into the detail of our practices – we can proceed to that once you get down to serious work with us – but suffice to say that what we try to do is engage with reality, with what life really means, perhaps even with the darker side of existence. We try to challenge convention, question hackneyed ways of acting and thinking. Get people to put aside their prejudices and preconceptions, so that they can see life as it truly is. We help people to draw back the veil, so to speak.'

'To see through the Matrix,' Greg offered from behind his laptop.

Kennedy stared at him for a moment. 'If you say so, Greg. I'm afraid that analogy means nothing to me.'

Clive was saved from immediate further discussion by the arrival of Eric Nolan bearing a tray containing an expensive-looking bottle of single malt whisky, two coffees, two glasses, milk, sugar and a small jug of water.

Rowan Wiseman and Charlie followed behind him, and took seats on a second sofa on the opposite side of the room.

Nolan placed the tray on the table in front of Kennedy with the delicacy of an old-school butler. It wasn't the first time he'd played this role, Clive thought. He realised now that Nolan made him feel uneasy. It was as if his urbane manner concealed something darker, more threatening.

'Please do help yourselves,' Kennedy said.

When they were finally all settled with their respective drinks, Kennedy said, 'I was just explaining to Clive the core principles behind our movement.'

'It's all very interesting,' Clive said. 'I'm looking forward to hearing more about the detail. How many followers do you currently have?'

Kennedy laughed. 'I have no followers. I'm not a leader in any conventional sense.'

Clive rather doubted that, but realised he'd expressed his question clumsily. 'Of course. I meant the movement, rather than you personally.'

'I have a little discomfort with the term "followers" even in that context,' Kennedy said. 'Again, we'll have to get your advice on how we might describe ourselves more appropriately. In a sense, the whole point of the movement is that people don't follow. We work collectively, as a network, if you like. We encourage people to seek their own paths, to challenge and test the established ways of doing things. By definition, this isn't for everyone. And, to be honest, we don't want just anyone joining us. People come to us through recommendations from existing members, and even then we have to ensure they're suited to the demands of the movement.'

'Demands?'

'We're looking for people who can buy into our principles, but also who will grow and develop both their own and our thinking. At the same time, we want people who will do this responsibly. We're not seeking sheep, but we're not seeking anarchists either.'

'Yes, of course.' Clive was still unclear what Kennedy was talking about. 'So what does that mean in practice? That you put people through some kind of selection process?'

'I suppose you might describe it like that,' Kennedy said. 'Nothing quite so explicit, of course. In most cases, to continue your analogy, people select themselves out. We help people to understand what will be expected of them, what personal challenges they will face if they choose to join us. We try to give people a taste of what we do. At that point, some simply decide that it's not for them, particularly if they've been looking for something more passive or if they are looking for someone else to give them the answers. If that's what they're seeking, then there are many conventional faiths that are more likely to suit their needs.'

'And if they still want to proceed but you don't think they're suited...?' Clive prompted.

'We give them a chance to progress, of course. Sometimes an individual who initially seems unsuited to us will ultimately prove that they can grow and develop in the ways we want. If not, then at some point – and usually sooner rather than later, so we don't waste their or our time – we make it clear to them that it's not working and that they'd be better off looking elsewhere.'

'This is absolutely fascinating, Robin,' Clive said. 'In terms of my involvement, how would you like to proceed? I suppose one of the key questions there is whether you're happy for me to publish the fruits of my research in due course.'

'In principle, we'd be delighted. As I say, one of our objectives in this is to try to present ourselves more effectively to the world out there.'

'Why do you want to do that, though?' Greg interjected. 'I mean, if you're so picky as to who you let join.'

Kennedy switched his gaze to Greg, his expression suggesting he had almost forgotten Greg's presence. 'As you say, Greg, we're not exactly proselytising for new members. On the contrary. We have too many people who approach us for the wrong reasons, who think we're something that we're not.'

'People who think you're satanists, for example?' Greg said.

'In the most extreme cases, we have had people harbouring those kinds of misconceptions, yes. But mostly it's more straightforward than that. It's people who think we offer the comforts of conventional religions. If we were better understood out there, then perhaps we'd find it easier to identify the people who really would benefit from what we can offer.'

'I explained to Rowan,' Clive said, 'and it probably goes without saying anyway, that I'm not a PR person. If you're looking for someone simply to present you effectively to the external world, then I'm not that person. I see myself as a researcher and a journalist. I'd be looking to represent you fairly but objectively.'

'I fully understand that, Clive. We're not looking for any kind of slick PR presentation. Indeed, that approach would seem more likely to attract precisely the wrong kind of person. We want someone who can present us accurately – warts and all, if you like. That's why we were so

interested when Rowan showed us samples of your work.'
He leaned forward and carefully poured himself another
finger of the whisky, then waved the bottle towards Greg
and then towards Charlie. Greg shook his head. Charlie
rose and helped himself to a large measure. Kennedy
watched him with apparent amusement.

Once Charlie had resettled himself, Kennedy went on,
'To return to your original question about how we'd like
you to proceed, to a large extent that's up to you. I see
tonight just as an opportunity for us to get to know each
other. We can confirm that you really are the man for us
– though I think that decision's already largely been made
from our side – and you can decide if you want to take
this on. Feel free to ask any questions you like. I can also
give you some reading material to take away this evening,
so you can absorb that also before making your decision.
It's important we all go into this with our eyes open.'

Clive was still unclear quite what he was being asked
to decide. His understanding from Rowan had been that
Kennedy would be able to provide access to individuals
and material pertinent to Clive's proposed research. But
it felt as if Kennedy was seeking some more exclusive
relationship. 'I suppose what I need to think about, on the
basis of what information you provide tonight,' Clive said
hesitantly, 'is what the nature and format of my research
might be. I'd originally envisaged some form of compara-
tive study looking at a range of so-called "left-hand path"
religions as a basis for highlighting the common themes
and principles, but also the differences in thinking and
approach. It sounds as if you're envisaging something more
focused on your specific movement?'

'Again, I think that's up to you, Clive. It's not my job to
tell you how to structure or conduct your research. But I

think you might also find that a more detailed study of our approach would pay dividends. But these are presumably decisions you can make at a later stage once you see how the work is progressing?'

'I suppose so,' Clive said. The truth was he didn't really have much choice. He was keen to pursue this particular topic because he thought it might help him establish his name, both among the rather esoteric audience who were interested in this kind of material and perhaps, through his tabloid contacts, to a wider public. Kennedy, like Rowan Wiseman, had been flattering about his work, but he knew he hadn't yet succeeded in achieving the profile he was aiming for. What he really needed was a themed series of articles that would really establish his credentials.

At the same time, he'd so far had little success in penetrating this world. Tonight was the first time that, with Rowan's help, he'd even managed to get through one of the right doors. Kennedy seemed to be promising him virtually unfettered access to their ideas and practices. He knew he'd be a fool to reject the chance.

'I'm very grateful to you for being so open, Robin. Obviously, I'll need to think carefully after this evening and I'll read whatever material you provide with great interest. As you say, we can perhaps decide later on the most appropriate ways of presenting my findings. But I'm certainly very attracted to taking this on. Very attracted indeed.'

'Good man,' Kennedy said. Clive fancied that Kennedy had exchanged a look with Rowan, but couldn't begin to interpret its meaning.

'Now,' Kennedy went on, 'can I finally tempt you to that single malt, Clive? Perhaps we should raise a toast to what I hope will be a fruitful and mutually beneficial collaboration. To us.'

'To us,' Clive echoed, feeling as if he'd just unwittingly signed up to something he still didn't fully understand.

Chapter Nineteen

'I don't reckon your hope's going to be fulfilled,' Zoe Everett said.

'What hope?' Annie Delamere glanced again at her watch, wondering how long they ought to give this. It was already gone six thirty and she didn't want to be too late getting back to Sheena. They'd arrived here just before six, but there'd been no response to her insistent ringing of Jonny Garfield's doorbell. She'd suggested sitting tight for a while on the basis that Garfield might still be out at work. She was keen to get this case moving, and Garfield was the only real lead they had.

'That Garfield Junior's place might be more pleasant than his dad's. Not judging from the neighbourhood.'

It was a fairly dismal inner city backstreet just outside Derby city centre, lined with narrow Edwardian terraces. Annie suspected that most of the houses were occupied by students. The tiny front gardens were mostly filled with overflowing wheelie bins, and few of the houses looked in decent repair. Garfield's had clearly been converted into flats, and his was one of four bells by the front door. Annie had tried all of them in the hope that someone inside might be able to give them some information on the likelihood of Garfield's return, but there had been no answer.

'Do you want to call it a night?' Zoe said. 'You ought to be getting back.'

'I checked with Sheena. She told me she'd be annoyed if I didn't carry on as usual.'

'But she didn't mean it, obviously,' Zoe said. 'Gary says stuff like that, and what he means is: if you're not back in the next fifteen minutes, I'm filing for divorce.'

'You don't know Sheena,' Annie said. 'She meant it. And she'd expect me to say the same to her. Although at the moment I'm not being very obliging. I'm telling her the last thing she should be doing is carrying on as normal.'

'Quite right. It's one thing accepting that your job carries risks. It's another to play silly buggers when those risks start becoming real.'

'That's exactly what— Wait, is that him?'

A tall, slightly gangling young man was approaching Garfield's house. He was probably in his early twenties, with an unkempt mop of black hair. There was no immediate resemblance to his father, but something about the awkwardness of his gait echoed his father's physicality. Sure enough, he turned in to Garfield's garden and began climbing the steps to the front door.

Annie and Zoe climbed out of the car and crossed the road towards him. 'Mr Garfield?'

Garfield had turned at the sound of the car doors slamming, visibly nervous. He had seemed to relax at the sight of the two women, but then tensed again as Annie called to him.

'Who?'

'Jonny Garfield.'

'Don't know him.'

'That's odd,' Annie said. 'We've just been talking to your dad, and he reckons you live here.'

'My dad…'

'You take after him, Jonny. Anybody ever tell you that?'

Garfield looked almost physically deflated. 'Not for a while, no. What do you want?'

'DI Delamere and DS Everett. We just want a little chat.'

Garfield had noticeably relaxed at the sight of Annie's ID. Whoever he was afraid of, it clearly wasn't the police. Or perhaps more accurately, Annie added to herself, he was afraid of someone else more. Some of his initial bravado seemed to have returned. 'You got a warrant?'

Annie sighed. 'We want a chat, Jonny. Not to ransack your house. We can do it out here in the street if you like, but that might attract interest from some of your neighbours. We could head back to police HQ and make it a lot more formal, but that'd be a waste of your evening. Or you could just invite us in and give us a cup of tea. What do you reckon?'

'This going to take long? I've got things to do.'

'That rather depends on how cooperative you are. Wouldn't want to interrupt your social life.'

'Chance would be a fine thing,' Garfield said. He pulled a set of keys from his trouser pocket. 'Come on, then. Let's get this over with.'

He led them inside, then up the stairs to the first floor. He unlocked the door of the flat and gestured for them to step inside.

Despite Zoe's earlier misgivings, the flat was a relatively pleasant surprise. It comprised essentially just three rooms, a decent-sized sitting room with a kitchen space and two adjacent doors that presumably led to a bedroom and a bathroom, though it was difficult to imagine how both had been fitted into the space apparently available. The sitting room, though, was immaculately tidy, the polar opposite of the equivalent room in the father's house.

There wasn't much to the room, except for a small sofa, a single armchair, a low coffee table and a large flat-screen television. Even so, Garfield had clearly made some efforts to personalise the place. There were pot plants scattered about, some pictures on the walls alongside a large Derby County banner, and even a small bookshelf containing a handful of books.

'Nice place,' Annie said.

Garfield looked genuinely pleased by the compliment. 'Not been here long,' he said. 'Now I've got it, I want to look after it properly.'

'You look to be doing a good job,' Zoe said.

'Thanks.' Garfield's initial frostiness towards them had thawed somewhat. 'Do you really want a cup of tea?'

'Just a figure of speech, Jonny,' Annie said. 'Okay if we sit down?'

'Yeah, of course.' He gestured towards the sofa. 'Make yourselves at home. What's this all about?'

Garfield wasn't what Annie had been expecting. From the descriptions given by his father and the others, she'd thought he would be some kind of truculent delinquent. In person Garfield came across as quiet, polite and relatively articulate, although Annie had been a police officer long enough to know that appearances could be deceptive. 'We're trying to gather information on someone called Darren Parkin. That name mean anything to you?'

The initial suspicion seemed suddenly to return. 'I'm not sure. Why?'

'We've heard you go way back.'

She could see Garfield hesitating, wondering whether to try to bluff his way out of this. 'Yeah, you're right. I knew Darren from school.'

'When did you last see him?' Zoe asked.

'Dunno exactly. A few weeks ago, I guess.'

'You're still in touch with him, then?'

'I suppose. We're not so close these days. We've both got our own circles, you know. But we meet up every month or two for a few beers.'

'You still get on?' Annie asked.

'Pretty well. You know how it is when you've known someone for a long time. What's this all about, anyway?'

Ideally, Annie would have liked to have kept Garfield in the dark for longer, expecting he might clam up once he knew the circumstances of their visit. But he really had been a friend of Parkin's, and she had no justification for withholding the information. 'I'm afraid it's bad news. Darren's been found dead.'

Garfield was clearly taken by surprise. 'Really?'

'I'm afraid so. We've got solid DNA and fingerprint matches, so there's not really any doubt.'

'Shit. How did it happen?'

'We're still really only at the beginning of the investigation. But we've reason to believe it was an unlawful killing.'

Garfield had dropped his head into his hands. Annie said nothing more, allowing his evident anxiety to build. Finally, he looked up at her. 'Can you at least tell me when it happened, then?'

'We're still waiting on the full post-mortem details. But we think within the last few days.'

'Christ.' He was staring past her, his eyes fixed on nothing in particular.

'I'm sorry we've had to break it to you like this,' Annie said.

He flicked his gaze back to her. His expression indicated that he'd given away more than he'd intended by his response. 'Well, you know. He was a mate. Like you said, we go way back. It's a shock.'

'Of course. It's always a shock when we lose someone who's been close to us, even if we don't see them very often.'

'Yeah, well, exactly.'

'And you said you last saw Darren – what, a few weeks back?' Zoe asked.

Garfield took a deep breath. 'Maybe more recent than that, now I think about it. Couple of weeks ago? Something like that.'

'I don't want to press you if you're finding this too distressing, Jonny,' Annie said. 'But would you feel up to answering a few more questions about Darren? The more information we have at this stage, the easier it'll be for us to discover who was responsible for this.'

Garfield's expression was sceptical. 'You reckon? You solve every murder then?'

'There's very little chance of whoever did this not being caught. The more information we have during the earliest stages of the investigation the better.'

'You've seen his nan and grandad? Don't suppose they told you much.'

'We've seen them, yes,' Annie said. 'But we need to know about Darren's recent life. Where he was living, what he was doing for work if anything, who his friends and associates were.'

'I don't know how much I can tell you,' Garfield said. 'Like I say, we weren't that close these days.'

'You've seen him more recently than anyone else we've spoken to,' Zoe pointed out. 'Do you know where he was living?'

'Somewhere in town. I don't know exactly.'

'He never invited you back?' Annie said.

'What? Like for coffee? He wasn't trying to pull me.'

'You've no idea of the area he lived in?' Annie didn't believe this for a second. 'What about work? What did he do?'

'Like all of us, I guess. Whatever he could to get by.'

'Such as?'

Garfield shifted uncomfortably in his chair, as if aware how unconvincing his responses sounded. 'Last time we spoke about it he was working as a kitchen porter in some cafe in town.'

'You know which cafe?' Annie allowed a note of scepticism to creep into her tone. 'Or was that another thing he didn't bother to discuss?'

Garfield was silent for a moment. 'Yeah, he told me.' He gave them the name of what Annie knew to be a fairly upmarket cafe-bar in the city centre.

'But he never told you where he lived?'

'I— No, not exactly.'

'What about friends? Who did he mix with apart from you?'

'I don't know. We were friends from the old days. He'd got a whole new bunch of mates now.'

'Any names you can give us?'

'Not really.' Garfield paused. 'He mentioned someone called Andy. Andy something.'

'Andy something.' Annie had ceased hiding her disbelief. 'I presume he never gave you any idea where Andy something might be living. Or how we might track him down.'

'Not really.'

'Not really.' Annie leaned forward. 'You know what I think, Jonny. I think you're lying through your teeth.'

Garfield looked as if he'd been physically struck. 'I don't know what you mean.'

'You know exactly what I mean. All this nonsense about not knowing where Darren lived, not knowing anything about his friends. Pretending that you didn't know who we were talking about, then claiming you last saw him a couple of weeks ago. You've given us nothing but bullshit since we arrived, Jonny. What is it you're trying to hide?'

'I'm not trying to hide anything.'

'You're certainly not succeeding. I can read you like a *Sun* headline, Jonny, and you're making about as much sense.' She leaned forward and stared directly into his eyes. 'Who are you afraid of, Jonny?'

'I don't know what you're talking about.' He sounded now like a truculent teenager.

'You know full well. When we got out of the car earlier, you looked scared to death. You're the only person I've ever met who was relieved to discover I was a police officer. So who else were you expecting?'

'No one. Nothing. I mean, you just startled me when you got out of the car.'

'What do you know about Darren, Jonny? What can you tell us that'll help us find the people responsible for this?'

'People?' Garfield spoke and then seemed to bite back the words, as if he'd said too much.

'Or person,' Annie said. 'You think it might have been more than one person?'

'No, I mean, you said—'

He was definitely rattled now, she could tell. Experience told her that this might just make him clam up more. Whatever Garfield was afraid of, he found it more frightening than any threat she might offer. They were more likely to make progress by allowing him to clamber back onto safe ground, hoping he might let his guard down as he relaxed. She gave Zoe an almost imperceptible nod.

'When you last saw him,' Zoe said, in her best emollient tone, 'did Darren seem worried or anxious?'

'I— Well, yes, he might have been. He didn't seem quite his usual self.'

'And how would you describe his usual self?' Zoe said.

'I don't know, exactly. You know, sort of relaxed...'

'Happy-go-lucky?'

'Yeah, I suppose.' Garfield's tone suggested he'd never heard the expression before. 'Things didn't usually worry him.'

'But this time you thought he seemed anxious?'

'A bit. As if there was something troubling him.'

'He didn't give you any idea what?'

There was another silence. Annie felt Garfield wanted to tell them something, to unburden himself, but couldn't find a way to do it. Or perhaps, she added to herself, a safe way to do it. 'No, not really. Like I say, it was just a feeling. Maybe I was wrong, or maybe it wasn't anything important.'

'What did you talk about?' Zoe said. 'The last time you met, I mean.'

'I don't know. What do you talk about with your mates?'

'Not the same things you do, I'm guessing.' Zoe smiled. 'You must be able to remember some of it?'

'The usual stuff, I suppose. Football. That kind of thing.'

Zoe gestured to the banner on the wall. 'You both supported County?'

'Yeah, for what it's worth. We'd both been at the match the previous Saturday. They'd been crap so we talked about that. That's probably what we spent a lot of the evening talking about.'

Annie could see Garfield was regaining some of his fluency now he felt on safer territory. Given the chance, he'd spout this kind of bollocks all day long.

'Did you go to the match together?' Zoe said.

Another pause. 'No. We did sometimes run into each other, but I hadn't seen him that Saturday.'

'So you talked about football. And what else?'

'I don't know. Some crap film he'd seen, maybe. And he had some story about work. Some customer who'd been behaving like an arsehole. It was just that sort of stuff.'

'And a couple of weeks later, or maybe less,' Annie said, 'he winds up dead. Any idea why that might have been, Jonny?'

'I don't know—'

'You don't know much, really, do you, Jonny? Do you know any reason why someone might have wanted to kill Darren? Any enemies? People he'd got on the wrong side of? People he owed money to?'

Garfield looked up at her, and she could tell he'd had to stop himself from responding. 'I don't know. He never talked about anything like that.'

'But?'

'It's how we live, isn't it? People like us. I do better than most. I do better than Darren did. But it's all hand to mouth. It's not difficult to end up in debt to the wrong people. Maybe that's what happened to Darren.'

It made sense, but Annie still didn't think Garfield was telling the truth, or at least not the whole truth. There was a lot more he wasn't telling them. 'Any idea who he might have been in debt to?'

'Like I say, he didn't say anything. But that might have been it.'

'And that's all you can tell us, is it? That he might have been in debt, but you've no real reason to think that and no idea who he might have been in debt to? Doesn't get us very far, Jonny.'

'I'm trying to help—'

Garfield flinched as Annie jabbed a finger in his direction. 'You've not given us an ounce of help since we arrived here, Jonny. The only piece of solid information you've given us is where Darren worked, assuming even that's true. You really expect me to believe you know literally nothing else about his life? You don't know where he lives. You don't know any of his friends. You don't know anything about his life, except that he meets up with you for a beer now and then. For Christ's sake, Jonny, the two of you went back years. Don't you want to help us find his killer?' Annie could feel her irritation spilling over. Other than learning who the victim was, they were getting precisely nowhere.

'I'm telling you everything I can.'

'What's the problem?' Zoe said, gently. 'What are you frightened of?'

'I'm not afraid of anything. I'm just telling you as much as I can.'

Zoe rose and walked over to stand beside Garfield. She placed a hand gently on his shoulder. 'We're not idiots, Jonny. You're scared to death of something. Or someone. If you tell us what or who, we can maybe help. That's our job.'

Garfield had visibly flinched at her touch. 'I've told you everything I can.'

Zoe looked back at Annie, who nodded. They'd worked together for long enough to have this routine off pat. Their version of good cop, bad cop. But it wasn't going to work for them today, Annie thought. If Garfield didn't want to confide in them, there wasn't much they could do. They could drag him back to the office and make everything more formal, but he'd just clam up still further. But it was worth pushing it as far as they could. If nothing else, Garfield would know that, when he was ready to talk, someone would be wanting to listen.

'Jonny,' Zoe said softly. 'Are you afraid of whoever killed Darren? Do you think they're coming for you next?'

Annie could see Garfield's body tense. 'Don't be stupid. I've no idea who killed Darren. I don't know why he was killed. Why would I be worried about that?'

'You tell us,' Annie said. 'You seem very frightened of something.'

'I've got you here. That's the only thing that's worrying me.'

'If you think you're in danger,' Zoe said, 'you need to tell us. We can give you protection. We can help you. Just tell us who it is.'

Garfield had closed his eyes, with the air of a child about to explode into a tantrum. 'There isn't anybody. I'm not afraid of anyone. I've just told you everything I can. Can't you understand that?'

Annie rose. 'You think it'll help you if you tell us nothing. But trust us, Jonny, that's not how it works. If someone's threatening you, they won't care whether you told us anything or not. They just won't trust you. If they are as dangerous as you seem to think…' She left the sentence hanging. 'I'll leave you a business card, Jonny. If you decide you want to talk, just call me. Any time. Believe me, if you're in some kind of trouble, it's the only way out.'

Garfield shook his head. 'You've really no idea, have you?'

'No idea about what, Jonny?'

'About what life's like for people like me. Or Darren.'

'You could try telling us.'

'I've nothing to tell you. There's nothing you can do for people like me.'

'If you say so, Jonny. But when you're ready to talk, just call me.' Annie placed the business card carefully on the coffee table. Garfield might throw it away as soon as they'd left the house, but she suspected somehow that he wouldn't. 'Come on, Zoe. We'll leave Jonny for the moment. He seems to be expecting some other visitors.' She turned her gaze back towards Garfield. 'We'll be back, though, Jonny. I just hope we're not too late.'

Chapter Twenty

As Annie turned the corner, she saw a black BMW parked under the streetlamp outside the cottage she shared with Sheena Pearson. She slowed her own car, immediately on her guard for anything untoward. As she drew closer she realised that the car was one of the unmarked vehicles belonging to the force. Jennings had confirmed earlier that a security operation was to stay in place for the time being and Sheena would be provided with as much protection as possible.

As she pulled up behind it, the driver and passenger doors opened and two uniformed officers emerged. She climbed out to meet them. 'Evening, boys. How's it going?'

It was clear that one of the officers had no idea who she was, but the other grinned and nodded. 'Evening. It's been very quiet, I'm glad to say.' He turned to his baffled-looking colleague. 'DI Delamere. She lives here.'

It took the other officer a moment to process this. 'Oh, right. Yes, of course.' It was evident that, as usual in the force, Annie's reputation preceded her.

'Are you two scheduled to be here all night?'

The first officer shook his head. 'Afraid not. We just don't have the resources. Chief Inspector Cowley asked us to hang around until you returned, but we'll have to head off shortly. We've arranged for a patrol car to come past every half-hour or so, and we're geared up to respond urgently to any requests for help, but that's about as much as we can do.'

Annie knew only too well the pressures the force was under, and she suspected Alan Cowley had already stretched his resources to the limits in allowing the two officers to remain here. Jonny Garfield had probably been right about one thing. If the police couldn't offer decent protection to a public figure like Sheena, they were never going to be able to do much for the likes of Garfield. 'Thanks for your efforts, anyway. Hope it's not been too boring.'

'Rather that way than the other,' the first officer said. 'Anything else we can do before we disappear?'

'Thanks, but we should be okay now. Or if we're not you'll soon hear from us.'

'Bit of a lonely spot,' the second officer observed.

'Thanks for reminding me.'

The cottage was actually only a couple of miles from the centre of Chesterfield, giving Annie an easy drive to police HQ while allowing Sheena to access the direct London trains. The nearest village, with a couple of decent pubs and a small scattering of shops, was only a fifteen-minute walk away. Even so, the cottage felt as if it could easily be a long way from anywhere. At this time in the evening, with the dark thickening, no other lights were visible and there were no other signs of human life. Normally, that was precisely what Annie loved about the place. Today, it felt as if they'd chosen to thumb their noses at the fates.

She waited while the two police officers climbed into the car and pulled out back towards the main road, then she turned her own car into the driveway. After a moment's thought, she backed out again and left her car parked across the front of the drive, where the police vehicle had been. That would make it easier for them to make a quick exit if necessary, with no risk of being boxed into the drive.

Christ, she thought, do I really need to be thinking like this?

Some of it was almost second nature, of course, the kind of caution that's drilled into you as a serving police officer. Just basic common sense. But for the moment she was going to have to exercise even greater caution. You tended always to assume it wouldn't happen to you. But it nearly had happened to Sheena twice in as many days.

She walked back to the front door and dug out her keys, finding herself now constantly glancing back over her shoulder. The front garden was relatively small, with nowhere for anyone to hide, other than a line of thick shrubbery along one boundary. The rear garden was more of a concern. It was potentially accessible from the woodland at the rear, and offered a number of places – thick bushes, a dense hedge and a row of trees at the far end – where an assailant could potentially be concealed.

The house itself was reasonably secure, and Sheena had further tightened up security when concern had initially surfaced about potential threats to MPs. They'd fitted CCTV around the property, installed an improved alarm system and installed security windows and doors on the ground floor of the house.

No doubt they'd tighten it up still further now. Sheena herself hated it. She hated the sense of being imprisoned in her own home. She hated the way these developments had inevitably distanced her even further from her constituents. Ironically, her contact with the protestors had been one of her few unplanned meetings with her constituents in recent months. Her surgeries now were appointment-only, and all local meetings were carefully vetted in advance.

Annie opened the door and stepped inside. 'Sheena?' She'd phoned before leaving to say she was on her way, but she didn't want her to suffer a moment's anxiety about who had entered the house.

'In the kitchen.'

Annie followed the sound of Sheena's voice into the farmhouse kitchen at the front of the cottage. Sheena was standing in front of the Aga, in the process of tasting what smelled like some kind of chicken casserole.

'You should have left that to me,' Annie said. 'You're only just out of hospital.'

'It's just displacement activity. Gives me something to think about other than that there's someone out there trying to kill me.' Sheena gestured behind her towards the large kitchen table. 'There's a bottle of wine opened. To cook with, you understand.'

'Did you put some in the casserole as well?'

'Very funny. Now you're here you might as well at least make yourself useful and pour us a glass.'

Annie did as she was told, placing one of the filled glasses beside Sheena on the corner of the Aga. She took a sip of her own. 'Sorry I'm so late back. We got stuck waiting to interview this guy, and then I made the mistake of going back into the office to drop Zoe off. Ran into the Assistant Chief, who clearly wanted to talk.'

'About me?'

'Partly. He'd already had the official line from Stuart Jennings and from Andy Dwyer, the guy in charge of the case, but I think he was looking for an inside track.'

'And did you give him one?'

'I told him what I knew. Not sure it was anything he didn't know already. I reckon he was just checking that Stuart and Andy were really on top of things.'

'Is he any good, this Andy Dwyer? You reckon he'll get whoever's behind this?'

'Dwyer's a decent cop, as far as I know. Ambitious sort, so he'll want this on his CV. We'll get this toerag soon enough.'

'I just hope that really is soon enough,' Sheena said. 'Before he has another go.'

'Amen to that.' Annie could sense that Sheena was looking for reassurance, even if she was reluctant to say so. 'He can't stay hidden for long. Either we'll pin him down through CCTV or someone will shop him.'

'You reckon it's a he?' Sheena asked.

'This kind usually are. But, no, I'm not assuming that. There's no practical reason why it couldn't be a woman.'

Sheena placed the lid back on the cast-iron casserole dish, then lifted it back into the oven of the Aga. 'Another half-hour or so.'

Annie topped up their wine, and they made their way back through to the spacious lounge. Sheena lowered herself on to the sofa, stretching herself its full length. She was dressed in jeans and a sweatshirt, as she invariably was at home. Her working image, by contrast, was carefully cultivated, as she'd explained to Annie – smart enough to be taken seriously by her more antediluvian colleagues, but not so smart that she seemed intimidating or elitist to her constituents.

'You wouldn't even have to think about that stuff if you were a man,' Annie had pointed out. She sometimes wondered how long Sheena would be able to put up with it. But she'd gradually realised how resilient Sheena was, and how determined she was to make Parliament work in the interests of her constituents. She was perhaps fighting a losing battle, but Annie knew she wouldn't give up easily. Even after a day like today.

Annie sat herself on the carpet beside Sheena and took her hand. 'What about you, though? How are you doing?'

'A bit shaken. Yesterday was bad enough, but today...' She'd closed her eyes, as if trying to block out the world. 'I don't like the thought that someone is actively targeting me.'

'I'm not keen on the idea either, funnily enough.' She squeezed Sheena's hand. 'I wish we could provide more protection for you.'

'I'm not sure I'd want it, to be honest. I'd feel bad if too much resource was being diverted to looking after me. You lot have enough on your plates.'

'You have to stop being so bloody selfless, you know. It doesn't help anything if someone in your position gets hurt.' For a moment, Annie found herself almost growing irritated with Sheena's apparent stubbornness. But she knew this was just Sheena's way of coping, of not allowing herself to be ground down by anxiety.

Sheena smiled. Her eyes were still closed but it was as if she'd read Annie's thoughts. 'Don't get me wrong. Just at the moment, I'm happy to accept whatever help you can provide. But having banged on about policing cuts for the last four years, it wouldn't be right for me to get special treatment. The guy who came today reckoned our security here was pretty decent already, and they're getting me this personal security device that connects directly to 999. There are a few more things they can do. Including installing some panic buttons and some more security lighting and cameras outside. Should be done in the next day or two.'

'And no doubt the *Daily Mail* will complain about you claiming it on expenses.'

'No doubt. Just this once, I reckon I can live with that. That's what really angers me about this. We've been playing with fire for years on this stuff. The tabloid press. Some of my less responsible colleagues. Even some of them on our side of the House. Stirring up anger and resentment. You'd think one death would have been enough to warn them, but even that got brushed under the carpet.' She pulled her mobile phone from the pocket of her jeans. 'You've seen the kind of stuff I get on social media. They've even been at it today.'

'You're joking.'

'Do I look like I'm joking? I mean, I've had loads of supportive messages, which is great. But plenty of abuse, even some threats. Unbelievable stuff.'

'You've told Dwyer's people?'

'They're monitoring the relevant feeds. Partly in case it gives them any leads into who was involved yesterday and today, and partly just for general nastiness.'

'Let's hope that one or two of the fuckwits out there get a bit of a shock when the police come calling,' Annie said. 'It's incredible that people can carry on spewing out that stuff after what happened today.'

'Amazing but true,' Sheena said. 'And apparently it should all be in a day's work for a conscientious MP.'

'You're sure you want to go on with this, Shee?' It was the question that Annie had been wanting to ask since the previous day's incident. It was a question that, in truth, she'd been asking since even before Sheena had been elected. 'Being an MP, I mean. After what's happened.'

'What else would I do?' It was her standard semi-serious response to Annie's recurrent question. She'd been a university lecturer in politics prior to her election. Her academic career had been relatively successful, and she'd been in increasing demand as a commentator and pundit. But Sheena had never been sure if it was a life she wanted to return to now she'd experienced politics on the front line.

'There's loads of stuff you could do,' Annie said. 'I know you feel you're doing something worthwhile as an MP, but there are roles where you could do even more.'

'Are there? Maybe there are. But I'm not sure I fancy sitting behind a desk driving some charity or campaigning group, however worthy they might be.' She eased herself up on the sofa and took another sip of wine. 'Anyway, it's academic. I'm not going to be driven out of the job by something like this. If and when I decide to move on, it'll be my own decision, not because I've been intimidated into it.'

Annie hadn't seriously expected her to say anything else. She knew she'd feel the same if their positions were reversed. 'Just take care, then, won't you?'

'I always do. As much as the job allows, anyway.'

'That's what worries me.'

Sheena pushed herself fully upright on the sofa. 'I know you think I'm a bit reckless sometimes, but I'm really not. I take as much care as I can. But if I lock myself away completely, I might as well not be doing the job. Shall we get some food?'

'By which you mean: will you just shut up about this? Fair enough. For what it's worth, I don't think you're reckless. I just worry about you.'

Sheena nodded and then grinned. 'I know that. And I know you mean well. Now, will you just shut up about this?'

—

They ate at the kitchen table. Generally, even after dark, they left the kitchen blinds open, untroubled by any thoughts of an intruder in the garden. Tonight, Annie noticed that Sheena had already lowered the blinds, as if she wanted to exclude as much of the outside world as possible. She seemed calm enough, Annie thought, but it was impossible to know what thoughts or emotions might be churning through her brain. Annie knew there was no point in pushing the issue further than she already had. She knew Sheena well enough to know she'd talk when she was ready to, if at all, and not before.

After supper, they returned to the living room. Without any open acknowledgement of what they were doing, both women returned immediately to work, sitting opposite each other with their laptops open on their knees. Annie had accessed the force's secure network and was checking her emails from the day. The vast majority were just routine administration that she could either ignore completely or at least disregard until some notional time when she was less busy. There were a few messages from various members of the team updating her and Jennings on various aspects of the enquiry, including a report on the second crime scene from the Senior CSI and a couple of long-shot leads relating to vehicles caught on traffic cameras in the areas surrounding the two killings. She dutifully ploughed through the material, sending responses where appropriate, knowing it would be one less task for the following day.

Sheena, opposite her, was working her way through her constituency emails. Annie had risked further wrath by asking whether she wouldn't be better taking a break at least for that evening. Sheena, in response, had gestured towards Annie's own laptop. 'I don't see you taking a break.'

'I've not been in hospital.'

'I was only in for observation. It's not as if I've been ill.'

'No, you've just been shot at. Twice. Some people might think you deserved a break.'

'Some people haven't seen the rate at which my constituency emails pile up.'

'That's because your constituents all know you're a soft touch.'

'Too ready to help them deal with unsympathetic government departments, dodgy landlords and the general problems of poverty and homelessness, just to take a few examples from today's mailbag. Is that what you mean?'

'You're just a do-gooder, that's your trouble.' It was an old joke between them, but tonight there was a slight edge to the banter.

'I guess it is. Anyway, if I don't deal with these tonight, they'll just keep coming. In fairness, the vast majority of today's are just messages of support, same as on the social media accounts. Interspersed with the odd bout of unimaginative abuse, obviously.'

'The police aren't monitoring the email account, presumably?'

'It's a secure account and a lot of constituents write in confidence about personal issues, so I can't give anyone else open access to it. But I've agreed to forward them any serious-sounding abuse, along with anything that might be pertinent to what happened yesterday at the protest.'

'You had anything of that sort?'

'Not since yesterday. When I originally made that statement about Mo Henley—'

'Our friend Bulldog.'

'That's the one. He really does think it makes him sound Churchillian. Anyway, at that point I got a load of stuff from those kind of groups. Britain Alone. England for the English. Even one who called themselves the Sons of Robin Hood, would you believe? But there's been a deathly silence since. I thought at least one of them might try to claim responsibility just to get a few inches in the local press, but nothing so far. Just the usual personal abuse from people without two brain cells to rub together.'

'Even the brainless stuff is probably worth forwarding on,' Annie said. 'It doesn't sound as if any of the people you were dealing with yesterday would exactly be *Master-mind* contenders.'

Sheena was still tapping at her keyboard. 'I normally resent wasting even a moment's thought on some of these numpties, but you're right. I suppose any of these might provide a lead—' She stopped suddenly, staring at the screen. 'Shit.'

'What is it?'

'I've just opened an email. Sent tonight. About an hour ago. Usual abuse. But then it says: "Saw your dyke partner arrive back around eight tonight. Then the police car drive away. So I guess you're both alone in there." There's a photo attached. Of the cottage. Looks like it was taken this evening.' She looked up at Annie. 'What do you think?'

'I think I call it in,' Annie said. 'And we get backup round here straight away. Then we have to make some decisions. It's probably just some arsehole trying to put the wind up us, but after today I'm taking no chances.'

It took Annie a few minutes to get through to the force enquiry desk. The call handlers had clearly been alerted to Sheena's case, so no lengthy explanations were required. She was told that a squad car would be there as soon as possible. They had moved back to the kitchen, pacing or absent-mindedly tidying, neither able to sit at ease.

'I'll feel such a fool if no one's out there,' Sheena said, when Annie had ended the call.

'Steel yourself then, because there probably won't be. If someone just wanted to kill you, they probably wouldn't announce the fact by email.'

'I'll bear that in mind. Very reassuring.' Sheena's defiant spark wasn't evident now. Instead of laughing she was quiet and, Annie thought, more than a little scared.

Annie went to her and put her arms around her partner in a loose embrace, touching her head to Sheena's. 'Sorry. I'm a bit shaken by this. What I mean is, it looks to me like whoever sent that email is mainly intending to scare you. At least for the moment.'

'You're not making this any better, you know.'

'I'm not sure sensitivity's my strong point. Not at a moment like this, anyway. I just shift into police mode.'

'I know. I've seen it enough times. I'm just joking. Well, kind of joking. Making light of it to avoid admitting how shit-scared I am. That kind of joking.'

'The point I was clumsily trying to make is that this person is playing with us. They may or may not want to kill you. They may or may not be the same person who shot at you today and yesterday. It might well just be some local fuckwit who thinks they're being funny. Whichever it is, they'll have made themselves scarce as soon as they sent that email. They're not going to hang around till the boys in blue show up.'

'So we're wasting police time?' Sheena stepped out of Annie's arms and leaned against the kitchen counter with her arms folded.

Annie sighed. 'Shee, just try to put your liberal conscience on hold for once and think about your own well-being. If there's the smallest chance there actually is someone still out there, we need to get that checked out. If nothing else, we need to get this incident formally recorded so the powers-that-be know there's a genuine and continuing threat. Nobody's going to begrudge taking a couple of uniformed officers off patrol to check it out. That's what they're there for. Take it from me, we're far more pissed off if something like this is ignored and we end up with a full-blown murder investigation on our hands.' She stopped as she realised the insensitivity of the remark. 'Sorry...'

'I suppose that's reassuring in its own way.'

'I do my best. The immediate question here is how this person got hold of our address.'

Sheena shook her head. 'I've always felt guilty at keeping it confidential. Now I'm glad I did.'

'You can probably blame or thank me for that,' Annie said. 'If I recall, I was the one who insisted on it.' Shortly before Sheena had been elected to Parliament, the law had been changed to allow prospective candidates to keep their domestic addresses confidential. In the wake of the MPs' expenses scandal, this had been a controversial move and a number of Sheena's fellow candidates had chosen to be open with the information. Annie had felt that the combination of her own and Sheena's roles potentially created an above-average security risk.

'As always, you were right,' Sheena said. 'Mind you, I think most of my colleagues agree with you these days. It feels different even from when I was first elected. So how could they have got hold of it?'

'I suppose it wouldn't be that difficult if you really wanted to find out,' Annie said. 'The media always seem to manage it. And, like I say, it might mean that our friend is based locally. I'm guessing our presence isn't exactly unnoticed in the local community.'

'Everybody knows everything in a place like this,' Sheena agreed. 'And they're usually only too happy to gossip about it.'

From somewhere in the distance, they could already hear the sound of a police siren. 'Even if our friend was still out there,' Annie said, 'they'll be off now my colleagues have announced their impending arrival. If I didn't know better, I'd almost think they did it on purpose to avoid meeting any trouble.' She smiled at Sheena. 'Come on, then. Let's go and waste some police time.'

Chapter Twenty-One

'I hope you've found the evening useful, Clive.'

They were standing outside the front door of the farmhouse. Rowan Wiseman and Charlie were already heading for the car, with Greg Wardle close behind them. Robin Kennedy had held Clive Bamford back in a characteristically proprietorial manner.

'Very much so. Thank you, Robin. And thank you for the loan of these.' He held up a large hemp shoulder bag that Eric Nolan, at Kennedy's request, had filled with a selection of books, pamphlets and other documents.

'As I said, you're welcome to keep most of them. A couple of the older books are rather rare and, to be honest, potentially valuable, so I'd be grateful if you could return those in due course. But not until you've finished with them, obviously.'

'I'll go through it all as quickly as I can. I'm really very grateful for all your help in this.' Clive was conscious he was on the edge of sounding obsequious. 'I hope I can do it all justice.'

'I'm sure you're just the man for that, Clive. We have every confidence in you.'

Clive had found the evening disconcerting. Kennedy had been consistently warm and welcoming, and had continued to be effusive about Clive's journalistic skills. Clive knew full well that he was being flattered and perhaps even seduced. He didn't particularly mind that, and for the moment he was quite happy to reciprocate if it helped him gain access to these people. He was confident that, when it mattered, he'd have sufficient independence to write fairly and objectively.

At the same time, Kennedy's charisma and charm were undeniable. If he paid attention to you, he had the knack of making you feel special, Clive thought, as if you were the only one who really counted. As if you were the only one who really deserved to be admitted into his inner circle. He made you want to try to please him, to sustain his respect and admiration.

But there was also something about Kennedy's manner that left Clive feeling uncomfortable. In the course of the evening, he had felt himself being drawn in, played off against Greg, whom Kennedy had continued to treat with some disdain. Clive had felt uneasy with that, even as he'd found himself helplessly playing along.

That was only part of the picture, though. For all Kennedy's charm and apparent openness, Clive still felt they weren't being given the full story. On reflection, this was what had left him feeling wrong-footed. Kennedy had continued to talk about the movement in broad abstract terms, but Clive had found himself unable to form any clear views about what its followers actually believed or practised. Whenever he felt he was drawing near to some kind of understanding, it would disappear into a cloud of Kennedy's verbiage.

He climbed into the rear seat of the car, taking his seat beside Greg, who was regarding him with a sardonic expression. 'Managed to tear yourself away, then?'

'He was just being hospitable.'

'To you, anyway.' Greg looked amused rather than offended.

Rowan Wiseman had started the car and, with a brief wave towards Kennedy, who was still watching them from the open front door, she turned the car back down the track towards the road.

'That's the way Robin works.' Charlie twisted in the front passenger seat to look back at Clive. 'Divide and rule. He's okay as long as you don't trust him too far.'

'You're just saying that because he doesn't trust you,' Rowan said. 'He's probably counting the spoons back there even now.'

'I wouldn't steal his spoons,' Charlie said. 'That nice malt whisky, maybe.'

'What did you make of him, Clive?' Rowan said over her shoulder.

Clive exchanged a glance with Greg. 'I'm not sure. I mean, he was very welcoming. And he gave me a load of useful stuff to take away. I felt as if he was holding some stuff back, but I suppose that's understandable. Given what he said about wanting to attract only the right kinds of people, I imagine he's probably just playing things close to his chest till he gets to know me better.'

'I wouldn't trust him an inch,' Greg said.

'I think that's a little unfair…' Clive had been surprised by the untypical vehemence in Greg's tone.

'Maybe I'm being oversensitive because he clearly had no time for me,' Greg said, 'but I just felt he was slippery. It seemed almost impossible to pin him down on anything.' He stopped. 'Sorry, Rowan, I'm being rude about someone who's a friend of yours.'

'He's not exactly a friend,' Rowan said. 'I've known him a long time and he's helped me out a lot. And Charlie too, even if Charlie sometimes has an odd way of showing his gratitude for that.'

Charlie snorted. 'Greg's got a point. Yeah, Robin's helped us out when we needed it. But Robin's mainly interested in Robin. As long as you appreciate that, you'll probably be okay with him.'

'Possibly,' Rowan conceded. 'It's never easy to understand Robin's motives. But that probably doesn't matter. What matters is what he does.'

'And what is that?' Greg said. 'That was part of the problem with tonight. Sure, he was very welcoming to Clive, but I'm not sure how much real information Clive got from him. My impression was that Kennedy can talk for England, but I'm not sure how much he actually says.'

'Be fair to him,' Clive said, finding himself feeling oddly defensive of Kennedy. 'It was the first time he'd met me. Like he said, we were really just sounding each other out tonight, seeing whether we could work with one another. I really wasn't expecting him to say too much.'

'Again, that's how Robin tends to work,' Rowan said. 'He can be cagey, but usually only when he has good reason to be. To be honest, tonight he was as open as I've seen him at a first meeting with someone. I think you made much more progress than you realise.'

'You think so?' Clive said. 'I really wasn't sure how to read him.'

'Like a closed book,' Greg said.

'He can seem a bit inscrutable when you first meet him,' Rowan said. 'But that's because he's sizing you up, deciding if he can trust you. If you go ahead with this, you'll find him much more open next time. Much more willing to discuss the detail.'

'I hope so,' Clive said. 'I'm really keen to get on with this. If Robin really can give me the information and insights I need, I really think we can make some progress.'

'You've just got to take it step by step with Robin,' Rowan said. 'Once you confirm that you want to go ahead and work with him, he'll immediately become much more open. He wants to make sure the choice is yours. Again, that's how he is. He doesn't coerce people—'

'No, he grooms them.' Charlie gave a sudden explosive laugh. 'That's Robin's way.'

'Charlie exaggerates as always,' Rowan said. 'But he's broadly right. Robin wants to bring you on board but he wants to make sure it's your choice.'

'Or at least that you think it's your choice.' Charlie grinned. 'I'm just winding Rowan up. She won't hear a bad word about Robin. I'm that bit more sceptical. Let's leave it at that.'

'You think you'll do it, Clive?' Rowan said. 'Work with Robin, I mean.'

'I think so.' Clive looked across at Greg. 'I mean, we'll give it a go, won't we, Greg?'

'If you say so.'

'There's a lot to explore here. If Robin can give us the information and contacts we need, we can produce a good piece of work.'

'The question is whether he's willing to be properly open with us,' Greg said. 'And whether he's prepared to tolerate me as your devoted assistant.' He placed an ironic emphasis on the last word.

'He'll warm to you if you give him a chance, Greg,' Rowan said. 'As Charlie says, it's just the way he works.

You'll probably find that next time it's you who gets the charm offensive. Keeps us on our toes.'

'I can get enough of that kind of thing at work,' Greg said. 'I don't want to have to tolerate tricksy behaviour in the evenings as well.'

'If you don't want to be part of this, Greg, I'll quite understand.' Clive knew from experience that the surest way to secure Greg's involvement was to threaten to with-hold it.

'No, I'm more than cool with it,' Greg said. 'I just want to be sure that our friend back there is equally happy about it.'

They were approaching the outskirts of the city now, leaving the dark of the country behind them. Charlie looked at his watch. 'Still pretty early, you know, folks. Anyone fancy another pint or two?'

Chapter Twenty-Two

'Where do you reckon?'

Annie was standing at the front of the cottage between the two PCs who'd responded to the call. These were different officers from the two who'd been keeping watch on the place earlier, and who'd now presumably completed their shifts. One was a young man called Paul Burbage, who had had some previous dealings with Annie. The other, a slightly older PC who'd already managed to acquire an impressively world-weary expression, had introduced himself as Ian Wharton. 'Must have been about here, I reckon.' She'd been peering through the camera of her mobile, trying to replicate the picture that had been attached to the email sent to Sheena. It was probably a waste of time, but at least it should give them an idea of where the author of the email had been standing.

Wharton shone his torch carefully across the grass beneath them. 'I don't know what I'm expecting to find,' he said, his tone an amiable grumble. 'Footprint of a gigantic hound, that sort of thing.'

Annie had warmed to the PCs almost immediately on their arrival. Her previous contacts with Burbage suggested he was a solid copper who could be relied on to do a decent job. Wharton clearly enjoyed playing the curmudgeon, but had provided a helpful and reassuring presence. Neither of them had shown any resentment at being called out, or any reluctance to search the gardens at the front and rear of the house. Needless to say, there had been no sign of any intruder.

'You're sure the photo was taken tonight?' Burbage asked, as Wharton continued to search the undergrowth.

'Can't be certain, obviously,' Annie said. 'But whoever sent that email knew when I got back and when your colleagues drove away.'

'Just wondering why they didn't take a picture of you arriving or the police leaving to prove they were actually watching. If they were looking to scare you, I mean.'

'Good point. It would certainly have made it even more unnerving.'

'Of course, they might have just been scared of being spotted if they came too near. Might have thought it was safer to wait till you were inside and the police had gone.'

'Maybe,' Annie said, thoughtfully. 'It's just…' She pulled out her phone. Sheena had forwarded the email to her, as well as to Dwyer's team. She opened up the picture again and held it in front of her, making another attempt to match it to the reality in front of them. 'It looks to me as if we're standing in roughly the right place, but the photograph was taken from somewhere above us. The elevation's not quite the same.'

Burbage squinted at the screen. 'I think you're right. I thought there was something funny about it but I couldn't put my finger on what.' He turned to his colleague. 'Ian, bring that oversized flashlight of yours over here.'

Wharton rejoined them. 'You just wish you had one, too. What is it?'

'Have a look up there.'

The edge of the front garden was lined with a row of trees, interspersed with bushes, which provided the cottage with some shelter and privacy from the public road. Wharton wafted the torch beam through the branches. Most were still bare, although the first spring buds were beginning to appear.

'There,' Annie said. 'The light caught on something. Among those lower branches.'

Wharton cautiously lowered the beam to where she was pointing. 'There's something. Hang on.'

As he moved to the left, the flashlight beam caught the object more clearly. A plastic box, strapped to the branch with what looked like gaffer tape. 'What the bloody hell's that?' Wharton said.

'I'm guessing it's a cheap security camera or something of that kind,' Annie said. 'That's how the photo was taken tonight.'

'You mean there was no one actually here?' Wharton said.

'Someone's been here at some point,' Burbage pointed out. 'If only to strap that up there.'

'They could have done that at any point. Sheena and I are out of the house a lot of the time. It wouldn't be difficult for someone to do that without much risk of disturbance.'

'It's not that high,' Wharton said. 'You'd probably only need a stepladder. Speaking of which, if you've got one to hand, I'll get it down so we can get it bagged as evidence.'

'There's one in the shed at the back,' Annie said.

'I'll go get it. Just in case there's anything nasty lurking in there.' Wharton handed the large torch to Burbage. 'Use it wisely while I'm gone.'

'We'll do our best. The question is…' Burbage began to shine the light up into the trees again.

'If the picture was taken remotely, how did they know what time I got back?' Annie was peering into the trees, following the movement of the torch beam.

'Exactly. Ah.' Burbage stopped, holding the torch steady. 'There.'

It was a second camera, apparently of a slightly different design from the first but similarly fixed to one of the lower trees' branches. This time the camera was pointing out to the road. 'That's how our friend knew when you got back. You were being monitored. Also explains why they didn't include an image of you arriving or the police leaving. It would have revealed that it was taken from here rather than by someone watching.'

'And we don't know how long the cameras have been there?' Annie said. 'Someone could have been monitoring our movements for days.'

'Hard to know,' Burbage said. 'They look like pretty cheap devices, and they still seem to be in decent condition. So they may not have been there long. On the other hand, some of these devices, even the budget ones, are designed for outdoor use, so they'd probably be okay for a while.'

There was a shout from the house. Annie whirled round to see Sheena standing silhouetted against the light in the hallway. For a moment, Annie felt a chill down her spine and wanted to tell Sheena to get back inside, not to leave herself so exposed. 'Everything okay?' Sheena called. 'I was beginning to feel a bit nervous in there by myself.'

'Sorry,' Annie said. 'Looks like we've found something, though.'

Sheena walked out to join them, wrapping her arms round her body against the cold evening air. 'What is it?'

'Cameras. Two of them. One monitoring the house. The other pointing out into the road, presumably monitoring our arrivals and departures.' Burbage shone the torch into the trees to allow Sheena to see the devices.

'You're kidding. So we don't know that anyone was actually out here tonight.'

'My guess is that nobody was,' Annie said. 'But someone was definitely out here at some point, probably in the last few days.' Her own initial instinct, on discovering the cameras, had been relief that there had been no intruder tonight. But somehow this felt almost worse. More calculated. It was as if the picture was shifting with each succeeding incident, so that what had seemed like a thuggish coincidence increasingly felt like a deliberate and carefully planned scheme. To what end, she couldn't imagine.

As if reading Annie's mind, Sheena gave an involuntary shiver. 'It gives me the creeps. How do we know there aren't more cameras about the house?'

'We don't.' Annie turned to greet Wharton, who was returning with the stepladder. 'This might just be a one-off, designed to enable tonight's little stunt. Or maybe we are dealing with some kind of – I don't know – voyeur.'

Wharton was setting the ladder under the trees, gesturing for Burbage to hold it steady. Between the two officers, they succeeded in removing the two cameras and securing them in evidence bags without risking any serious compromise to their potential value as exhibits.

'Not sure they'll tell us much,' Burbage said. 'I'm no expert but they look to me like the kind of thing you'd pick up for a few quid on the internet. Probably not possible to track down who bought them.'

'They must link back to a user, presumably?' Annie said.

'Probably through some kind of app. Whether you can track back from the camera to its user I've no idea.'

Annie nodded. 'And even if you can in theory, my guess is that it wouldn't be difficult to cover your tracks if you know what you're doing.'

'Usually the way,' Burbage agreed. 'Though some of your IT people are pretty smart.'

'Worth a try,' Annie agreed. 'You'll deal with getting those logged in? Andy Dwyer's the SIO. I want to make sure everything's done by the book.'

'I'll take care of it,' Burbage said. 'You reckon you'll be okay for tonight?'

'Reckon so. Especially as it looks like we never really had an intruder. Not tonight, anyway.'

'You think whoever did this expected us to suss the cameras so quickly?'

'That's a good question,' Annie said. 'I'd guess not. Having gone to the trouble of installing them, you'd think they'd want to get some use out of them first. Send us a few more unnerving emails at least. Maybe they didn't expect us to be quite as smart as we were.' She shrugged. 'Or maybe they did expect it, and this is just another in a series of stunts intended to intimidate us.'

'But why would they do that?' Sheena said. 'What are they trying to achieve?'

'I doubt whether even they know,' Annie said. 'There's a lot of pent-up anger out there, but a lot of them don't even seem to know who they're angry with or what they're angry about. You think this is connected with that Bulldog guy? What's his name?'

'Mo Henley, supposedly. Though I've seen suggestions that even that's not his real name and it's something double-barrelled. It seems likely. Not directly, maybe. But he attracts the kind of people who might do this.'

'That's the danger with people like Henley,' Annie said. 'We treat them as a joke, but they have some nasty people working with them. And sometimes some even nastier people behind them.'

Burbage had returned from replacing the stepladder in the shed and had joined Wharton, ready to leave. 'Is that this Bulldog guy you're talking about? If so, you're not wrong.'

'You know him?' Annie said.

'I wouldn't touch him with a twenty-foot bargepole,' Burbage said. 'But my mam and dad lived round the corner from his parents. He was a few years above me in school, and he had a nasty reputation even then. I always steered well clear, but he bullied a couple of my mates. His mam and dad were decent types, by all accounts. His dad worked in the pits, back in the days when we still had pits. Big union and Labour man, which is funny when you consider the son's politics. From what I've seen of him, he's not the brightest. Like you say, I reckon he's being used by some pretty unpleasant people.'

'Used in what way?' Annie said.

'To stir up trouble, mainly. It's all difficult to prove. We usually just end up dealing with results of it. But I've heard rumours there's nasty stuff associated with Henley. Loan sharks. Drugs. Protection rackets. Mobster stuff, really. Small-time mobster stuff, maybe, but nasty all the same.'

'You think Henley's deliberately working with these people?' Annie prodded.

Burbage was beginning to look as if he was regretting his outburst. 'I don't imagine he's much of a clue what he's doing. He just likes being the centre of attention. He was like that at school. He didn't care what he did, even if it got him excluded, as long as people were noticing him. But I reckon he's being used. Not that he'd care.' He shifted awkwardly, and Annie noticed that Wharton was half-concealing a grin. She imagined this wasn't the first time he'd had to listen to Burbage.

'I get the impression this is important to you,' she said.

'Sorry,' Burbage said. 'I know I need to avoid talking politics in this job. It's just that people like Henley make me angry. I've seen how people in those communities are being ripped off, and they look at Henley as if he was some kind of hero. But he's part of the problem.'

'You're entitled to your views,' Annie said. 'And I'm not saying I disagree with them. As long as you're objective in the job, eh?'

'I try to be. It's only people like Ian who have to put up with my ranting.'

'Tell me about it,' Wharton said.

Annie smiled at Burbage and Wharton. Clearly they worked well together. 'Thanks for all your help, anyway. I'm sorry if we've wasted your time.'

'You've not wasted anyone's time,' Wharton said. 'Those cameras are real enough. We'd better get on, if you're sure you're okay here. But if anything else happens tonight, just call it in.'

'Trust me, we will.' Annie's face turned serious. 'Sheena can play the hero all she likes. But I'm only too happy to admit that this scares the hell out of me. And I'm not easily scared.'

Chapter Twenty-Three

'You're doing what?'

Annie Delamere could see a couple of her colleagues in the open-plan office look over in curiosity at her semi-yelped question. She reminded herself yet again that it was best to lower your voice in this environment. Though that was often a challenge when she was on the phone to her mother.

'It's just a pilot. They may never show it.'

Annie could almost envisage the expression on her mother's face as she spoke those words. She knew exactly how much she was succeeding in winding up her daughter, and she was no doubt enjoying every minute.

'Mum, it was one of Mo Henley's supporters behind what happened to Sheena the other day. He's just a racist thug.'

'He may well be but he's entitled to his views.'

'Not if he's inciting racial hatred, he isn't. You know all this better than I do.'

'He won't be inciting racial hatred on any programme I'm involved in. And the whole point is to challenge his opinions.'

'While giving him a platform to express them.'

'You know my views on de-platforming, or whatever idiotic term it is they use for silencing free speech.'

They could go round this loop all day, and Annie knew there was no point. As always, her mother would do what she wanted to do and nothing could be done to stop her. 'You're really doing a television series?'

'It's not a series. It's just a pilot for a possible slot on the local politics programme. The idea is to do challenging interviews with provocative political figures, which is why they've gone for Henley for the pilot. They're looking to liven things up, and because I've appeared on there a few times, they thought of me. But it could be the start of a whole new career, even at my age.'

Annie sighed. There were countless reasons for her to dislike this idea. The ribbing she'd no doubt get from her colleagues here. The glee that her mother would take in adopting positions she knew would cause her daughter maximum embarrassment. The fact that so many people here still assumed that Annie had only reached her current rank because of some behind-the-scenes influencing from her mother. That assumption would become even more prevalent if her mother's public profile continued to grow.

But there was nothing she could do to prevent her mother doing this. It might sometimes seem as if her mother's sole motive was to embarrass her daughter, but Annie didn't really believe that was really the case. She was doing this because she wanted to. And why shouldn't she? She was retired. She was divorced. She probably needed a hobby. But why the hell did it have to be this?

'I just hope you know what you're doing, Mum. I don't want you to end up making a fool of yourself—'

She regretted the words as soon as she'd spoken them, and sure enough her mother's retort was immediate. 'You always know how to fill me with confidence, Annie. You seem to think it's your life's work to undermine me and my reputation. Can I just remind you that I progressed further in the force than you're ever likely to...'

Annie had repeatedly told herself that her mother's accusations at moments like this were nothing more than what psychologists call 'projection', but that didn't prevent her from feeling guilty. 'You know that's not what I mean. It's just that this is all new to you—'

'And that's why it's exciting. I don't know why you can't just be pleased for me.'

'I am. Congratulations. Look, Mum, I've really got to go now.' There really was no point in yet again pointing out why this kind of development was less than ideal for Annie.

'Of course you have. Far too busy to talk to me.'

This from the woman whom Annie Delamere had barely seen throughout her childhood. The woman who was always too busy to be there for her bedtimes or to come to school performances. The woman whose career had always come before everything, including her daughter and her marriage. 'I'll give you a call tonight, okay?'

'How is Sheena, anyway? I hope she's okay.'

Typical of her mother to finally mention Sheena's welfare, as an afterthought when Annie was trying to wrap up the call. 'She's fine. A bit shaken but fine. I'll pass on your good wishes.' The last sentence came out as more sarcastic than she'd intended, but she was almost past caring. 'I'll call you tonight. Bye, Mum.'

She ended the call before her mother could say anything more, then looked up to see Stuart Jennings standing in front of her desk, grinning broadly. He'd obviously arrived at some point while she'd had her head down, struggling to hold onto the last threads of patience with her mother. She didn't know how much of the conversation he'd actually overheard.

'The blessed Margaret, I assume?'

'The one and only.'

'What's she up to?'

'This and that.' She had no intention of sharing her mother's news with Jennings. 'Like she always is.'

'Busy woman. Talking of which, I hear you had an eventful evening.'

'You might say that.'

'Just been talking to Andy Dwyer. He's heading out to talk to Sheena today. You've no problem with that?'

'Why would I have? The sooner we get this sorted, the better.'

'He wanted to have a chat with you first. Just informally to get a bit of background. He's going to call you, but I thought I'd give you the heads-up in advance. Just so he doesn't catch you on the hop.'

'Happy to talk to him, formally or otherwise. But I don't know how much I'll be able to tell him. Sheena's the one he really needs to talk to.'

'To be honest, I think he's mainly concerned about the sensitivities of the investigation. He's aware how high-profile it is and he doesn't want to screw up. He just wants to pick your brains to make sure he doesn't say anything out of turn.'

'To Sheena?' Annie laughed. 'She wouldn't care what he said. She's not exactly the high and mighty type.'

'You know that. Andy doesn't. To him, she's a public figure who's in a position to make a lot of capital about any aspects of the investigation she's not happy with. He just wants to get it right.'

'All she wants is for us to catch the bastard who did it. She's honestly not too fussed about the niceties.'

'That's what we all want. Andy especially. Anyway, he'll be in contact with both of you this morning.'

'Sooner the better as far as I'm concerned—' She was about to say something more when her mobile buzzed on the desk. She glanced at the screen. 'Zoe. I'd better take it. She's been out talking to Darren Parkin's employer. The only lead that Jonny Garfield was prepared to give us.'

'I'll leave you to it.' Jennings rose and waved a vague farewell as she picked up the phone.

'Zoe? How'd you get on?'

'It's been interesting. The manager was around, fortunately, and she was as helpful as she could be. Darren did work there for a while, but not for some time. She reckoned he seemed a decent-enough lad, willing worker, all that, but not the brightest. His employment record was patchy, she said, but it looked as if it was mainly because he'd been laid off or made redundant rather than through any fault of his. No real qualifications, so the world wasn't exactly his oyster. He'd made noises about wanted to get on in catering, and she'd tried to encourage him in that. But he didn't turn in a few months back and they didn't see him again. She'd been a bit surprised because he'd been pretty reliable up to that point, but he wasn't the first who'd let them down.'

'Goes with the minimum-wage territory, I'm guessing.'

'That's more or less what she said, though a bit more diplomatically. But she'd been particularly surprised in this case because the owner had apparently taken a bit of a shine to him.'

'Really?'

'Name meant nothing to me, but he's apparently a guy with a few bars and clubs around the area. Does very well for himself, she reckoned. She said he's always looking for employees with potential and she'd mentioned Darren as someone who seemed to want to get on. The owner had had a few chats with him, and she'd thought Darren appreciated the attention.'

'Poor kid. When the biggest opportunity in your life is being a kitchen porter in a cafe.'

'Some people don't even get that,' Zoe pointed out.

'How did she react when you told her what had happened to Darren?'

'As you'd expect. Shocked. Couldn't believe it could have happened to someone like him. She couldn't imagine why anyone would have a reason to harm him. Just the usual, really.'

'And she had no idea what might have happened to him since he'd stopped working there?'

'So she said.'

'Doesn't take us very far, does it?'

'Not really, other than filling in his background. The main thing I got out of it was his home address. Guess what?'

'I'm not sure I've got the brainpower for all this guessing, Zo. Go on.'

'It's just a few streets from Jonny Garfield. There's no way Garfield couldn't have known where he lived.'

'Not a surprise that Garfield was lying. I'm just wondering why he bothered. He must have known we'd find out.'

'I didn't get the impression that he was being particularly rational yesterday.'

'That's one way of putting it. We'll have to pay him another visit. Keep the pressure on. He'll talk to us eventually. When he realises that we're probably the closest thing he's got to a friend.'

'You want me to go and check out Darren's address?'

'Why don't we go together? Don't know if we'll be able to gain access, but we'll cross that bridge when we come to it. You go and grab a bite to eat, and I'll head into the city centre. I've just got to see a man about an MP, and I'll be on my way.'

'A man about an MP?'

'Andy Dwyer.'

'Ah. How's he getting on?'

'That's one thing I want to find out.' She'd already told Zoe about the previous night's developments. 'I don't know if we're still in lone fanatic territory or somewhere even more sinister, but the sooner we sort this, the more comfortable I'll be.'

Chapter Twenty-Four

'Morning, Andy.'

Dwyer peered over his computer screen. 'Annie. Was just about to give you a call.'

Dwyer was located in an open-plan office almost identical to her own but one floor lower in the building. 'Stuart told me. I was just heading out, so I thought I'd grab you on my way past.'

'Always delighted to be grabbed by you, Annie.' Dwyer was a year or two younger than Annie but had the air of being prematurely middle-aged. He'd obviously been an athletic type once, but was now running slightly to fat, with incipient baldness and jowls. He'd make an ideal Chief Constable one day, she thought. He certainly made no effort to conceal his ambition.

'You'd better not try that kind of talk with Sheena. She's been known to castrate a man for less.'

Dwyer looked mildly startled before realising she was joking. 'That's really what I wanted to talk to you about.'

'Your fear of castration? Don't worry. She only does it figuratively.' She allowed him a smile. 'Seriously, happy to help you in any way I can. We just want to get this sorted.'

'Trust me, I'll pull out all the stops. I just thought it might be helpful to know a bit more about Ms Pearson before I talk to her. In case, there's any useful background you can give me.'

'Not sure what I can tell you. I've known her for years. We were at uni together. Before she was an MP she was a politics lecturer. She'd always been active in Labour politics, but she never really thought she'd become an MP. The party half-expected her to lose in 2010. She was very different from her predecessor and the majority was getting squeezed.' She shrugged. 'I'm just throwing facts at you. Probably not very useful.'

'It's helpful just to get a feel for the kind of person she is. I looked her up online but it didn't tell me too much.'

'She tends to avoid controversy. Until now, anyway. She's very driven, conscientious, wants to do the best for her constituents. Takes it seriously.'

'I don't share her politics,' Dwyer said. 'But we could do with more MPs like that. From what I've read, she strikes me as a decent sort.'

'She's that all right.'

'Not sure if I should be asking this, but did it cause any problems? Her becoming an MP while you were a serving officer, I mean.'

'I got it all cleared through the right channels.' Annie was conscious that she could sound defensive in responding to questions like this, though she wasn't sure what she had to be defensive about. 'Even when she was first elected as a councillor, in fact. Everything we both do is transparent and above board, and we have a kind of "Chinese wall" arrangement on anything political. We just don't discuss it, in the same way I don't discuss police business with her. Everybody seems happy with that.'

Dwyer held up his hands. 'Didn't mean to imply anything different. I was just curious, that's all. How's she taken all this?'

'As you'd expect, really. Very shaken, but she's pretty resilient. The main challenge will be to stop her getting straight back to work.'

'This may be a daft question given her line of work, but do you think there's anyone who'd have a reason to want to hurt her? She seems to do a fair bit of campaigning.'

'Well, that's part of her job. She stirred a bit of a hornets' nest with her comments, hence the protest outside her office. And like a lot of MPs, particularly female ones, she gets more than her fair share of abusive messages and correspondence.'

'I've seen her social media timelines,' Dwyer said. 'Some nasty stuff.'

'And, in fairness, some very nice stuff. And a lot of the abuse is just from lonely men who get their kicks from trying to scare what they imagine to be a vulnerable female. Most of it you can disregard. The trick is trying to spot the tiny percentage you need to take seriously. But, like I say, Sheena's not really the provocative type. She speaks out when she feels strongly about something, as she did on the Bulldog thing, but she doesn't go looking for trouble.'

'What about last night's developments?' Dwyer said. 'Someone had clearly been into your garden to place those cameras. Have you seen anyone suspicious hanging around?'

'Not that I can recall. But Sheena and I are out of the place a lot. You know the kind of hours we can work in this job, and Sheena's down in London for most of the week when Parliament's sitting. It wouldn't be difficult or particularly risky for someone to get into the garden. I assume you'll be speaking to some of the neighbours? There aren't that many houses around us, but there are one or two neighbours who tend to notice any comings and goings.'

'We're on to that. You have any security cameras at the house?'

'We do, actually. But they're trained on the front and rear doors, so they wouldn't pick up anyone who was just in the garden.'

'Worth checking, though. And we'll do a search around the garden just in case there are other cameras.'

'What about the shootings? Are you making any progress with those?'

'Surprisingly little with yesterday's, to be honest. I'd assumed we'd pick someone or something up on CCTV. There are plenty of cameras around the hospital site. But our friend seems to have neatly eluded all of them.'

'Almost as if they knew what they were doing?'

'Exactly. Looks to me like someone who'd fairly carefully sussed out where the cameras were and did their best to avoid them. I've got someone going through the footage for the last few days to see if we can spot anyone acting suspiciously but it's a long shot. And so far no strong leads from any of the CCTV or other cameras on the surrounding roads, either. My guess is whoever did it was parked discreetly somewhere outside the site, but the main roads round there are busy, so it's difficult to pick out anything useful. As you know, we issued a warning in the media that the shooter or shooters remain at large, along with an appeal for any information. We've had the usual small deluge of calls but there are only a handful of even potentially promising leads.' He paused. 'Wish there was more. But it's early days.'

Or, alternatively, the Golden Hours, she thought. The early days of an investigation when you were most likely to make a breakthrough. It didn't always work like that, of course. Many cases were cracked simply through long hours and sheer hard work. But it was discouraging to have so few leads at this stage. She knew Dwyer would be leaving nothing to chance but she felt frustration, tinged with fear. 'What about the previous day's shooting?'

'We're making more progress with that.' She could see Dwyer visibly relax as they moved on to more comfortable territory. 'Got some decent CCTV footage of the protestors and we've identified a few of them from the system. Small-time thugs, most of them. We've also had a couple shopped by their friends or family. So we're following up on all those. The challenge will be identifying who actually fired the shot. So far, they're all denying any knowledge. Claiming they didn't know that anyone on the protest was carrying a gun, and they wouldn't have allowed it if they'd known. Thing is, it might even be true. The first part, anyway.'

'You think so?'

'We've been checking the ballistics of the shot. We've now found the bullet, so we've an idea of what sort of gun it was and where it was fired. I don't pretend to understand the technical details but it was fired from some distance away from the protest itself, probably from near the corner of an adjacent street. The ballistics guy even reckoned that it might not have been intended to hit at all. The angle suggests it was probably intended to be fired over the heads of the protestors and Ms Pearson. One possibility is that, because the crowd had drawn closer, the shooter misjudged the angle and aimed too low.' He shrugged. 'But that's just guesswork, really. The real question is whether the two shots were fired by the same individual, or whether the second was a more calculated attempt to feed off the publicity. We're waiting for confirmation, but now we're able to compare the bullets, it does look as if both shots could have been fired from the same weapon.'

Annie nodded. 'The other question is whether the intention was actually to kill Sheena or just intimidate her.'

'Exactly. That feels marginally more likely at the moment, but that's really nothing more than gut instinct.'

'You mean that if they'd really wanted to kill Sheena, they'd have succeeded by now?'

'I wouldn't have put it quite like that,' Dwyer said.

'For what it's worth, I think you've got a point. We both know only too well that it's not too difficult to kill someone if you've got the means and the will. Whoever's doing this – if it's one person – obviously has the means. So either they lack the will or they've just been unlucky. But last night's email suggests it might be more about intimidation than a serious intent to kill.'

'Which doesn't mean she shouldn't take the threats seriously. But you know that.'

'I know that. And I'll make sure Sheena remembers it. Any luck with tracing the email?'

'Not so far. I'm not too hopeful, to be honest. It's a bit like the CCTV at the hospital. Whoever sent the email knew what they were doing. The IT people are giving it their best shot but they didn't seem too optimistic. They're also trying to see if it matches any of the other emails sent to her in recent days, but most of those seem to have just been from idiots who made no serious attempt to conceal their identities.'

Annie looked at her watch. 'I'd better be getting on. I've got Zoe Everett waiting in town for me.'

'This the sacrificial bodies case? Weird stuff.'

'Don't know about sacrificial, but it's weird all right. We certainly seem to be getting them at the moment, don't we?'

Dwyer gave a grim smile. 'It's because the fates discovered that Stuart Jennings thought he was transferring over here for a quiet life. That'll teach him.'

'Something like that.' She pushed herself to her feet. 'Good luck, Andy. You heading out to Sheena this morning?'

'That's the plan. If you think she's up to it.'

'She's more than up to it. We both just want to go back to our normal lives. If there's anything else you need from me, just let me know. I don't want to do anything inappropriate, but I'm happy to give all the help I can.'

'Thanks, Annie. We'll put everything into it, you know. We're not going to let this bastard get away.'

'Yes,' she said. 'I know that.'

Chapter Twenty-Five

'Nice place,' Annie said. 'Characterful.'

'It's a hidden gem,' Zoe agreed. 'They do a mean bacon roll and tea you can stand your spoon up in. You want anything?'

Annie looked around them. Zoe had directed her to this backstreet greasy spoon on the outskirts of Derby city centre. It looked like the kind of place that would serve hefty, unpretentious food, much of it deep-fried, at rock-bottom prices. Not that there was much wrong with that, she thought. It was clearly an opinion shared by the diverse clientele filling most of the other tables. 'The bacon roll sounds enticing, but I'll pass for the moment. This a regular haunt, Zoe?'

'Used to be, funnily enough, back when I was on the beat. I'd sometimes pop in for a coffee at the beginning or end of a shift. If you want to know what's going on in this neighbourhood, Georgio's your man.' She gestured towards the middle-aged man with slick black hair who was standing behind the counter. 'He still gives me a discount.'

'Fair enough. I knew there had to be a reason we were here.'

'Apart from the fact that it's just round the corner from where Parkin lived? That was my main motive. Thought Georgio might be able to give me some background.'

'And could he?'

'Didn't know Parkin, or at least didn't know the name. But he knew the street and he knew the house. They're all terraces that have mostly been converted into flats or shared residences. Georgio reckoned they're mostly owned by one company, let mainly to students or young professionals. Decent places, he said. Better than they looked from the outside. When I described Parkin's circumstances, he seemed surprised that Parkin would have been able to afford to live there.'

'It's not exactly the most upmarket area,' Annie said.

'One of those the estates described as "up-and-coming". But it's getting more expensive, apparently, partly because it's relatively close to the city centre.'

'Did Georgio know anything about the landlords?'

'Not really. But I was thinking about what you said about access, and I've done a bit of digging while I was waiting for you. Took a walk down there and saw a couple of the flats had "To Let" signs on them. They all seem to be managed by the same agency. Including Parkin's. So I took the liberty of calling them to see if someone could give us entry.'

Annie raised an eyebrow. 'Good work. What did they say?'

'I told him we were police and that we had reason to believe that something might have happened to the occupant. Said we didn't want to force an entry if we could avoid it, so if they were able to send someone round…'

Annie smiled. 'So they think something might have happened to the occupant actually inside the flat?'

Zoe shrugged. 'I didn't say that. But I suppose it might be possible they assumed it.'

'Certainly quicker for us than taking a more formal route. You've got hidden depths, Zoe, you know that?'

'If you say so. We'd better get round there, actually. The guy reckoned he'd be about fifteen minutes.'

Annie shook her head. 'Just remind me never to buy a used car from you.'

–

Spring was on its way, but it was still a chilly afternoon. The young man wore no overcoat over his cheap-looking suit. He was standing outside the house, hopping from foot to foot in an effort to keep warm.

Zoe called out, 'Bryce?'

The young man blinked. 'Yeah. I'm Bryce Scott. From the agency. I was expecting the police.'

'We are the police,' Annie said. 'DI Annie Delamere and DS Zoe Everett.'

The two women held out their ID for Scott to check. He peered closely at the cards for a minute and then looked up. 'It's just that I was expecting—'

'That we'd be in uniform? We can explain once we're inside.' Annie was determined not to lose the opportunity Zoe had created.

'Yes, of course.' Scott pulled out a large bunch of keys and began fumbling with the lock. 'You said that you thought something might have happened to Mr Parkin…'

'Best to wait till we're inside.'

'It's just that I don't want to intrude on Mr Parkin's privacy without knowing—'

'Trust me, Mr Scott. Mr Parkin won't mind.'

Scott finally succeeded in opening the door, leading them into a narrow hallway. The house was a tall, narrow terrace, not dissimilar to the place where Jonny Garfield was living. It looked relatively well-decorated and maintained.

'Mr Parkin's is the ground-floor flat,' Scott said. He looked nervously at the door in front of them. 'You think he might be…?'

'You can open the door,' Annie said. 'You don't need to worry.'

Clearly unsure how else to respond, Scott did as he was told. He stepped back as Annie and Zoe made their way past him into the interior of the flat.

The door opened directly into the living room. Annie stepped inside and then stopped, staring around her. 'Zoe. Come see.'

As in Garfield's flat, the room had a small kitchen area at one end. The remainder of the room was relatively sparsely furnished, with just a sofa, a small television, a low central table, a small dining table under the window and a couple of high-backed dining chairs. The difference was the walls. They'd been decorated with an array of posters and artwork. Annie recognised some of the prints as copies of artwork by Bosch and Brueghel. Others were clearly similar classical artworks, some of them vaguely familiar, though she couldn't name the artists.

All appeared to be depictions of hell.

Interspersed among them were pictures of various symbols. There were pentagrams and similar symmetrical symbols, some apparently runic symbols, and even a couple of ornate swastikas.

The dining table held a number of books. Judging from their covers and titles, they appeared to relate to similar esoteric material to that implied by the wall decorations.

None of this was remotely what she'd expected from everything she'd heard about Darren Parkin.

'Jesus,' she heard Scott say from behind her. 'What's he done to the place?'

She turned to see Zoe staring at the display open-mouthed, her face ashen as her eyes darted between the various images. She looked as if she was on the point of fainting.

'You okay, Zoe?'

Zoe looked at her as if she'd barely understood what Annie had said. 'Do you mind if I go outside for a breath of air? I just feel a bit…' She left the sentence hanging if she had no idea how to finish it.

'No, of course. I'll have a look round in here.'

Zoe stumbled back to the front door and stood on the step, her back to the interior of the house.

Annie returned her attention to the room, sure now that Zoe's reaction had been a response to these images. There'd be time to explore that later, but for now she was wondering more about the significance of what they'd found.

As if echoing her thoughts, Scott said, 'So what's this all about?'

'The first thing to tell you, Mr Scott, is that Darren Parkin is dead.'

'Dead? But your colleague—'

'He's dead, Mr Scott. We believe he was murdered.'

'Jesus.' He stared past her at the display of posters. 'But all this stuff— I mean…'

'Your guess is as good as mine, Mr Scott. I'm afraid I'm not yet at liberty to give any more information about the cause and nature of Darren Parkin's death.'

Scott gestured towards a door at the far end, which presumably led to a bedroom. 'He's not…?'

'No, he's not. He was killed elsewhere. It's taken us a short while to identify him and obtain his home address. How long's he been living here?'

'Couple of months. He seemed okay. Didn't quibble about the deposit. Was all a bit academic anyway, because he was recommended as a tenant by the landlords.'

'By the landlords? Is that common?'

'It's a happened a few times. They've got their fingers in a few different pies and they employ a fair few people. Sometimes they're looking for accommodation for people who work for them. I guess this was one of those. Anyway, they were willing to act as guarantors so it's easy for us. If anything goes wrong, they can't really complain. The only pain for us is that they're usually on shorter leases than our regular clients, but again we can't really do much about that if the landlords are happy with it.'

'What about Parkin? Was he on a short lease?'

'Just three months. We usually insist on at least six.'

Annie nodded. 'I'll need to get details from you once we finish here.' She pointed towards the bedroom door. 'Do you mind if I have a look?'

'Be my guest.'

She pushed open the bedroom door and peered inside. The bedroom was tiny and, at first sight, much more conventionally decorated than the living room. There was a Derby County poster, similar to the one they'd seen in Garfield's flat, but few other decorations. Beyond that, the room contained nothing but a single bed and a small bedside table. A further door led into what she assumed to be a shower room.

The bedside table held a pile of books that appeared similar in content to those on the table in the living room. There was also a small framed print of one of the pentagram-style symbols depicted on one of the living room posters. Whatever its significance, it had clearly meant something to Parkin.

She stepped across the room and pushed open the door of the shower room. It contained a shower, a small sink and a lavatory, and seemed unremarkable. She didn't want to disturb the scene any more than she could avoid, in case it should yield any useful forensic material, but she paused for a moment to take a photograph of the bedside table and books before returning to the living room. Again, she stopped and carefully took photographs of the walls and the books on the table. She'd get the place properly searched later. For the moment, she just wanted an opportunity to find out more about these various esoteric materials.

'We're going to have to get this place sealed off and properly examined by our forensics team,' she said to Scott. 'We can get authorisation for that, but it's easiest if everyone just cooperates.'

'I'll tell them back at the office. We'll need to inform the landlords.'

'Might be better if we do that, Mr Scott. If Parkin was working for them, we'll need to talk to them in any case. If we can come back to the office with you, we can get the details.' She followed Scott back out into the hallway. Zoe was still standing outside the front door, her back to them. 'Anything else you can tell us about Darren Parkin, Mr Scott?'

'Not really. I only met him a couple of times. Once when he came in to sign the various documents and once when he collected the keys.'

'What was your impression of him?'

'Not much, really. He was very quiet. Hardly said a word when he came in. I'm not being disrespectful, but he didn't strike me as the brightest. Not the type to be interested in all that kind of stuff, anyway.' He jerked his thumb in the direction of the room behind them.

'People are full of surprises, I guess. Okay, we'd better get this place locked up. How far's your office?'

'Just round the corner really. Five minutes.'

While Scott locked the flat behind them, Annie crossed to the front door. 'You okay, Zo?'

Zoe turned to greet her. 'Yes. Fine. Just a bit stuffy in there.' She was making an effort to smile, but the expression in her eyes belied her words. The vivaciousness evident at the cafe just a short while earlier was nowhere to be seen. Now, Zoe was closed down.

'Just want a quick catch-up with my colleague,' Annie said to Scott. 'We'll be over in a few minutes.' She gestured up at a 'To Let' sign on a neighbouring house with the agency name on it. 'Assume that's you?'

'That's us. We look after most of these. It's all the same landlords.'

'The same as Parkin's place?'

'It's a sizeable operation. We're starting to get a bit nervous they'll set up their own management function. They're probably getting big enough to justify it. But don't let them know I suggested it.'

'Must be raking it in,' Annie said. 'Okay, we'll be along in a few minutes.'

'I'll have the info waiting.' Scott waved to them, then set off down the street, whistling tunelessly.

Annie turned back to Zoe. 'You sure you're okay, Zo? I don't want to be rude, but you don't really look it.'

'I'm fine. Really. Just a bit tired.'

It didn't feel like this was really the moment, standing in the cold on this featureless backstreet, but Annie felt she'd already delayed the conversation too long. 'You're not yourself, Zo. It's obvious. Even Stuart Jennings has noticed, and he's about as sensitive as a comatose rhino. What's wrong?'

'I—' For a moment, Zoe looked as if she might be about to answer the question, but she stopped. 'I don't want to talk about it. Not here. Not now.'

'Not to me?'

'I didn't say that.'

'You've a point, though. I'm your boss as well as – well, your friend, I hope. I have to juggle both roles. As your boss, I'm concerned because I can see this, whatever it is, could affect your performance.'

'It won't—'

'It already is, Zoe. You didn't want to stay in the room back there. Stuart reckoned you behaved oddly when the two of you were out on the moors. Whatever is going on is already affecting your ability to do your job.' She paused, wondering how best to phrase all this. 'So, as your boss, I'm concerned about that. As your friend, I just want to help you deal with whatever the issue is. Because I've got to wear both hats, I know I might not be the best person for this. But you've got to talk to someone.'

There were tears welling in Zoe's eyes. 'I can't talk about it. I'm not even really sure what it is.'

'But you were affected by the images that Parkin had in there?'

'I don't know. Look, Annie, I know you want to help. But it's not something I can talk about. Certainly not here or now.'

'Have you spoken to Gary about it?'

'He couldn't help. He means well, but…'

'Do you want me to try to arrange some counselling?'

'No. It's nothing to do with work. I don't want to start bringing my problems into the office.'

Annie wanted to say that it was a little late for that, but she knew that would get them nowhere. 'I can't force you to do anything, Zoe. But I don't want to reach a point where I have to take formal action. I'm here to listen and I'm here to help, if I can. That's all I can say.'

'I know. And I'm grateful. But this is something I've got to work out for myself. I won't let it undermine my work.'

'Okay. It's your choice.' Annie felt as if she'd pushed it as far as she could for the moment. She'd made it clear that she could only protect Zoe so far if she compromised the case because of whatever was going on with her. There was nothing much more she could do except keep an eye on Zoe, and hope that, in a more appropriate time and place, she might eventually be prepared to open up. At least she'd acknowledged there was a problem, which felt like a step forward. Annie pulled her coat more tightly around her, conscious of the chill of the bright spring afternoon. 'Right, let's go and visit an estate agent's. Never say I don't show you a good time.'

Chapter Twenty-Six

For perhaps the twentieth time that evening, Clive Bamford picked up the business card Robin Kennedy had given him and stared at it, as if it might be about to reveal some information it had previously withheld.

It was a handsome affair, he thought, much better than the cheap cards Clive had had printed by some online company and which, to date, he'd barely had reason to use. Kennedy's card was made of stiff, expensive-looking card that had been textured in some way to create an even more imposing effect. His name was embossed in a cursive script with the address of Kennedy Farm below. There was no indication on the card of Kennedy's occupation, another contrast to Clive's rather optimistic description of himself as 'Author/Commentator'.

Kennedy's occupation was something that had intrigued Clive since their meeting. Perhaps the 'movement' or whatever it was had proved sufficiently lucrative for him to need no other source of income, or perhaps, like those characters in Edwardian novels, he had 'independent means'. Or perhaps he had some occupation distinct from his leadership of the movement.

Clive imagined that a building of that size and style in the middle of the Peak District would not have come cheap. It would be expensive to run and maintain, too. Clearly, there was some money behind this, and Clive was intrigued to know where that money might be coming from.

He'd already decided he wanted to continue working with Kennedy. The whole thing was just too fascinating to leave alone. Clive had started to make some progress with the wealth of material that Kennedy had given him. It was, as Kennedy had warned him, a very mixed bag. There were a couple of very old books – the ones that Kennedy had suggested were potentially valuable – published by arcane-looking presses, which appeared to recount that early history of what Clive took to be Kennedy's movement. Clive had given them a cursory skim, and had initially found them largely incomprehensible. There were lengthy descriptions of what seemed to be highly abstract ideas and Clive had found his head spinning even trying to parse some of the sentences. He'd need to give them a serious go, though, if he was to have any credibility with Kennedy.

The other materials seemed more straightforward, if still not entirely enlightening. These were mostly pamphlets or booklets, setting out various 'new paths' to spiritual truth. Intriguingly, all of the pamphlets seemed to be published anonymously, as if from some generic source, and there was nothing relating explicitly to Kennedy's 'movement'. There was much talk of 'dispelling illusion', 'grasping corporeality' and 'testing the boundaries', but again Clive had found himself struggling to extract much concrete meaning from them.

Perhaps, he thought, this was part of the process. Perhaps he hadn't yet succeeded in 'dispelling illusion' to the point where he could begin to gain insights into this new world. It was possible that he was approaching this from the wrong perspective, trying to impose some kind of inappropriate mundane meaning on the words rather than allowing himself to be swept away by the abstract ideas.

Maybe. But what he thought of as the more rational part of his brain still resisted that conclusion. The point of words was to communicate, and so far these words were failing to communicate anything much to him. But it was early days. He suspected the answer might lie, as it so often did, simply in hard work. He had to keep reading and rereading this material and whatever other relevant writings he could find until it all finally began to release its secrets.

In the meantime, he was wondering whether he should already be contacting Kennedy to confirm that he wished to continue. Kennedy had told him to take a few days to make up his mind, and he was nervous about seeming overkeen. It was important that Kennedy saw him as a dispassionate, objective journalist, not some fan-boy straining at the leash to be involved.

On the other hand, he didn't want Kennedy to think he was uncommitted to the project, or that he'd had serious doubts or second thoughts about being involved. He didn't want Kennedy to have any concerns about the time and effort Clive would be prepared to devote to the work.

After a few moments, he picked up the phone and dialled the landline number given on Kennedy's card. There was a mobile number, too, but it somehow felt presumptuous to use that at this early point in their dealings. It occurred to him that his own business card didn't even include a landline number.

'Kennedy Farm.'

'Is that Robin?'

'It's Eric Nolan here. How can I help you?'

Clive felt taken aback and, he realised, slightly disappointed. He didn't know why he'd expected Kennedy to answer the phone directly – after all, Nolan was supposed to be his PA or some such – but he was already feeling oddly wrong-footed.

'Oh, Eric. It's Clive Bamford here. We met yesterday evening.'

'Of course. I trust Rowan guided you safely back into town.'

'Very smooth journey, thanks. Glad I wasn't trying to navigate in the dark.' He took a breath, realising he was talking too quickly. 'I was just wondering if Robin was around for a brief chat.'

There was an almost imperceptible pause before Nolan said, 'I'm afraid he's a little busy at the moment. Can I help you at all?'

Clive's initial mild disappointment was already growing into something more substantial. He realised that, when he'd decided to make the call, he'd been looking forward to hearing Kennedy's enthusiastic approval of his decision to take on the work. He didn't want Nolan to deliver the news on his behalf. 'Probably not. I just wanted to check on something with Robin.'

'I might be able to help you. To be honest, Robin's very busy over the next couple of days so I'm not sure how quickly he'll be able to get back to you.'

'It's not urgent. If you can let him know I called, he can ring me back when he's got a moment.'

'If you're sure. Do you think you'll be working with us, then?'

The direct question caught Clive by surprise. 'I— Well, yes, I think so. That's really what I wanted to talk to Robin about. Just a couple of points of clarification.'

'I'm sure Robin will get back to you as soon as he can. But great to hear you'll be working with us. I'll let Robin know.'

'I—' Clive stopped, conscious that he could hardly now claim he hadn't yet made up his mind. That would certainly convey the wrong impression. 'Thanks. I hope he'll be pleased.'

'I'm sure he'll be delighted. He speaks very highly of you.'

Clive ended the call with a sense that he'd been manipulated. It wasn't a feeling he could justify rationally. After all, he'd called Kennedy with the intention of confirming that he wanted to continue the work, so he could hardly complain that he'd been somehow tricked into making that decision. Yes, he'd hoped to tell Kennedy directly, but it would be childish to make an issue of that. Even so, he was left somehow feeling that he hadn't been fully in control.

It didn't matter, he told himself. The outcome would be the same. Kennedy would ring him back before too long, and would no doubt still greet the decision with the same enthusiasm. Clive's own intentions remained the same – to approach this with the necessary level of objectivity and independence. If he was going to do his job properly, the last thing he should need or want was Kennedy's approbation.

He wondered whether to call Rowan Wiseman to break the news of his decision to her. She'd perhaps give him some of the response he'd been hoping for from Kennedy. But as he reached to pick up his phone, it began to ring. He snatched it up, hoping that it would be Kennedy already calling back.

But it was only Greg Wardle. He took the call, by now feeling utterly deflated. 'Evening, Greg.'

'Hi, Clive. Just wondered if you felt like meeting up for a beer. I've had something cancelled on me so just at a loose end.'

Clive's first instinct was to say yes, even though it was hardly the most flattering of invitations. In any case, Clive had dragged Greg off at short notice the previous evening, so he could hardly complain. Then he looked at the large pile of documents from Kennedy that were awaiting his detailed attention. 'Sorry, Greg. I'm a bit busy myself this evening.'

'Are you?'

'I've got all that stuff from Robin to work through.'

'Oh. Right. How's it looking?'

'There's a lot of it, for a start. Some old stuff – books and the like. And a lot of recent and current booklets.'

'All about this so-called movement of Kennedy's?'

'Pretty much. A lot of it's more general, but I assume this is really just background. There's some interesting-looking stuff but it's going to take some effort to get my head round it all.'

'If it's as lucid as Kennedy was last night, I don't envy you.'

'Thought that was just me being a bit dim. You felt the same, did you?'

'Seemed to be a lot of words without too much substance, but I'm guessing that's how he works.'

'How'd you mean?'

'Draws you in. Gets you interested. A sort of drip-by-drip approach. He struck me as a good salesman. Knows how to close the deal.'

Clive could feel himself bridling at the depiction of Kennedy. 'That's a bit unfair. I don't think he's that cynical.'

'I didn't say it was cynical. He's selling an idea, after all. He does it well. Have you decided to go ahead with it?'

'I—' For the second time that evening, Clive felt as if he'd been somehow outmanoeuvred. 'Yes, I have, as it happens. I just called Robin to tell him.'

'How did he react?'

'I didn't speak to him directly, as it happens. I spoke to Eric Nolan.'

'Of course.' Greg sounded amused, as if this had been exactly what he'd expected.

'Kennedy was a bit tied up, that's all.'

'I'm sure. Anyway, sorry you can't make the pub. But I'll drink a pint on your behalf in celebration of Robin Kennedy and his movement.'

'Take the piss all you like, Greg, but could be a real opportunity for me.'

'I don't doubt it. And I'll be happy to help you, if you want my support.'

Clive took a breath, conscious that he'd been growing increasingly irritated with Greg's flippancy. But he knew they worked well together – partly because they were opposites in many ways – and he didn't want to lose Greg's friendship. 'That would be good, Greg. Sorry I can't make it tonight.'

'No worries. There's no way I can compete with one of Robin Kennedy's leaflets. Have fun.'

Clive eyed the large pile of papers in front of him. 'I'll do my best.'

Chapter Twenty-Seven

Annie and Zoe had followed their visit to Parkin's flat with a fruitful half-hour in the estate agent's offices. Bryce Scott had been joined by a woman, seemingly scarcely older than himself, who'd introduced herself as Lauren Ransome, the branch manager. They'd gone through the predictable expressions of shock at the news of Parkin's death, and questions from Ransome about the implications for the tenancy, which Annie had skilfully fobbed off. Finally, they'd got down to some useful discussions about the ownership of Parkin's flat.

The buildings were owned by a company called Werneth Holdings, with a business address in the city centre. 'I don't know a lot about them,' Ransome said, 'except that they've been good for our business. They've gradually been buying up a fair number of properties around the city. Mix of usage, mainly depending on the location. Some student lets. Some, like Mr Parkin's, more aimed at the professional market.'

'Do they buy properties and do them up?' Annie asked.

'Again, it's a mix. A lot of the student properties they've just bought as they are, usually from individual landlords who've been looking to realise their investment. In those cases, they haven't generally done much more than a bit of renovation where necessary and the usual maintenance. But somewhere like Mr Parkin's place would have been a conversion. They'd have bought a house and then turned it into flats. It's amazing how much you can fit into some of those terraces.'

Zoe had seen the size of Parkin's and Garfield's flats, so she didn't doubt it. 'They must be investing a fair amount in all this?'

'Must be. Property in Derby's cheaper than a lot of places, but the city-centre places aren't exactly going for peanuts. And the costs of the conversions won't be cheap. For the professional ones, they seem to have done a good job, at least superficially. But then if you can attract the right clientele, there's a lot of money to be made. You can build it up gradually if you're smart, reinvesting the profits as you make them. It's good business if you've the capital to kick it off.'

'Bryce said that Parkin had been introduced to you by Werneth Holdings,' Annie said. 'Must be unusual for a landlord to recommend their own tenants.'

'Well, sort of. It's an odd set-up,' Ransome agreed. 'I don't know the detail, but Werneth seem to have their fingers in a lot of pies. They're got various hospitality interests around the county – bars, cafes, that kind of thing. And there are some other related businesses I don't know much about. Every now and then, they ask us to sort out accommodation for one of their employees. Parkin was one of those.'

'Generous of them,' Zoe commented.

'Up to a point,' Ransome agreed. 'But they charge them commercial rents, so I suppose it's more a case of making best use of the assets they've got. If there's a flat available and they've got a candidate for it, why not? Helps out the employee, and the money's going back to Werneth rather than to some third party.'

'Wouldn't it be simpler for them just to provide free accommodation and deduct it from the salary?'

Ransome shrugged. 'You'd have to ask them why they do it like this. I think it can become complicated in terms of the minimum wage because you're only allowed to offer a fixed amount for free accommodation. My guess is that they just want to keep it simple. Parkin's employer was some restaurant that was run as a separate company, though part of the grand Werneth empire. But, like I say, you'd have to ask them. We just do what they ask us.'

Afterwards, as they were walking back to their respective cars, Annie said, 'Parkin seems to have been oddly popular for a lad with not much going for him.'

'That's what I was thinking,' Zoe agreed. 'Boss at the cafe takes a shine to him. Then he apparently walks out and finds himself a job where the employers find accommodation for him. All seems a bit weird.'

'The other question,' Annie continued, 'is how he was able to afford that flat. Ransome reckoned he was paying a commercial rent. Okay, it was a tiny place, but it was fairly upmarket. Even if he'd found himself something better than kitchen porter, catering at that level's not the most lucrative of trades.'

They'd obtained contact details for Werneth Holdings from Lauren Ransome, and their first priority in the morning would be to visit their offices up in Chesterfield. Annie had felt that, given their unanswered questions about Parkin, it might be better to visit the landlords in person. 'See the whites of their eyes,' she'd said, 'when we ask them where he was working and why they were so keen to have him as a tenant.'

Now, hours later, Zoe Everett was wondering what state she'd be in for that meeting. She looked over at the clock on the mantelpiece. It wasn't yet 4:00 a.m., but she'd already been sitting here for more than an hour, idly searching the internet for something to catch her interest. She'd woken in the small hours, her sleep disturbed by some nightmare she couldn't recall. Knowing she wouldn't sleep again and not wanting to disturb Gary, she'd pulled on her dressing gown and made her way downstairs to make herself a coffee.

Through the kitchen window she'd seen it was a clear spring night, an almost full moon shining down on their small rear garden. It was a time of year she normally enjoyed – the clusters of bright spring flowers, the first green shoots appearing on the trees, the days gradually growing longer. It was a season when she normally felt optimistic, ready to face whatever new opportunities the year might have to offer her. Now, she just felt flat, bleak, empty. And anxious. Above all, anxious. With an indefinable sense that something bad, something serious, was lurking just over the horizon, just around the next corner.

She'd made the coffee and wandered back through to the sitting room. Her laptop was sitting on the small table she used as a desk when she worked from home, and, not thinking about what she was doing beyond killing some time, she booted it up and began searching aimlessly on the internet.

At first, she'd found little to interest her – just the latest news headlines, the weather forecast for the morning, a couple of forums she participated in. She'd logged into the force secure network and dealt with a handful of routine emails, wondering whether any of the recipients would notice the timing of her responses. She was conscious that, with the heating off for the night, the house felt cold, and she pulled her dressing gown more tightly around her.

Finally, with nothing much else to do, she started searching on Werneth Holdings. Slightly to her surprise, they didn't appear to have a dedicated website. From the way that Ransome had described the company, she'd assumed they'd be large enough to have some kind of web presence. But perhaps there was no particular need for it. If their properties were all let and managed through the agents, they'd have no other obvious requirement for marketing themselves. If they owned bars or cafes, as Ransome had said, those would no doubt have their own sites.

She found a Companies House link for the company, and followed it through to see what information might be in the public domain. There were various sets of accounts, which were up to date. Zoe opened up the most recent set, but they meant little to her untutored eye except to indicate that the company appeared to be in robust financial health. Finally, she clicked on the list of people associated with the company.

The key directors were names she didn't recognise, all with addresses in the county. She scrolled further down till she came to previous officers of the company, and then she paused.

It took her a moment to place it. A name that struck her as familiar, but she couldn't immediately recall why or how. It was only when she looked at the address below it that she remembered.

Thomas James Miller.

Higher Wenlow Farm.

Higher Wenlow Farm was where they'd found the second body. Tom Miller had been the farmer they'd spoken to.

It seemed a hell of a coincidence. Unless of course it wasn't. When she'd first transferred to CID, her DI had always been insistent that, in police work, there was no such thing as a coincidence. 'If you stumble across a potential link,' he'd said, 'start from the assumption that it's significant. Then work out why.'

Like most of the advice she'd received as a young copper, it was an exaggeration. Sometimes a coincidence was just that. But her gut was telling her this felt odd. It was strange enough that the investigation into Parkin's death should have spiralled round so directly to link to the second body. But it also raised other questions. Like why the hell a sheep-farmer should ever have been a director of a property development company in the first place.

Her first instinct was to call Annie to let her know about the discovery. Annie had always insisted she was available day or night if it helped to progress an investigation. But Zoe looked at her watch and hesitated. It was only just after four. This was almost certainly something better left for the morning. She'd be feeling more clear-headed, and maybe in the cold light of day she'd see some more obvious explanation for the connection. In any case, nothing was going to change in the next few hours.

Even so, there was no chance now of her getting more sleep tonight. She might as well make the best use of her time. She returned to the kitchen and topped up her coffee, and then sat back down at her laptop, wondering what else it might be possible to discover about Tom Miller or any of the other current or past directors of Werneth Holdings.

Chapter Twenty-Eight

Annie Delamere woke suddenly, with the sense that her sleep had been interrupted by some external factor. A loud noise, or some similar kind of disturbance.

She was generally a sound sleeper but she'd had this kind of experience occasionally before. A couple of times, she'd been briefly certain on waking that she'd been roused by a loud hammering at the front door of the house. She generally had these kinds of experience when she'd been under abnormal stress, usually due to some work-related issue. After everything that had happened over the last few days, she was under even more stress than usual. Even so, this did feel different.

This time she had no distinct recollection, even in the moments when she'd first woken, of what might have disturbed her. Now, lying in the darkness, it felt almost as if the echoes of whatever it had been were still dying away. As if she could almost still hear it.

At first, the only sound she definitely could hear was that of Sheena's soft breathing beside her. Then, as she lay motionless, holding her own breath, straining her ears, she thought she heard it.

A movement in the garden below their bedroom window.

She slipped silently out of bed, dragged on her dressing gown and made her way over to the window. She pulled back the edge of the curtain and peered out into the night.

The sky had remained clear, and an almost full moon was shining down into the garden, creating a shifting vista of black and silver. There was a stiff breeze blowing, and the trees at the rear of the house were swaying rhythmically. Was that all she had heard?

It seemed unlikely that that sound alone would have woken her. The rush of the wind in the trees had become part of the familiar nocturnal soundscape. There had to be something else.

She peered through the narrow gap between the curtain and the wall, trying to discern anything in the shifting half-light. Then she saw it, or she thought she did.

It was scarcely anything. Just a glimpse of movement in the very corner of her eye. Something that, for reasons she couldn't have explained, was different in quality from the steady shifting of the trees and bushes. The movement of someone hurriedly leaving the scene.

She left the bedroom and crossed the landing to the guest bedroom. The room offered a view of the front driveway, the trees in which they'd found the camera yesterday and the open moorland beyond.

She stood at the uncurtained window and peered out. It took her a moment, but then she spotted two figures near the gates, little more than black shapes scurrying out into the road. A moment later, there was the sound of an engine starting and then, through the trees, she saw the dark shape of an unlit vehicle heading away.

'What is it?'

Sheena's voice in the darkness behind Annie almost stopped her heart. 'Jeez, Sheena,' she said, turning to face her, 'you made me jump.'

'What is it, though?' Sheena asked again. She was generally a light sleeper, and Annie was unsurprised she'd been disturbed.

'There was someone in the garden. A couple of them, I think.' Annie returned to the main bedroom, turned on the light, found her phone and dialled 999. Within a few moments, she'd received a commitment that a car was on its way. There was no point in trying to trace the intruders' vehicle. It had been parked out of range of their own security cameras and she had no description. That would be a question for tomorrow, when they might be able to identify possible suspects on the CCTV and other cameras in the surrounding area.

She ended the call and turned to see Sheena standing in the doorway.

'They were actually in the garden?'

'The rear garden,' Annie confirmed. 'Somehow it woke me. Christ knows why. I can usually sleep through a thunderstorm, but this must have been some sixth sense.'

'What were they doing?'

'I've no idea. Planting another camera. Setting up something to scare us. God knows.' She could already see the pulse of a blue light through the landing window behind Sheena's head. 'Looks like support's already here. You're obviously privileged.'

'Neurotic MP who calls out the police on a nightly basis?'

'Cautious MP who's already experienced two attempts on her life. Let's get some clothes on and head down.'

Annie was relieved to see the familiar faces of Paul Burbage and Ian Wharton on the other side of the front door. At least she wouldn't have to go through another round of explanation.

'We'll have to stop meeting like this,' Burbage said.

'You've drawn the short straw again, then,' Annie said. 'Sorry.'

'Don't be. It's just a fluke really. You got us at the start of the shift last time. Tonight's been a quiet one, so we were kicking our heels a bit.'

'Relatively speaking, you understand,' Wharton added with a grin. 'Don't want you to think we were slacking.'

'Thought never crossed my mind. Just glad you were able to get here so quickly.'

'You've had an intruder this time?'

'In the garden. Two of them, I think, though I only glimpsed them as they were leaving the front gate. They had some kind of vehicle parked on the road outside.' She shook her head. 'And before you ask, sorry, I can't give you any description of the vehicle. It was behind the trees and gone before I could do anything. Best bet would be to see if there are any cameras in the vicinity that might have caught anything. I'll take that up with Andy Dwyer in the morning.'

'You want us to check the garden?'

'I think we should. They were here for a reason. I don't think they could have been aware that I'd spotted them – it was only luck that I woke up and I didn't turn on any lights – so they must have finished whatever they came here to do.'

'And you've no idea what that might have been?'

'Not a clue. We've had no more email contact since we found the camera. No threats. Or at least none that appear to be connected with the last incident. Andy Dwyer had the garden thoroughly searched today after he saw Sheena, but they found nothing.'

'We'd better go and see then,' Burbage said.

'I'll grab my coat and come with you,' Annie said. 'I already feel as if I'm not pulling my weight here.'

'You're not on duty,' Burbage pointed out. 'But I'm guessing I can't stop you, given that you outrank me.'

'I wouldn't even try if I were you.' Annie grabbed her waterproof from where it was hanging beside the front door. She turned to Sheena, who was watching from the doorway of the living room. 'We'll just be a few minutes.'

'Take care.' Sheena spoke in a small voice, a long way from her usual assertive tone. Annie hated seeing her that way.

'Trust me, I will.'

Annie turned back to the two officers. 'They were at the rear of the house when I first glimpsed them. We might as well start there.'

She led them through the house into the kitchen and opened the back door. Outside, the wind had risen and the swaying trees were noisier than ever. She stepped outside and stood back while Burbage shone his flashlight around the garden.

At first, they could see nothing but a dark tangle of rocking branches in the trees and shrubbery surrounding the narrow lawn. The rear garden was not large and in the summer provided a cosy suntrap. On a night like this, in circumstances like these, it felt threatening, as if the trees themselves were closing in on them.

'There's something,' Annie said. 'In the trees over there.' She pointed towards a corner of the garden to their left. 'If they came down the side of the house, that's the nearest point.'

Burbage took a few steps forward, directing the torch beam at the point Annie had indicated. 'Jesus.'

'What is it?'

Burbage hesitated. 'I was going to tell you not to look, but I'm guessing you've seen it all before.'

Annie moved to stand beside Burbage, Wharton close behind her. As they saw the object caught in Burbage's torchlight, she heard Wharton utter an expletive behind her.

'I've definitely seen it all before,' Annie said to Burbage, keeping her voice steady. 'But I've seen this all too recently.'

It was another body.

The same type of victim, a young white male left naked among the trees. The same slitting of the throat. The same neat incisions made across the skinny chest. Another offering, she thought. This time, though, she knew very well who the victim was. She'd seen and spoken to him just the previous day.

Jonny Garfield.

Chapter Twenty-Nine

'You think it's the same?' Stuart Jennings said.

'It's looks identical to me, except he wasn't killed on site, presumably because they didn't want to risk waking us. Danny Eccles and his team are in there now.' Annie gestured towards the crime-scene tent that had been erected in their garden. 'But as far as I could tell it looked to be exactly the same MO. Naked white male. Throat cut. Incisions on the chest.'

'But this time in your garden.'

'Tell me about it. Takes a lot to knock Sheena back, but this has done it.' Annie wasn't ready to admit to Jennings that she too was shaken, though he could probably guess. 'The trouble is, we've always seen this place as our shelter from the world. Sheena, especially. It's where she comes to get away from the crap of Parliament and the stuff she has to deal with in the constituency. She'd never put it that way but it's a world away from how she grew up, and it means a lot to her. The stuff with the email and the camera was bad enough, but this...'

Andy Dwyer had been talking to one of his team and now walked over to join them, catching the tail end of the conversation. 'She struck me as the resilient type when I spoke to her yesterday. I was surprised by how unfazed she was. But this is a whole other thing.' He paused. 'Apart from anything else, I don't know if we can assume she's safe here. The security's tight and I know you're looking to make it tighter still, but if this place has been targeted it might be better to get her away somewhere where she's less conspicuous.'

Annie nodded. 'I'll talk to her. No idea where she'd go, though. I know Sheena. She wouldn't want to be seen to be running away. She'll want to stay in the area. I wondered about speaking to some of the local party members or constituency staff, but I think it would be difficult to keep under wraps. She's a public figure, particularly round here. It won't be easy.'

Jennings had been peering around them, as if expecting that the garden itself might give them some answers. 'I can't get my head around this. We've been working on the assumption that we had two cases, but this suggests we may only have one. It's too much of a coincidence otherwise. Why the hell else would anyone place a body here? Apart from anything else, it's a hell of a risk given we're already keeping an eye on the place.'

'Maybe not if you're aware how limited our resources are,' Dwyer observed. 'But I take your point. What do these killings have to do with Ms Pearson? And how are they connected, if they are, to the attempts on her own life?'

'Search me,' Annie said. 'But how do we know this is about Sheena? I was the one who interviewed Garfield. Maybe it's some kind of warning to me.'

'Again, it seems a hell of a coincidence,' Dwyer said. 'You've already had an intruder planting a camera in the garden, sending threats to Ms Pearson. Then you get another intruder who dumps a body as a warning to you? Either you're the world's unluckiest couple, or there's something more behind this.'

Annie nodded, considering the implications of what Dwyer was saying. 'I knew Garfield was scared. I knew he was afraid of someone from the moment Zoe and I met him. He clammed up because he was more afraid of them, whoever they are, than he was of us.'

'Looks like his judgement was sound on that, anyway,' Dwyer commented.

'I shouldn't have just left him, though. We were getting nowhere, but I thought he'd be more likely to talk if we let him stew for a few days. Turns out the poor bugger didn't have a few days. I should have pushed him harder.'

'You can't blame yourself for that.' Despite his words Annie could detect a faint note of smugness in Dwyer's tone. If he was as ambitious as everyone said, he'd be happy to chalk this up as another instance of a potential competitor screwing up. 'You couldn't have predicted this.'

She wanted to tell him to bugger off, that she wasn't interested in defending herself. 'Who knows? If he was scared enough…'

'Andy's right, though,' Jennings said. 'He clearly had good reason to be scared. My guess is that he'd never have talked to you unless we'd somehow been able to guarantee the threat would be removed. There's nothing else you could have done.'

'I could have tried,' she said.

Jennings was clearly keen to move the conversation on. 'So we know now that two of the victims, Darren Parkin and Jonny Garfield, knew each other. That should start to close the net a little. We presumably still don't have an identity for the second victim found at the farm.'

'Not yet,' Annie said. 'This might make it easier, though, if we start from the assumption the third victim also knew Parkin or Garfield.'

'There's one other thing about Garfield,' Dwyer said. 'I was just checking with one of the team because I thought the name rang a bell. He's one of the names who's come up in connection with that mob outside the constituency office. We've managed to ID a few of them, one way or another. It was one of the calls that came in when they showed the CCTV footage on TV, so we were due to follow it up today. Bit of a different context now.'

'You know who identified him?'

'Not offhand. We had a lot of calls, and not everyone was prepared to give their name. I'll check.'

'We'll have to break the news to Garfield's dad, too. Maybe he'll be a bit more forthcoming now. Had the sense he was hiding something as well.' She turned to Jennings. 'How do you want us to handle this, Stuart? We still don't know for sure that the two enquiries are linked. If Garfield's body was dumped here as a warning to me rather than Sheena, maybe the apparent links to her are nothing more than coincidental after all.'

Jennings frowned, clearly uncomfortable with being forced to make the judgement call. 'I think for the moment we continue to treat them as two investigations. I don't want us to jump to conclusions and start seeing conspiracies where they don't exist. But we've got to keep an open mind. As Andy says, if it's a coincidence, it's a big one, especially if Garfield was present when the first attempt was made on Sheena's life.' He paused. 'The other question, Annie, particularly if there's a possibility that the two enquiries might be converging, is whether you're too close to all this.'

Objectively, she knew he was right. If the two cases were linked, her relationship with Sheena should rightly preclude her involvement. At a more personal level, though, the question felt like an attack on her integrity or her capability. She took a breath before responding. 'I take the point. But if we're continuing to treat the enquiries as separate, I think I should continue with the murder investigation. If that seems to risk any possible conflict of interest or if the enquires do merge, we can review the situation then.'

Jennings seemed almost relieved by her response. She knew he wasn't exactly overwhelmed with resources, and at least this way he could defer making a decision. 'Okay, we'll keep it under review. But just bear it in mind. For now these remain two separate cases but I want both of you to share information. If anything comes up to confirm a link I'm to be told immediately.'

'Understood.' She turned to Dwyer. 'Can you find out for me if we've a name for the person who identified Jonny Garfield? Garfield was one of the few real leads we had. If he's out of the picture, we're almost back to square one. If there's anyone out there who knows more about him or Darren Parkin, we need to find them.'

'I'll let you know.'

'Thanks.' She gestured back towards the house. 'I'll have a chat with Sheena about trying to get her away from here.'

'She's a proud woman,' Dwyer said. 'Maybe too proud in this case.'

Annie gazed at him for a moment, then shook her head. 'It's not a question of pride. It's her job. She can't be seen to be running away in the face of intimidation. As far as she's concerned, she owes it to her constituents.'

'I didn't mean—'

'No, I know, Andy. And I'll do what I can. But I can't promise anything.'

She left Dwyer talking to Jennings, and made her way back into the house, checking her phone as she went. To her surprise, it was already nearly 8:00 a.m., and she was conscious she hadn't informed Zoe yet, and she didn't want Zoe to think she was being sidelined after their conversation the previous day. After they'd found the body, everything had moved too quickly. Jennings had turned up unexpectedly with the rest of the crew, Dwyer in tow, and for the last couple of hours she'd found herself swept up in the activity.

Zoe had already left her a couple of voicemails. Steeling herself for a potentially awkward exchange, she dialled her number.

Zoe answered almost immediately. 'Annie? I've just got into the office and heard the news. Is everything okay?'

'As okay as it can be. Sorry, Zo, should have called you before. It all just got a bit hectic after we called it in. Then Jennings turned up…'

'That never helps.' Zoe sounded more cheerful than she had the previous day. 'No worries. I was more concerned about you and Sheena.'

Annie had closed the back door of the house behind her and was standing in the kitchen. She kept her voice low, knowing Sheena was in the living room. 'It's really knocked Sheena back. She's pretty tough but this feels like the last straw. I'd like to get her away from here. Problem's finding somewhere suitably discreet for her to go. I don't want anything that's just going to result in a media scrum.'

There was silence for a moment at the other end of the phone. 'This is probably a stupid idea, but she could stay with us.'

'Oh, God, Zo, I wasn't suggesting—'

'I'm serious,' Zoe said. 'We've got room. Gary wouldn't mind. We're about as low-key as we can get. No one would think she'd be staying there. And you could trust us to be discreet.'

'I know that. But if there's any risk involved then I couldn't impose that on you and Gary.'

'There's no risk if no one knows she's there. And I'm a cop, after all. If there should be any problems, I'm better qualified than most to deal with them.'

'That's what I thought about myself,' Annie said. 'And I've not done a great job so far.'

'Please think about it, Annie. The offer's there. See how Sheena feels.'

'Thanks, Zo, I will. It's good of you.'

'Actually,' Zoe said, 'I didn't call you about any of this stuff. Not the first time, anyway. There was something else I wanted to share with you.'

'Go on.'

Annie listened as Zoe recounted what she'd discovered about Tom Miller and his historic links to Werneth Holdings. 'I did a bit more digging,' she said. 'There seems to be a whole network of companies linked to Werneth. Various permutations of the same group of directors. Some shared registered offices. Some dormant. Some active. Miller's name occurs a couple of times as a past director, though I couldn't see any sign he was currently involved.'

'It's intriguing,' Annie said. 'Another odd coincidence, and we seem to be finding rather too many of those at the moment. Speaking of which, Dwyer reckons that someone's identified Garfield in that protest outside Sheena's office. Maybe it's just highlighting how small this community really is, but it feels as if we might be starting to join a few dots even if we've no idea what we're drawing.'

'You think it's worth talking to Miller again?'

'Yes. Though the first priority is to break the news to Garfield's dad. There's just a chance he might have more to tell us now.'

'You think he'll care?'

'Who knows? They hardly seemed close, but there seemed to be some paternal spark there.'

'So Garfield's dad. Miller. Any other priorities?'

'I'm conscious we haven't seen Carl Francis yet. I suspect he'll be a dead end from what his mum said, but he's one of the remaining leads we've got on Parkin and Garfield.'

'Impression I got was that he wouldn't be part of their circle any more.'

'That was my impression too, but mums don't always know everything. If Francis had been as much under their influence as she said, maybe he was still in contact with them. Worth a shot, anyway, given we've contact details for him.'

'Is that our morning sorted, then?'

'Sounds like it. There's not much I can do here till the CSIs have done their business, and that'll take some time. I'll head back in and do the morning debrief with the team, then we can get started.'

'I'll have a coffee waiting.'

Annie ended the call, relieved that any lingering tensions from the previous day seemed to have dissipated. That didn't mean that the issue was resolved, of course.

She had no idea of Zoe's real state of mind, but she'd sounded more energised than she had for a while.

She walked through into the living room. Sheena was sitting on the sofa, apparently sorting through some papers, but even at first glance Annie could see that Sheena's eyes were unfocused, her mind elsewhere.

'How are you doing?'

'Oh, you know. As well as can be expected after two apparent attempts on my life and finding a body dumped in the back garden. You?' Her voice was toneless, with no trace of her usual humour or enthusiasm. Annie couldn't recall seeing her like this before, even in the most stressful moments.

Annie smiled. 'Yeah. Same. Look, I was thinking...'

'That I should get away from here?'

'You MPs have scary telepathic powers.'

'I need them, given how some of my constituents clam up. But it's written all over your face. You're worried.'

'Obviously I'm worried. But what do you think?'

'Where would I go? I mean, to be honest, I had the same idea. I've no desire just to be sitting here waiting for something else bad to happen. Someone literally knows where I live, and they're making the most of it.'

'There's a good possibility the body might have been a message to me rather than you.'

Sheena gave a mirthless laugh. 'I didn't realise it was a competition. But, no, Annie, it doesn't make me feel any better that someone might be targeting both of us.'

'So what about it?'

'Like I say, where would I go? I couldn't think of anywhere I wouldn't be conspicuous. I was wondering about staying with someone we know, but most of the possible candidates have kids, and it wouldn't be right to bring any kind of threat into their homes.'

'I've had one offer.'

'From who?'

'Zoe. She reckons she and Gary would be delighted to have you.'

'That's a relief. For a moment, I thought you were going to say your mum.'

'There are some limits to what I'd inflict on you. What do you think?'

'I've no idea, really. Wouldn't she feel uncomfortable?'

'There'd be a bit of awkwardness. But you know each other quite well, and you've always seemed to get on.'

'No problem in that respect. I've always liked her. But it's different being under someone's roof.'

'We're only talking a few days. If we don't get this sorted by then, we're going to have to rethink anyway.' She paused. 'To be honest, I get the impression that Zoe might be glad of another person there. Not that there's any problem between her and Gary, as far as I'm aware. But there's something going on with her at the moment that she doesn't want to discuss. You're good at listening and giving advice. Zoe might be more willing to talk to you than she was to me. She'd trust you not to say anything to me without her agreement. I've been wondering if that's why she made the offer. For herself as much as for you.'

Annie wasn't sure if this was true but she was desperate to keep Sheena safe. Staying discreetly with another police officer was probably the best she could hope for. And if she could stop worrying so much about Sheena, Annie could get on with her job and maybe prevent more threats.

'You think that's likely?'

'There's no knowing with Zoe. I think she needs some help and she might just see you as the ideal compromise. Not a stranger, but not too close, either. Someone she trusts. Someone who's experienced enough to give her some advice.'

'But you don't know what any of this is about?'

'I haven't a clue. All I know is that it seems to be affecting her state of mind, and that at the moment she's not doing the job she's more than capable of.'

Sheena finally smiled. 'You're a cunning bugger, Annie Delamere.'

'How do you mean?'

'Don't come the innocent with me. I know you too well. You know exactly which buttons to press to get me to take up Zoe's offer. I'd be reluctant to do it just for my own sake, but you know I can be persuaded to do it for hers. And if I do, you'll have someone inside the tent keeping one eye on Zoe. Okay, I'll have a think about it, assuming Zoe really is serious. And I'd want to give her some kind of recompense.'

'Treat her and Gary to a weekend away once this is all over,' Annie said. 'She deserves it.'

'Too right she does, if she's prepared to put up with you at work and me at home. Speaking of which, what about you?'

'What about me?'

'If I get out of here for a few days, you don't think I'm going to leave you here? Like you say, that body might have been a message to you rather than me.'

'I can't come to Zoe's. That really would be too awkward. And it wouldn't allow her to talk to you freely, if that's what she wants.'

'So where will you go?'

Annie hesitated, then gave the answer that she knew she'd already resigned herself to. 'I could always go to my mother's, I suppose.'

Chapter Thirty

Clive Bamford was collecting his belongings ready to leave the house when his mobile rang. He'd been tempted to ignore it, conscious he was already running late for work. Then he glanced at the screen and saw the caller's name. Robin Kennedy.

It wouldn't actually be Kennedy, of course. It would be Eric Nolan passing on some message from the great man. That was if Kennedy hadn't already relegated him to someone even lower in the pecking order.

Even so, he couldn't ignore the call. If he really did want to undertake this work, then there was no point in risking offending Kennedy so early in the process. He dropped his bag, sighed and took the call.

'Clive.' It was unmistakeably Kennedy's voice booming down the phone. 'Really sorry I missed you last night. I can only offer you my most sincere apologies. Just got caught up in something that ran on much longer than I'd expected.'

'No problem, Robin,' Clive found himself saying. 'I appreciate you're a busy man.'

'Never too busy to find time for you, Clive. In fact, I was slightly annoyed Eric didn't come to find me last night. Not his fault, of course. I'd told him I didn't want to be interrupted. But if I'd known it was you…'

'Don't worry, Robin. Really. Eric was very helpful.'

'I'm sure he was,' Kennedy said. 'And he was able to pass on the good news that you do want to work with us. That's really why I'm calling. To let you know that I'm delighted and that we're privileged to have you working with us.'

'Likewise. That was why I wanted to let you know straightaway.' Clive looked at his watch. His drive to work took forty minutes minimum. He was already running late because he'd become caught up in reading the material that Kennedy had given him.

'I was just wondering whether there was any chance you might be able to pop over to see us today.'

Clive took another look at his watch. 'Today? What time?'

'This afternoon, if possible. We've got a meeting going on. We call it a symposium, but that's a rather grand name for it. It's essentially just a convocation of some of the more senior figures in the movement, in preparation for developing our next clutch of neophytes.'

'Neophytes?' Clive remembered just too late what the word meant.

'The newbies, if you like. People who've joined us in the last few months and are beginning to take the first steps to enlightenment. Anyway, I thought that if you could join us, it would provide you with an immediate and very rounded insight into what we're about.'

'It sounds very interesting.' Clive was already trying to work out the possibilities. He was due at work in – well, less than forty minutes now, he realised. He couldn't take annual leave at this kind of notice, and he knew that once he went in he'd struggle to find any convincing excuse for taking the afternoon off. On the other hand, he was keen to attend the meeting. Partly because it did sound potentially invaluable in informing his understanding of the movement, and partly simply because he didn't want to be appearing unhelpful or uncooperative.

'I'm not sure, Robin. I've got various commitments today, and I don't know—'

'I do appreciate it's very short notice, Clive. It's my fault for not mentioning it before. But we don't open these meetings up to just anyone, so until you were safely on board, I didn't think it appropriate to raise it with you. But now you are, it would seem a tremendous pity for you to miss it. We don't run these often, and the attendees are all people I'd want you to meet.'

'I'll see what I can do, then.'

'Of course, Clive. Fully appreciated.'

'What time do you start?'

'If it's possible for you to get to the farm by around two thirty, that would be perfect. We'll have kicked everything off by then, so you can see us in full flow.'

Kennedy was already beginning to sound as if this was a done deal, Clive thought. 'Just give me a few minutes, then, Robin. I'll see what I can do. Shall I call you back?'

'Just heading into another meeting before the day kicks off, so might be better if you text me to confirm your attendance.'

'Will do. Thanks for calling, Robin,' Clive said, but the call had already ended.

He thumbed through his phone contacts and found his manager's mobile number. 'Mark? Clive here.' He gave a cough that, to his own ears, sounded anything but realistic. 'Really sorry about this, but I've woken this morning feeling like death. Hoping it's just a bad cold, but it feels like it might be flu. Temperature, aching joints, the lot. Barely been able to drag myself out of bed. I was trying to struggle in, but not sure I'm up to it, and I don't want to risk infecting others…'

He ended the call having secured grudging acceptance of his non-attendance. He was already feeling guilty. He'd never skived off work before. He'd never even missed a day through genuine illness, which was presumably why his boss had accepted the story relatively readily.

He texted a short message to Kennedy: *Managed to rearrange other commitments. Will be there at 2:30.*

A moment later, the phone buzzed with a return text. Just a single word. *OK.* Clive would have liked a bit more appreciation but perhaps Robin Kennedy would express his gratitude in person later.

If he didn't have to be at Kennedy's till 2:30, he should at least make best use of the time. It would give him another opportunity to focus on the documents Kennedy had given him. He walked back into the kitchen to make himself another coffee.

He was beginning to reconcile himself to what he had done. Somewhere in the back of his mind, though, he felt conscious that, without even realising he'd done it, he had somehow crossed a line.

Chapter Thirty-One

The bright morning sunshine did little to improve the appearance of Pete Garfield's house. The peeling paint-work and filthy windows were even more apparent than before, and the scene had been further enhanced by an overflowing wheelie bin by the front door.

At first, there was no response to the doorbell. Annie glanced at Zoe and pressed again, holding the bell down longer this time. She could hear its insistent ringing from somewhere inside the house.

Finally, the door opened and an unshaven face peered out at them. 'Christ, Cagney and Lacey again. Thought you'd done with me.'

'Good morning, Mr Garfield. I'm afraid we have some bad news.'

The door opened fully to reveal all of Pete Garfield. He was dressed in a worn dressing gown that was barely long enough to protect his modesty. It was past 10:30 a.m., but Annie guessed they'd dragged him out of bed. 'What bad news? This about Darren Parkin again?'

'May we come inside?'

'Yeah. If you're sure you want to.'

The room looked and smelled much the same as on their previous visit. Garfield again swept the sofa clear of debris and pushed open the windows to dilute the fetid atmosphere. Annie lowered herself cautiously onto the sofa, Zoe taking a seat beside her.

'What's this about?'

'It's about your son, Mr Garfield. And I'm afraid it's bad news.'

'Jonny? What's the little bastard—?' He stopped. 'What's happened to him?'

'He's dead, Mr Garfield. I'm very sorry.'

'Dead?' Garfield spoke the word as if the concept was new to him.

'We believe unlawfully killed,' Annie went on. 'In a very similar manner to Darren Parkin.'

'Shit!' Garfield slammed his fist hard into the side of the armchair. 'I told them—'

'You told them what, Mr Garfield?'

Garfield looked up as if he'd almost forgotten the two officers were there. 'I— It doesn't matter. I told them to be careful.'

'Mr Garfield,' Annie said slowly. 'I've every sympathy for your loss, and this isn't the moment for me to pressurise you. But if you know anything that might help us find the killer of your son and of Darren Parkin, I implore you to tell us. I can't go into the details at this point, but we have good reason to believe your son may not be the last victim.'

When Garfield finally looked up at them, Annie was surprised to see there were tears in his eyes. She'd envisaged him as the kind of would-be hard man who'd resist crying in front of a woman, even at a moment like this. He was silent for a long moment. 'I don't know much. All I know is that Jonny and Darren were mixed up with some pretty nasty people. They'd been tangled up in that sort of stuff for a long time. Since they were at school.'

'What sort of stuff?'

'You name it. Mainly drugs when they were at school. I know how they were enticed into that. But it wasn't just soft stuff. They were dealing the hard stuff. Even to schoolmates.'

'They never got caught?'

'Not for that. They had a few scrapes with the law, but only for trivial stuff. No one ever laid a finger on them for the serious business.'

'You knew about this?' Annie tried hard to keep any note of accusation out of her tone. She wanted Garfield to keep talking.

'Some of it. I suspected more.' He shrugged. 'What can I say? I was a single father. But that's not an excuse. I was also a crap one. It was easier to turn a blind eye.'

'And it wasn't just drugs?'

'One thing leads to another, doesn't it? It was the people they were mixing with. I don't know the details and I don't want to. But they'd do anything that would earn them a few quid.'

'Your son didn't have a regular job?' Annie said.

'Not that I'm aware of. We weren't in regular contact. Or much contact at all. We never exactly had a falling-out, but I wanted to steer well clear of whatever he was involved in.'

Annie decided to try another tack. 'Your son was identified at a far-right political protest a few days ago. Were you aware that he was involved in that kind of politics?'

'That the one where the MP was shot?' Garfield didn't wait for a response to his question. 'No, I didn't know about that. But it fits. Something where he can be the big I-am while being told what to do.'

'You don't share those politics?'

'Me? Christ, no. I'm not that much of a moron. I suppose I'm still Labour if anything. I don't think any of that lot have much interest in the likes of me. Certainly not the tinpot little fascists. But Jonny would have gone for that stuff.'

'Why do you say that?'

'Acting tough surrounded by his mates. That's why he got caught up in all this crap. It wasn't the money, though he developed a taste for that. He just wanted to be part of the gang, even if they were just using him.'

Annie frowned. 'So who was using him?'

'Early days, it was older kids at school. They were the ones who first got him and Darren caught up in bad stuff. But there were people running them, too. There are always plenty of people out there only too keen to exploit kids like Jonny and Darren.'

There was something about the way Garfield talked about the two young men that had been bothering Annie, though she hadn't been able to pin down what it was. 'Can I ask you about Darren's mother?'

Garfield looked up, clearly startled by the unexpected question. 'Darren's mother?'

'Did you know her?'

'I— A little.'

'The identity of Darren's father seems to be a mystery. Is that right?'

There was a long silence before Garfield said, 'I suppose so.'

'We've already got Darren's DNA on the system. Jonny seems to have escaped our attentions in the past, but I imagine if we were to check his sample against Darren's it would give us an indication of whether they were related.'

'I don't understand—'

She was aware she was perhaps pushing this too far and too hard given the circumstances. 'When we were last here, Mr Garfield, we had the sense there were things you weren't telling us. I was just wondering whether one of those things might have been that you were Darren's father?'

Garfield looked bewildered and initially she thought he was going to deny it. Finally he said, 'I don't know. It's possible. I – had an affair with Cathy.' He laughed. 'Though "affair" is probably a rather grand term for it. And I wasn't the only one. When she found out she was pregnant, let's just say I was one of several candidates.'

'She didn't try to make you take responsibility for the child?' Zoe asked.

'She didn't seem interested in anything from me. I was still married at the time, though it wasn't the first time I'd played away.' He gave a mirthless laugh. 'Or the last. Which is why I'm no longer married. But, no, Cathy never spoke to me about it.'

'Darren seems to have been brought up mainly by her parents,' Zoe said.

'Pretty much. Cathy was always a handful. Did things her own way. Didn't take responsibility for much. A born troublemaker.'

'Then she vanished?'

'Got bored here, I'm guessing. She liked to stir things up and, well, you've met her parents. She was already up to her ears in trouble.'

'What kind of trouble?'

'Drugs again, mainly. But she mixed with the wrong types. My guess is she was on the game at that point. That was how she paid for the drugs. I don't know when that would have started, but it might have been another reason why she didn't know who Darren's father was. She took a hell of a lot of risks.' He shook his head. 'Christ, it's all such a mess, isn't it?'

It wasn't clear to Annie whether he was talking specifically about Cathy Parkin or life in general. Pete Garfield was a long way from the cocksure man they'd met the previous day. 'I'm sorry. I appreciate this is a difficult time for you. We're just trying to put together as many pieces of the jigsaw as we can. Some of them may be relevant, some won't be. But we need all the facts we can get.'

'Yeah, of course. I wasn't hiding anything from you. I genuinely don't know if I was Darren's father, and it didn't seem relevant when I spoke to you before.'

'We need all the leads we can get, however tenuous. You don't know anything about where Cathy Parkin went after she left here?'

'She's still around,' Garfield said. 'Or at least she was until fairly recently. Not here, obviously, but I've clocked her a couple of times in Derby. Just on the street.'

'Did you speak to her?'

'No. What would I say? Both times I just saw her across the street. You don't miss her easily. She still looks pretty amazing. Same bright-red hair. Like I say, you notice her.'

'You don't know if she was still in contact with Darren?'

There was another slight hesitation before Garfield responded. Another question that had caught him by surprise, Annie thought. 'I think she might have been. I don't know. Just some remark of Jonny's once that gave me the impression they'd both spoken to her.' He paused, rubbing his temples as if trying to force his brain into action. 'I'm trying to remember what he said. It was something about a potentially good deal that Darren's mum had put in their direction. Something that might change things for them. To be honest, I didn't take a lot of notice. Jonny was always talking bullshit about some great deal he had in the offing.'

'When was this?'

'Not long ago. Couple of months, maybe. It was really only the reference to Cathy that caught my attention. To be honest, if Cathy had involved them in something, my guess is it would have been bad news.'

'You think it's possible it could be linked to what's happened to them?'

Garfield stared at her, red-eyed, as if until that moment he'd forgotten about his son's death. 'She was bad news. She was always bad news. But I can't believe she'd have deliberately involved them in anything – well, anything harmful. Not her own son. Not even Cathy.' He sounded as if even he scarcely believed what he was saying.

Annie nodded. 'Thank you for your honesty. It gives us another line to pursue. And you've no idea where we might find Cathy Parkin?'

'I'm sorry. I've no idea at all. I'm sure her parents wouldn't have a clue, and I wouldn't know where else to begin.'

'That's a job for us. We've already pressed you too hard on all this. I'm very sorry for your loss, Mr Garfield. Sincerely.'

'It's a shock. We weren't close but, well, a son's a son, isn't he?'

'Of course. You're sure you'll be okay?'

'I'll be fine. As fine as I ever am, anyway.' He looked around, as if seeing the room for the first time. 'I'm a fucking mess, aren't I? Got nothing, going nowhere. I've screwed up my life from start to finish.' He gave a faint smile. 'But I'm still here, I suppose. That's all I've got going for me. Maybe this'll give me a kick up the backside. Or maybe not.'

'We won't take up any more of your time,' Annie said. 'If anything else occurs to you, however minor it might seem, please give us a call. I don't know if we'll need to talk to you again.'

'Talk to me as much as you need,' Garfield said. 'It's not like I'm busy. If I can do anything to put the bastard who did this behind bars, I'm only too happy to help.'

Chapter Thirty-Two

'What do you think?' Annie asked.

They were driving through the dales, heading west towards Tom Miller's farm. The landscape was largely moorland, given over primarily to sheep-farming, the rolling hills majestic in the morning sunshine. On a day like this Annie could appreciate the reasons why she'd chosen to stay in the county.

Zoe was driving, and Annie had just finished an extended telephone debrief with Jennings, which she suspected had added little to either's knowledge but had at least reassured Jennings some kind of progress was being made. The CSIs were still busy back at the house, but so far there was little of substance to report. Annie had followed her call to Jennings with a brief call to Sheena, who had seemed a little brighter than earlier.

'About Garfield?' Zoe's eyes were fixed firmly on the road. 'He seemed to be telling the truth this time, anyway.'

'That was what I thought. Whether it gets us anywhere is another question.'

'This Cathy Parkin sounds as if she's worth tracking down. If nothing else, she might be able to give us some more insights into what Garfield and Parkin were involved in.'

'I'll get someone on to it. If she's still calling herself Cathy Parkin it may not be too difficult. If she's going by any other name, it'll be harder. But, yes, worth a shot.' Annie paused. 'You still serious about offering Sheena a place to stay?'

'Definitely, if she's up for it. Spoke to Gary about it, and he's fine with the idea. Think he's quite excited about the prospect of having a celebrity about the place.'

'She's hardly a celebrity.'

'She is by our standards. I told Gary that that's fine as long as he doesn't start blabbing about her being there.'

'Is he likely to?'

'Not Gary. He plays the fool sometimes, but he's pretty switched on. And he knows when to keep schtum.'

'He's welcome to the bragging rights, such as they are, once it's all over.'

'Sheena's up for it, is she?'

'She is. I thought she'd resist and say it was a bit too much like running away. But this turning up almost literally on her doorstep really shook her up. So emotionally she wants to get away, and rationally she knows she might not be safe there.'

'That's great, then. Bring her over later this afternoon, once we've done.' Zoe hesitated. 'What about you, though? You can't stay in that place on your own. Not if dumping the body there was intended as a message to you. You're welcome to stay too.'

'I don't think that would be fair on you or Gary. I can't expect you to take on two people, and I just think, well—'

'That it would be awkward, you being my boss and everything.'

'Something like that. Anyway, I've made the ultimate sacrifice and asked my mum if I can stay there. She's jumped at the chance to lecture me whenever she feels like it.'

Zoe laughed. 'Thoughts and prayers for you, then. But if it doesn't work out...'

'It's all only a few days,' Annie said. 'If this isn't all sorted one way or another by then, we'll need to come up with another plan anyway.'

'Good luck then.' Zoe squinted at the road ahead. 'We're nearly there.'

Another mile brought them to the farm turn-off. Zoe pulled into the narrow lane that led to the farmyard.

They drew up in front of the farmhouse and climbed out into the chilly morning. Somewhere beyond the house, Annie could hear the sound of sheep and a faint breeze was rustling through the trees, but otherwise the morning was silent. 'Nice place.'

'Looks much less sinister than on my previous visit. Surprising what a bit of sunshine can do,' Zoe said. She stepped forward and pressed the doorbell. They'd agreed that, since Miller had met Zoe previously, she should take the lead in talking to him now.

There was no immediate response to the bell, and Annie was about to conclude that Miller was out, perhaps working elsewhere on the farm. Then she saw a curtain in a window to the right of the front door flick back as someone peered out at them. A few moments later, they heard the sound of bolts being drawn back and the front door was opened. Annie raised a quizzical eyebrow to Zoe, who nodded.

Tom Miller peered out at them suspiciously. He was unshaven and looked as if he hadn't slept. Annie thought that, even from some feet away, she could detect the smell of alcohol on his breath.

It clearly took him a second or two to place Zoe, then his gaze flicked between the two women in surprise. 'I wasn't expecting a return visit,' he said. 'What can I do for you?'

'I'm sorry to have to bother you again, Mr Miller. I just wondered if you could spare us a few minutes to answer a few more questions. This is my colleague, DI Delamere.'

Miller was silent for a moment, as if considering whether to refuse the request. 'Yes, of course. Come in.'

He led them through into the living room. 'Can I get you a tea or coffee? I could do with something.'

Annie nodded. 'Thanks. Coffee for me. Just milk.'

'Same for me. Thanks.' Zoe lowered herself on to the sofa.

As Miller disappeared into the kitchen, Annie whispered, 'He seems jittery.'

'We had all the security stuff with the front door when we were here before. But that wasn't surprising given what he'd just found. He didn't particularly strike me as the nervous type. But he looks awful today. As if he's ill.'

'Or hung-over.' Annie fell silent as they heard Miller returning with a tray laden with mugs of coffee. He placed the tray carefully on the low table between them, then slumped down on to one of the armchairs. As he reached to pick up his own mug, Annie noticed his hands were trembling slightly.

'What can I do for you?' Miller asked.

'It may seem a slightly odd question,' Zoe said, 'but we wondered if you could tell us about your connections with a company called Werneth Holdings.'

'Werneth Holdings? Why?'

'We've just come up against some references to them in connection with our enquiry, and we noticed that you were listed as a former director.'

Miller frowned. Annie could almost hear his mind working. 'I don't understand,' he said after a moment. 'What connection could Werneth Holdings have with your enquiry?' He had the air of someone playing for time, Annie thought, perhaps trying to discover how much they knew.

'I'm afraid we can't go into any detail in respect of the enquiry, Mr Miller,' Zoe said. 'But we came across the company through another source and then noticed your past involvement.'

'I still don't see why it's important.'

'We'd be grateful if you could just humour us, Mr Miller,' Annie said. 'You'll appreciate that in the course of an investigation we follow numerous lines of enquiry. Many of them lead nowhere but we still need to pursue them until we're sure.'

Miller seemed to hesitate. 'There's not really much to tell. This goes back a few years. Werneth was set up by an acquaintance of mine. Entrepreneurial type. Much more than I am, anyway. Had his fingers in various pies. Property development. Couple of pubs. Various other bits and pieces I didn't entirely understand. Which was part of the trouble, really. He gave me an opportunity to invest some money in the business. I had some cash available because he'd already bought a plot of land off me. My parents had obtained planning permission for residential building on it, but hadn't done anything with it by the time my dad died, so it was worth a fair bit. I'd planned to invest the money back in the farm, but he persuaded me that I'd get a much better return if I invested some of the money back in his business. It seemed a decent punt given that farming isn't exactly the most lucrative business at the moment. So I put the money in, took a shareholding, and in return he made me a director.'

'And did it work out?'

'Not the way I expected, let's say. It was all a bit beyond me. I was supposed to be a director, but I didn't really feel in control in the way I'd have liked. There was a network of companies linked to Werneth, and I didn't really understand how cash was being transferred between them. My fault, I'm sure. I'm just not really cut out for that kind of thing. I have enough trouble with the accounts here. Anyway, I began to feel more and more out of my depth, and I wasn't really seeing the kind of returns I'd been promised. So in the end I just bailed out.'

'What about your investment?'

There was a silence before Miller said, 'I got some of it back. But there were supposedly all kinds of good reasons why my shareholding wasn't worth what it had been when I'd invested.'

'You think you were ripped off?' Zoe said.

Miller shrugged. 'You live and learn, don't you? It was probably my naivety. We didn't exactly part on the best of terms. I've made a few attempts to get recompense through various channels. But I guess I have to accept it.' He sat up straighter in his chair. 'That's really all I can tell you. I hope I've not wasted your time.' He had the air of wanting to end the conversation.

'Not at all. That's been very helpful,' Zoe said. 'Just for the record, can we ask for the name of your acquaintance? The person who persuaded you to invest, I mean.' They already had a list of the directors of a number of the businesses, drawn from the Companies House submissions, but it would save them some time if they could identify who was really behind the web of companies.

Miller appeared surprised by the question. 'Does it matter? I mean, it's water under the bridge now.'

'Just for completeness, Mr Miller,' Annie said. 'As I say, we have to follow up all these leads, just in case.' She decided to leave Miller dangling for a few moments longer. 'You must have known this man quite well, if you trusted him with your money?'

'I—' He stopped, and again Annie could sense that he was trying to align his story, unsure what information they already had. If only he knew, she thought. 'It's a bit of a long story,' he said, finally. 'I went through a bit of a rough time, psychologically, after my parents died. They both died of cancer within a couple of months of each other. I was introduced to him by a friend, and he helped me through some of that. I felt I owed him something.'

'I'm not sure I follow,' Annie said. 'You said he was a businessman?'

'He was. Is. But there's another side to him. He's involved in – well, I suppose you'd call it a spiritual movement. That was how I initially got to know him. Everything flowed from there.' He stopped, as if conscious that he'd said too much. 'Anyway, that was it. Look, I need to get on...'

'Yes, of course,' Annie said. She started to rise, then paused. 'Oh, I don't think you told us his name. Your friend, I mean.'

Miller looked up at her, his expression unexpectedly anxious, as if he'd been caught out in a lie. 'Yes, of course. Not that it matters. He's a man called Robin Kennedy.'

Chapter Thirty-Three

'Another intriguing encounter,' Annie said.

'Very.' Zoe was taking the road back into the city on their way to complete their final task of the morning, which was to try to track down Carl Francis. By now, it was feeling almost like a waste of time. As far as they were aware, Francis had had no recent contact with Parkin or Garfield and there was no strong reason to think he'd be able to tell them anything useful. Annie had more than enough to deal with and had been tempted to delegate the task, but, after Garfield's death, part of her felt some responsibility that Francis was another loose end they'd left dangling. He was still one of the few people who might be able to give them some insights into what Parkin and Garfield had been involved in. At worst, they'd waste half an hour.

'He was in a state,' Annie went on. 'Looked scared of something.'

'It was like when we saw Jonny Garfield. The way he seemed almost to be expecting someone else at the door.'

'Everyone seems to be running scared of someone or something. But what?'

'I don't know. I just hope Miller doesn't end up in the same condition as Garfield.' Zoe paused while she overtook a slow-moving van. 'You think it's worth following up this Kennedy character?'

'I recalled the name from the directors of Werneth Holdings,' Annie said. 'He was the major shareholder and MD of the parent company, I think. We need to talk to him anyway about the links between Werneth and Parkin. Strikes me it might be worth throwing Miller's name into the pot when we do. There's obviously a story there, and I got the impression Miller might not have been telling all of it.'

'Once you've done this afternoon's briefing, that's likely to be the day sorted, then. When do you want to bring Sheena over?'

'I'll give her a call. Might be better to do it this afternoon if she's up for it. If we leave it till later presumably more of your neighbours will be around. More risk of her being spotted.'

'Fine by me. I'm good at the cloak-and-dagger stuff.'

Annie laughed. 'It's really good of you to do this, Zo. You're sure it's not too much on top of – well…?'

'On top of what we were talking about yesterday? Or what we weren't talking about because I wouldn't. Yes, I'm fine. Really.'

It was clear that Zoe had no intention of saying more. Annie decided not to press further. She just hoped that Sheena would have more success in getting to the bottom of what was troubling Zoe.

They made their way back into the city centre, caught up in the slow-moving morning traffic, and Zoe eventually found a parking place in a side street close to the address they'd been given for Carl Francis. A short walk brought them to the location of Francis's flat, part of a conversion of what looked to be an Edwardian terraced house.

'If Francis wasn't in contact with Parkin and Garfield,' Annie commented, 'he was living interestingly close to them.'

'Not only that.' Zoe pointed to the 'To Let' sign on the neighbouring house. 'Same agents. Looks like these might be another part of the mighty Werneth empire.'

'Curiouser and curiouser.' Annie studied the array of doorbells alongside the front door of the building and pressed the bottom one. Francis's mother had told them he was sharing the ground-floor flat.

After a moment, the speakerphone by the bells buzzed and a voice said, 'Who is it?'

'Police. We're trying to contact Carl Francis.'

'Police?' There was a moment's pause, then the front door clicked open. 'You'd better come in.'

Annie stepped into the narrow hallway beyond. At the end of the hallway there was an open door, with the figure of a young woman silhouetted in it. 'In here,' she said.

The decor and feel of the flat was similar to those in the flats where Parkin and Garfield had been living, but this was larger, clearly designed to accommodate several people. The room was tidy but felt more personalised, with an array of pot plants and a vase of flowers on the table.

'I don't understand what's going on,' the woman said. 'Do you know anything about Carl?'

Annie frowned, surprised by the question. 'We were hoping he might be here. Or at least that you might be able to tell us where he was.'

'But that's it,' the woman said. 'I don't know where he is. We haven't seen him for ages.' She shook her head. 'I'm sorry. I'm Ellie. Ellie Jordan. One of Carl's flatmates.'

'Good to meet you,' Annie said. 'I'm DI Delamere. This is DS Everett. Are you saying that Carl hasn't been here for some time?'

'It's probably getting on for a couple of weeks. He just didn't come back from work. At first, we thought he was just away for the night. But he hasn't been back since.'

'Have you tried to contact him?' Zoe asked.

'Yes, of course. We've tried his mobile repeatedly but it just goes to voicemail. We've left messages but he's not called back.'

'Have you tried his work?'

'That's the other thing. He'd told us he worked in the local Tesco. But I called them and they claim they've never heard of him. Those were the only contacts we had.'

'Who else lives here?'

'There are three of us including Carl. Ged's at work at the moment. I can contact him if you want me to.'

Annie shook her head. 'It doesn't matter for the moment. You've not reported Carl missing, presumably?'

'It just seems stupid, doesn't it? I mean, he's an adult. He's not obliged to be here. For all I know, there could be countless places he might have gone. I hardly know him.'

'How did you end up sharing a flat with him?'

'Just answered an advert on one of those websites. I was really looking for an all-female place but this was the best flat I saw for the money, and Carl seemed pleasant enough. He'd just started renting the place and was looking to split the costs.' She added, 'It was all done through the agency. They were okay with it, and Carl wanted to do it all properly. So it's a three-way split. The rent's very reasonable for the quality of the flat. To be honest, that was one reason we were concerned about Carl. If he doesn't pay his share of the rent, me and Ged have to cover it.'

'It's a decent place.' Annie was gazing round the room, trying to spot any items that might have belonged to Carl Francis. Anything that would give her a sense of what the young man had been like. 'Do you mind if we take a look at Carl's bedroom?'

'No problem as far as I'm concerned,' Jordan said. 'And Carl's not here to object.' She paused, realising what she had said. 'Do you think something's happened to him?'

'We honestly don't know,' Annie said. 'We wanted to contact him in connection with one of our ongoing enquiries. We expected him to be here or at work. So we really know no more than you do just yet. Which is Carl's room?'

Jordan led them across to one of the rooms off the living room. 'In here. It's not locked. Carl never locks it.' She pushed open the door and stood back to allow them to enter the room.

It was little more revealing than the living room had been. It was clear that, whatever the reasons for his absence, Francis had expected to return. The wardrobe and drawers were full of clothes, and a couple of pairs of shoes were tucked under the bed. There were football posters on the walls, but otherwise little effort had been made to personalise the room. There was a row of books on the top of the chest of drawers, most of them apparently gaudy-looking thrillers. Annie walked across the room and looked more closely at the selection. Tucked among the thrillers there were a couple of more sombre-looking volumes. *The Left-Hand Path* and *Another Route to Enlightenment*. Unexpected reading for a young man, and very similar to the books in Parkin's flat. Annie felt a sense of disquiet.

She turned back to Jordan. 'I don't suppose you've a picture of Carl?'

'I probably have on my phone. Hang on...'

Jordan spent a few seconds skimming through her photo library, then held the phone out to Annie. 'That's the best I can find. We went to the pub for Ged's birthday a few weeks back and got someone to take it for us.'

Annie gazed at the image for a few seconds, then handed the phone over to Zoe, who nodded. They'd clearly both had the same thought and their fears were confirmed. The photograph was clear and the likeness unmistakeable, even compared with the stark images prepared by the CSIs. The first body they'd found, the body on Beeley Moor, had been that of Carl Francis.

'Could you let me have a copy of this image, Ellie?' she said. 'We won't take up much more of your time. Is there anything else you can tell us about Carl? Any close friends you're aware of?'

'Not really. Like I say, I hardly knew him really. I was even wrong about where he worked, though I'm sure that was what he told me. He said he had a few friends locally, but I've no idea who they were. He never seemed to bring anyone back here. He was away a fair bit, sometimes overnight, but he never told us where he'd been. He seemed a very private individual.'

Annie had had a quick look through the drawers in Francis's bedroom, but had found no sign of an address book or mobile phone. There was little evidence of anything that might have shed any further light on Francis's life. Once his death was confirmed, they'd get the flat searched properly, but she had little expectation that they would find much more.

She handed Jordan one of her business cards. 'If you think of anything else that might help us track him down, please let me know. But we'll take care of it now.'

'Do you think I should have reported him missing?'

'It probably wouldn't have made much difference.' That was true enough, she thought, given that Francis would most likely already have been dead. 'As you say, he's a grown man. You had no real grounds for concern about his well-being. Nobody would have given it a high priority.'

'You'll let us know if there's any news?' Ellie said.

'Of course. We'll take your number before we leave. But thanks again, Ellie. You've been really helpful.'

–

Annie waited until they were well away from the house before she spoke. 'Shit. I'm not wrong, am I?'

'I don't think so,' Zoe said. 'It looked like him.'

'We should have followed up Francis earlier.'

'It wouldn't have made any difference, would it?'

'Who knows? It might have helped prevent Garfield being killed.' She shook her head. 'No, you're right. It almost certainly wouldn't have made any difference. I just feel bad because I'd more or less dismissed Francis as a lead.'

'It was what his mum told us,' Zoe said. 'All that "butter wouldn't melt" stuff. We assumed he was out of the picture.'

Annie had stopped walking. 'She was lying to us, wasn't she? I mean, it wasn't just the usual thing about mothers only seeing the best in their children.'

'Maybe she was just relaying what Carl had told her. He must have told her the stuff about working at the supermarket, just like he told his flatmates. Though why lie about that anyway?'

'Because the real story was less pleasant or more complicated, I'm guessing. But that wasn't what I meant. His mum told us that he phoned them every few days and came to see them regularly. But if he's been missing for a couple of weeks, and if we're right about what's happened to him…'

'Then she wasn't telling the whole truth.'

'Doesn't necessarily mean much, of course. Maybe Carl didn't contact her as frequently as she wanted us to think. Maybe she had an inkling he was back involved with Parkin and Garfield. Perhaps she was just trying to protect him. I had a sense that she didn't want us to be there when her husband got back. It's possible she was afraid he might have given us a more accurate picture.'

'Which suggests that we need to speak to them together,' Zoe said.

'If we're right about Carl we'll have to break the bad news to them in any case, and that's best done when they're both present. We'll need to handle it with some sensitivity, but that might be the moment for a bit of truth-telling.' She gave a mirthless laugh. 'Christ, there are times when I think this job has turned me into an utter callous bastard.'

'The job needs doing, though. And we have to do it in whatever ways we think will work best. If their son has been murdered, they'll want us to catch the killer.'

'And that's me told.' Annie laughed again, this time with more humour. 'Okay, let's head back to HQ. I need to get an update on how everything's going. Especially how everything's going back at my place. And we can double-check those photographs against the one that Ellie

Jordan copied across to me. Then I guess we need to deal with Sheena.' She glanced at her watch as they continued walking. 'It's turning into a hell of a day. And it's not even lunchtime.'

Chapter Thirty-Four

Clive Bamford was already running late by the time he finally found the track leading up to Kennedy Farm. The postcode on Robin Kennedy's card had taken his satnav only to an apparently random point on the main road, and it had taken him longer than he'd expected to identify the route that Rowan Wiseman had then taken on his previous visit.

He had assumed the place would be thronged with cars, but there were no other vehicles parked in front of the house. The other attendees were presumably parked somewhere at the rear. Perhaps, Clive thought, some of them were already staying at the farm.

The truth was that he had no idea what to expect. He had no sense of what kind of people might attend these sessions or how the process might work. He'd spent the hour or so before setting off searching through the various leaflets that Kennedy had given him in the hope of finding some further information, but there was nothing that seemed relevant.

All he could do was go with the flow. Kennedy would presumably be aware he would be approaching this with no prior knowledge and treat him accordingly. After all, that was presumably the point of this. To immerse him as soon as possible in the activities of the movement so that he could develop a full understanding of what they were all about. Today was the first step on what he expected to be a very exciting journey.

He was still feeling guilty at missing work. He kept telling himself no one would really miss him or his contribution today. Some of his colleagues pulled sickies all the time. And this was likely to be far more important to him in the longer term than anything he might achieve in his mundane office job. Even so, he still had the sense he'd crossed a line, however trivial it might seem. He couldn't decide whether that idea was terrifying or exhilarating.

He toyed with taking his own car round to the rear of the house but couldn't immediately see how to do so. Finally, he parked in the same spot that Rowan Wiseman had used on their previous visit. As before, he was afraid of making a fool of himself, but he reasoned he was more likely to do so trying to navigate his way around the house. If Kennedy preferred him to move the car elsewhere, he'd presumably say so.

He climbed out of the car and stood for a moment in the chill afternoon sunshine. The place felt eerily silent. On his way over here, he'd been envisioning that the house would be a hive of activity, with substantial numbers of people attending. But perhaps the symposium was a more intimate affair than that.

There was no immediate response to the doorbell. Clive pressed it again and waited, wondering if he could have somehow misunderstood Kennedy's invitation. But surely it had been clear enough, unless the symposium was taking place somewhere else on site. Clive looked around in case he'd missed some sign or other indication, but as far as he could see there was nothing. He looked at his watch. It was already nearly 2:30. If he didn't find the location of the meeting soon, he'd be late. He pressed the doorbell one more time, telling himself that if there was still no response he'd try the rear of the house in the hope of tracking down the other attendees.

But this time, finally, he heard a movement from within and the door was opened. To his slight surprise, Robin Kennedy himself was standing inside. Clive had been expecting the door to be opened by Eric Nolan or some other member of the team.

'Clive, welcome! We're delighted that you were able to come at such short notice.' There was, Clive noted, no apology for keeping him waiting or even an acknowledgment of the delay in opening the front door. 'Come in.'

Clive had half-expected that the symposium would be held in some conference room, but instead Kennedy led him along to the same living room in which their previous meeting had taken place. Kennedy pushed open the door and ushered him inside.

Clive took a step forward and then froze. 'I don't understand.' He looked back at Kennedy. 'What's going on here?'

'Welcome to our symposium, Clive. You're our guest of honour.'

Clive looked around at the small group gathered in the room and blinked. It was, essentially, the same group who had been here on his previous visit, although there was no sign of Eric Nolan. Rowan Wiseman. The man known only as Charlie. There was only one newcomer, whose face looked vaguely familiar.

'I wasn't expecting—'

'No, we appreciate you weren't, Clive. I'm afraid we haven't been entirely honest with you.' He paused. 'But then I feel you haven't been entirely honest with us.'

'I don't know what you're talking about.'

'Please do take a seat.' Kennedy gestured to an armchair that had been moved to the centre of the room. The remainder of the seats had been arranged in a circle around it. Clive lowered himself on to the seat, acutely conscious of the others' gaze fixed upon him. He'd expected to be here as an anonymous observer. He had no idea of what role he was now being asked to play.

Kennedy took his own seat directly opposite Clive. He was still dressed casually in an open-necked shirt and expensive-looking trousers, and he looked as relaxed as he had on Clive's previous visit, It struck Clive for the first time that Kennedy's appearance and image were very carefully cultivated. The full but neatly trimmed beard, the swept-back mane of hair. A man who was out of the ordinary, but fully in control. 'I had read some of your material, Clive. Some of the articles you've produced.'

'Yes, I know. You told me—'

'I told you I'd been impressed by them. Yes, I know. That was one of the areas in which I haven't been entirely honest with you. I'm afraid I didn't really like them.'

'I don't—'

'Don't misunderstand me, Clive. They seemed well-researched. Thorough. Perhaps even well-written, though I'm not the best judge of that. But far too sceptical. Far too muck-raking.'

'I try to make them objective—'

'We believe you also have contacts on the national tabloids, Clive. That you've fed sensationalist titbits to in the hope of furthering your own journalistic career.' The last word was spoken with an edge of irony. 'We've also read the sensationalist pieces that resulted.'

'I've never done anything inappropriate.' He had no idea how Kennedy had found out about his tabloid contacts. But he didn't understand anything that was happening here.

'We all have different ethical standards, Clive, and I'm not interested in judging yours. But I do know that we became a little uneasy when we discovered that you were sniffing around ours and some similar organisations. We really don't want that kind of publicity.'

'But I thought—'

'I'm afraid we gave you the impression we were interested in working with you. We really aren't. I wanted to meet you to see if I was misjudging you, to see if you were the kind of person we might work with. But I quickly realised that your knowledge and understanding was very superficial. I think you'd be interested only in presenting a sensationalist view of our activities.'

Clive knew he ought to be feeling furious at the deception. But even now he felt as if this was all his own fault, as if in some way he'd let Kennedy down. Yes, he had considered whether any of his findings here might be of interest to the national media, although he'd never intended to misrepresent or sensationalise anything. But somehow he still felt as if he'd been caught out.

'You see, Clive, our range of work here is complex. The movement is small and discreet and works very well for us. We achieve enlightenment through materialism and that involves expanding our material resources. We do that in a variety of ways, some of which the authorities might disapprove of. So we demand loyalty from our inner group, and we have ways of establishing and enforcing that.'

Clive still wasn't really following what Kennedy was saying, but he realised the final sentence carried an undertone of threat. 'Look, I'm sorry if I've misunderstood what you wanted from me. But perhaps I should just go now.'

Kennedy shook his head slightly. 'I don't think so, Clive. We have some other plans for you.'

Clive began to rise from his seat, but Kennedy nodded to Charlie, who immediately rose, walked over and pushed him back down. Charlie stood over Clive, glowering down, his hand firmly gripping Clive's shoulder. 'I think you'd better show a little respect, Clive,' he said, 'and listen to what Robin's telling you.'

'You can't just—' Clive began but stopped as Charlie's grip on his arm became even tighter.

'Please don't make things difficult, Clive,' Kennedy said. 'I do want to tell you a little about how the movement works, so you can understand why this is so important to us. I suspect that some of it will go over your head, but that can't be helped.'

It was finally beginning to dawn on Clive that he really was in some kind of trouble. He didn't understand how or why, or what any of this was about. But Charlie's physical grip on his arm had convinced him that this was no longer a game. 'Look, you can't just—'

Kennedy smiled. 'I think we can, Clive. And I'm sure you'll be gratified to know that, despite our differences, you'll be able to do your bit to help us on our way.'

Chapter Thirty-Five

Back at police HQ, Annie Delamere had spent an hour or so briefing the team and hearing updates about the ongoing investigation. She could sense a renewed sense of purpose among those working on the case. A further comparison of the CSI images of the body with the picture provided by Ellie Jordan had confirmed Annie's view that the third body was that of Carl Francis. That meant they now had identities for all three victims and a link between them. It felt as if they were finally beginning to make some progress, and Annie had directed the team to various new lines of enquiry. They were looking at the personal finances of the three victims, conducting detailed searches of their flats, trying to track down Cathy Parkin and gathering more information on Werneth Holdings.

Even so, Annie herself remained frustrated that, as yet, they still seemed a long way from finding a killer or even a motive. For all the activity, they had too few real leads, and it still wasn't clear where or how they might make a real breakthrough, even now they'd identified the first body as Carl Francis. Ellie Jordan had apparently known little about her flatmate's private life, and Annie couldn't imagine that the third flatmate would provide many additional insights. They'd need to talk to Francis's parents but, despite the mother's apparent lies, they might have little more to offer. Perhaps she'd lied to them simply because she was a mother who wanted to think the best of her son.

Time was passing. While it was true that the new lines of enquiry combined with the continuing painstaking work of conducting interviews, examining CCTV footage and reviewing forensic data might eventually throw up some lead that would open up the case, every day that went by made their work that much harder.

'What's the plan?' Zoe said, when they finally reconvened later in the afternoon.

Annie was chewing on a belated lunch of a tuna sandwich while trying to catch up with her overflowing in-tray of emails. It was the first time she'd sat down since they'd returned to the office. 'Wish I had one. Or at least a more inspired one. There's a lot going on, but we still need a real breakthrough.'

'We're making progress,' Zoe said. 'We've identified the victims. We've got a clear link between them. We've got some new leads.'

'I know. And we're doing all the right things. We just need that one break.'

'It'll come,' Zoe said. 'Any word on how they're doing at your place?'

'CSIs are still there, though I'm told they've nearly finished. I had a quick chat with Danny Eccles, but it doesn't look as if there's anything very new emerging. And I spoke to Sheena, who's only too keen to get away from the place. She's been okay this morning because there've been plenty of people milling about, but I'd like to get her out of there before the CSIs pack up.'

'Do you want to do that first, then?'

'Why not? Then we need to pay a visit to Francis's mother and father. Break the bad news.'

'Always my least favourite part of this job.'

'Tell me about it. Especially when it's someone so young. I'm dreading this one even more than most. We need to keep things moving. We'll have to press the mother because we really need to know why she lied to us before, and find out if there's anything useful she can tell us about Carl.'

'Doesn't feel like the moment to be interrogating her,' Zoe said.

'Sadly, it may be the best possible moment. That's why I want to handle this one myself. Like I said in the car, this job sometimes turns me into a person I don't much like. But given we've now had three identical murders, I don't think we can afford to waste any time. Jennings has told me five times that the media office's phone is ringing off the hook and the nationals are sniffing round.'

Zoe nodded. 'I guess we'd better get going then.'

—

They completed their first task relatively straightforwardly. Annie had phoned ahead and Sheena was waiting for them. She'd packed a small bag with a few changes of clothes, and was sitting at the kitchen table, drumming her fingers anxiously on the wooden tabletop.

Annie had been outside for a brief conversation with the CSIs, who confirmed that they were in the process of packing up and would be gone within the next hour. The remaining police presence had largely been removed, and, with darkness already beginning to fall, Annie was becoming conscious again of the isolation of the house. Even when this was all over, they might have to rethink whether this was the right place for them to be living.

It had been such a happy place for them but now it felt tainted.

'It's really good of you to offer to do this,' Sheena was saying to Zoe as Annie returned from the garden.

'No worries at all,' Zoe said. 'We'll be delighted to have you. Gary's quite star-struck.'

Sheena laughed. 'I hope I'm not a sad disappointment to him. But it really is just for a few days. I'll do my best not to be a burden.'

'I've told Andy Dwyer where you're going,' Annie said, 'but asked him not to spread the word too widely. I don't trust some bugger not to leak it to the media. Dwyer's going to keep any security pretty low-key. I'm hoping your biggest safeguard will be that no one knows you're there.'

They left the house with Sheena dressed in a heavy waterproof with a hood that would help conceal her face when they reached Zoe's house. The chances of anyone spotting her arriving in the middle of a suburban housing estate were limited, but Annie didn't want to risk any nosy neighbours blabbing to the press. Whether she liked it or not, Sheena's features were only too familiar from her frequent appearances on local media.

With Sheena safely in the car, Annie went through the routine of locking up the house behind her. Her own bag for her stay at her mother's was already packed and stowed in the back of the car, so there'd be no need for her to return here tonight.

The process of locking up and departing felt oddly final, as if they were moving away permanently. Perhaps they were, she thought bitterly, or at least perhaps this was the beginning of that process. The events of the last few days felt as if they'd changed everything. Sheena had been insistent that her determination to continue her work was as strong as ever, but Annie could sense there'd already been a change. What the impact of that change might be she had as yet no idea, but it felt as if their lives were at a point of transition.

Zoe lived in a relatively anonymous estate on the edge of the city. It was the kind of place that Annie would normally have found soulless, with its rows of largely identical 'desirable' houses. She knew Zoe liked it for precisely that reason. For her, it provided a low-effort normality, a place where she could just lose herself once she'd finished dealing with whatever the job might throw at her. Tonight, Annie could understand what Zoe meant.

As soon as they reached the house, Zoe jumped out to unlock the front door while Annie retrieved Sheena's bag from the rear of the car. Their aim was to minimise the amount of time Sheena would be exposed to any potential public gaze. The whole thing felt absurdly cloak-and-dagger, particularly as it was already almost dark, but Annie wanted to take no chances.

Minutes later, Sheena was inside, and Annie was already feeling more relaxed. It was only then that she realised how anxious she'd been feeling on her partner's behalf. She'd been trying not to think about what had happened over the last few days, but the attempts on Sheena's life had been close calls. The dumping of Garfield's body, whatever the motives, had brought it all even nearer to home. It had shaken Annie more than she'd understood. Sheena had always seemed extraordinarily resilient, but Annie wondered what the impact on her had really been.

'I've just spoken to Gary,' Zoe said as she returned from the kitchen with a welcoming coffee for Sheena.

'He's on his way back from work. Reckons he'll be about thirty minutes. Do you want us to wait till he's back before Annie and I head off?'

'You go,' Sheena said. 'I've already wasted enough of your time this afternoon. I'll be fine for half an hour. Nobody even knows I'm here.'

'You're sure?' Annie said.

'Annie, I'm not an idiot. I fully appreciate what's happened and the risks. But we've got to continue with our lives. I'm as safe here as I can be.'

Annie hesitated. She knew Sheena was right, and she also knew that the last thing Sheena wanted was to make any concessions to those who had tried to harm her. It wouldn't help Sheena's state of mind if they continued to treat her like some kind of invalid. 'Well, okay. But you'll call me straight away if there are any problems.'

'Like what?'

Annie shrugged. 'I've no idea. But you'll call. Promise.' More than anything, she wanted to embrace Sheena – for her own sake as well as Sheena's – but she knew Sheena would feel self-conscious in Zoe's presence.

'If there are any problems, I'll call. I promise. Now, bugger off, both of you.'

Chapter Thirty-Six

'Let me explain a little about how we work, Clive.' Robin Kennedy had begun to walk around the room, with the air of a professor delivering an extemporised lecture. 'I can't expect you to understand or follow all of it, and you will probably misinterpret our motives as so many do. But I'd like at least to try to explain. In the circumstances, you deserve at least that.'

Clive still had no idea what Kennedy was talking about. He had begun to wonder if Kennedy was simply insane, but he suspected that the truth was simpler and more mundane. For all his superficial charisma, Kennedy was just an articulate con man, peddling the twenty-first century equivalent of patent medicine. Clive didn't consider himself to have much of an intellect, but perhaps that was why he could see through this stuff. If he'd been brighter, he'd have made more effort to try to engage with what Kennedy was saying and after a while he'd no doubt have begun to find some spurious meaning in it. As it was, it just sailed above his head, leaving him convinced it was all just vapid nonsense.

Unless, of course, Kennedy was right and he was just too dim to understand. But that was the anxiety that people like Kennedy played on. Nobody wanted to admit that they didn't understand, so they fooled themselves into believing they did.

Even so, Clive was scared. He didn't know where this was leading or what a man like Kennedy might be capable of. It was already clear to Clive that he was being held against his will. Although he'd made no further efforts even to rise from his seat, let alone leave, he had little doubt he'd be stopped forcibly if he tried. Charlie had returned to his seat but was watching him closely. Clive had also now managed to place the semi-familiar face of the man sitting in the corner of the room. He'd seen him on TV a few times, usually in the middle of some filmed altercation. Today, he was incongruously dressed in a dark blue business suit rather than his usual T-shirt and jeans, but Clive recognised the short muscular body, the close-cropped hair, the air of barely contained steroid-fuelled aggression. It was that far-right thug, the one who risibly called himself Bulldog. Mo Henley. Clive considered the man a joke, but he didn't doubt that he'd be more than capable of real violence.

The real question, of course, was why Kennedy was associating with someone like that in the first place. And why Rowan, who had seemed so warm and likeable in their previous encounters, now remained blank-faced and silent. Clive was beginning to realise how flawed his perceptions had been from the start. Next time, he thought, he should perhaps pay more attention to Greg Wardle's scepticism.

That was assuming there would be a next time. Clive still couldn't really believe he was in any physical danger here, but he also couldn't see where this was heading. Was Kennedy just going to deliver some lecture and then let him go? Even for a man with Kennedy's outsized ego, that seemed odd behaviour.

Clive had decided that for the moment he had little option but to play along. He'd sit and listen to whatever Kennedy might have to say, make some polite noises, express his regrets that Kennedy didn't want his services, and then try to find a way to get the hell out of there. If they tried to stop him – well, surely in the end they wouldn't. No one really behaved like that. Not someone like Kennedy anyway.

He was conscious Kennedy was still talking, though Clive had no real idea what he'd been saying. He tried to force himself to concentrate on Kennedy's words.

'You see, Clive, the key to our movement is materialism. Some religions try to divorce spirituality from the real world, but they're simply deluding themselves. Denying the reality all around them. But, for us, material wealth isn't something to be embarrassed about or ashamed of. None of that nonsense about camels and needles' eyes for us. Acquiring wealth is part of the path to enlightenment. I see myself, in effect, as a spiritual entrepreneur.'

In other circumstances Clive would have laughed out loud at the preposterous phrase. But he felt he had no choice but to engage with Kennedy's arguments until he could see where the hell this was going. 'So how do you do that?'

'In any ways we can. And that's the other point. We don't worry about the supposed ethics of what we do. Those kind of small-minded constraints are what prevent people from genuinely embracing the material world. We simply do what we need to. Breaking free of those hypocritical shackles is one of the keys to achieving true enlightenment.' He paused and moved to stand beside Clive, gazing down at him. 'That was why I knew you could never be one of us, Clive. You're a creature of convention, aren't you? A rule-taker, not a rule-breaker.'

'I'm not a believer in anarchy, if that's what you mean.' Clive intended the words to sound defiant, but he knew they merely sounded petulant.

'We're not anarchists, Clive. But we believe in a higher set of laws. Something beyond the pettifogging limits that you accept.'

'Like what?' Clive felt as if he needed to puncture this airy nonsense. He still had no real idea of what Kennedy was talking about. 'How do you make your money?'

'In a number of ways, Clive. Some of them are straightforward and perfectly legal. We have a substantial property business, for example. Mainly private rentals. A very lucrative business if you have the capital to invest. And we obtain and build the capital in a variety of ways, some of them less straightforward. Drugs. Money laundering. Various financial… arrangements, let's say. We have a substantial network.'

'This is a joke, isn't it? I mean, if any of this was true, you wouldn't tell me about it. You wouldn't talk about it so openly.'

Kennedy gestured expansively at the group seated around him. 'We have one key rule in the movement, Clive. One iron law above all others. Whatever we do, we do it collectively. We involve all our more senior members in all decisions. That way, we're all involved. And we're all complicit.' He smiled. 'The thing is, Clive, I'm not really talking to you. Not primarily. It's amusing to treat you as my audience, and I'll enjoy explaining what we have in store for you. But, frankly, I wouldn't waste my time simply on an intellect like yours. It's important that everyone here fully participates in our acts and understands their implications.' He looked around the group, as though seeking their approval, although it was clear that he expected no interruption. Rowan Wiseman nodded slightly. The others continued to sit in silence. 'If you'd really read and understood the material I gave you, you'd already have grasped this, Clive.'

'I've no idea what you're talking about,' Clive said. 'Look, I've had enough of sitting here being insulted by a tinpot tyrant like you—' He made a move to stand, but saw that Charlie and Henley were already rising from their seats. 'You can't just keep me here.'

'I think we can, Clive. Just for a little while. Just for as long as it takes.'

'As long as what takes?'

'Patience does not seem to be one of your virtues, Clive. Just wait and all will be revealed.'

Kennedy stopped as a mobile phone buzzed on the low coffee table behind him. Without turning, he said, 'Can someone get that? It'll be Eric.'

Rowan Wiseman picked up the phone and took the call. She listened for a few moments, and then held out the phone to Kennedy.

Kennedy took the phone. 'Everything going to plan?' He stopped, listening. 'Okay. But make sure you're really on top of this. We can't afford a fuck-up.'

The change in tone was noticeable, Clive thought. The smooth urbane manner had briefly evaporated, replaced by something much less polished. It was only momentary, but Clive suspected he'd briefly glimpsed the real Kennedy. The rest of it was nothing but a performance. Kennedy wasn't just a con man. He was a thug. Suddenly the association with Mo Henley made much more sense.

The thought was far from reassuring. Up to now, despite everything that had happened, Clive had found himself almost seduced by Kennedy's manner. He'd told himself that, whatever nonsense he might be talking, Kennedy was essentially a civilised man who, ultimately, would behave in a civilised way. But the man who had just been revealed seemed like a very different beast.

Kennedy ended the call and then turned back to Clive. He was smiling and the mask seemed to have slid back into place. 'All more or less going to plan,' he said. He sounded as if he was talking to himself as much as Clive. 'They have the target in their sights. Eric has it all under control, I'm sure.'

'Target?'

'Target, Clive. Your target, in fact, though you don't yet know it.'

'I don't understand.'

'No, of course you don't. In due course I suppose you'll have a very small place in history, though you'll never be aware of it.'

'Are you sure about this, Robin?' The unexpected intervention came from Rowan Wiseman. Apart from Charlie's earlier threats to Clive, it was the first time any of the assembled group had spoken. 'Eric sounded a bit unsure about how reliable—'

'Nothing's gone wrong, Rowan. The situation's under control and Eric is more than capable of dealing with it.' It was clear that Kennedy regarded her comment as unwelcome.

'It's not Eric I'm worried about.'

Kennedy glared at her. His tone and manner were as smooth as ever, but Clive once again detected the uglier personality beneath the surface. 'You know how we work,

Rowan. You know how we initiate neophytes. That's how we gain their commitment.'

'I'm just saying it's a risk. It's one thing to bump off some two-bit toerags who've tried to go freelance. This is an entirely different—'

'Rowan.' Kennedy had barely raised his voice but the threat was unmistakeable. 'If you want to continue this conversation, we do so at another time.'

Rowan clearly wanted to say more, but lapsed back into silence. Kennedy turned back to Clive, who had been listening to the exchange with mounting anxiety.

'Now, Clive,' Kennedy continued, as if Rowan's interruption had never taken place, 'let me finally put you out of your misery.'

Chapter Thirty-Seven

'Looks like Carl's dad is back,' Annie said. 'Time to break the news.'

Zoe pulled the car in to the kerb outside the house. There was a superannuated-looking Volvo estate parked behind the white van. In the late afternoon, the house had lights showing in all its uncurtained downstairs windows.

The two women climbed out of the car and walked up the drive to the front door. As they approached, the door opened.

'Police?' The man standing on the threshold was middle-aged but looked as if he worked out frequently. He was dressed in jeans and a paint-spattered white T-shirt that was perhaps a size too small for him.

Annie nodded. 'How did you know?'

The man shrugged. 'You can always tell, if you know what to look for.'

Annie decided not to pursue that one. 'Mr Francis?'

'That's me. Jim Francis. You've come about Carl, I'm guessing.'

'You seem to be a step ahead of us, Mr Francis. I'm afraid we're here with bad news.'

'Of course you are, if it's about Carl.' He nodded, his expression weary. 'That kind of bad news, then. I'd better speak to Kelly first. It'll come better from me.'

'He's dead, Mr Francis. I'm very sorry.'

'It's a shock, but not a surprise. Look, do you mind waiting here for a moment? I'll go and prepare the ground and then you can come in.'

'If you're sure—'

'Trust me.' Francis made his way back into the house, leaving the two women standing on the doorstep.

Annie exchanged a look with Zoe. 'Not the textbook approach.'

'I don't know what else you could have done. It's as if he was waiting for us.'

'Perhaps he was.'

It was a few minutes before Francis returned. 'Okay, you'd better come through. I've broken the news.'

They followed Francis through into the living room where they'd spoken to his wife previously. Kelly Francis was sitting on the sofa, sobbing. At first she seemed unaware of their entrance, then she looked up. 'It's true, then?'

Annie took a seat on the sofa opposite where Kelly Francis was sitting. 'I'm very sorry.'

'Can you tell us how?' Jim Francis said.

'We believe it was murder.'

Jim Francis nodded. 'I knew it would be something like that. Or drugs,' he added.

'Why do you say that, Mr Francis?'

'Because those were the kind of people he mixed with. It was only a matter of time.' He shrugged. 'I'm sorry. I sound heartless. I'm not. We both loved him, and it'll hit me properly later. But I've had so many fights with him about this stuff. So many times I've had to bail him out.' Francis was pacing up and down the room, as if trying to walk off his emotion.

'This isn't really the moment for me to be asking this,' Annie said, speaking to Kelly Francis. 'And if you're not up to discussing it at the moment, we'll understand. Does your husband know we spoke to you about Carl a few days ago?' She'd have preferred to have raised this privately with Kelly Francis, but it felt as if the time for that kind of discretion had passed. Too many people had already failed to tell them the whole truth.

Kelly Francis looked up, her eyes red. 'I told him. Eventually. I thought about not saying anything because I thought if he knew the police were looking for Carl—' She stopped. 'I lied to you. I told you Carl was doing well. That we were in regular contact. You seemed more interested in the other two, Darren and Jonny, so I thought you might leave Carl alone.'

'That's not how it works, love,' Jim Francis said. 'You can't keep denying these things.'

'Was Carl still associating with Darren and Jonny?' Zoe asked.

'As far as we know,' Jim Francis said. 'I was in contact with Carl. But only because every now and then he'd come to sponge money off me. Or ask me to get him out of some scrape or other. But he was still mixing with the same crowd. And Darren and Jonny were at the heart of that.'

'He wouldn't talk to me.' Kelly Francis had begun to cry again. 'Reckoned all I did was lecture him. He was probably right about that. Not that it ever did any good.'

'Again, this may not be the moment,' Annie said. 'But is there anything you can tell us about Carl's recent circumstances? What he was up to, who he mixed with. Mrs Francis told us he worked in a supermarket but—'

'That wasn't true either,' Jim Francis interrupted. 'He did for a while when he first moved out but they sacked him. Recurrent lateness, absence, all that. That was six months ago. I don't know what he's been living on since then, though I'm willing to bet it wasn't anything kosher. He's had the odd sub from me, but only to tide him over when he was short. Or that's what he told me.' Francis paused. 'There was one thing, though.'

'Go on.'

'Last time I spoke to him was probably four or five weeks ago. He seemed pretty chipper. Reckoned he and some mates had got this big opportunity. One of the things about Carl was that he couldn't resist shooting his mouth off. He'd told me a while before that they'd been doing some good business with some local outfit. Now, he was telling me they'd found a way to cream off some of the profits for themselves. He wouldn't tell me the details, but it all sounded deeply dodgy to me. I told him not to be so fucking stupid. He just laughed and said that it wasn't as if the people they were ripping off would be going to the police.'

It was the third time Annie had heard mention of a big opportunity in relation to the dead men. 'What do you think he meant by that?'

'I took it to mean that he was already up to his ears in something criminal and now he was trying to do some double-dealing. I told him that, if these were the kind of people who wouldn't go to the police, they'd have their own ways of dealing with anyone who crossed them...' He tailed off.

'Was that why you weren't surprised to see us today?'

'Maybe. I didn't want to tell Kelly, but I had a really bad feeling about it. Carl was trouble, but he was just a naive kid really. He never really seemed to understand what he was getting involved with.'

'Do you know what kind of thing he was involved with?'

'They were dealing drugs at school. I mean, the hard stuff. They were small fry, being exploited, but they never realised. But from hints that Carl dropped, I think they were gradually sucked into some pretty nasty stuff. Loan sharking, protection stuff. There's plenty of potential victims round these parts, believe me. And there's plenty prepared to prey on them.' He shook his head. 'Mind you, people like Carl, kids with no prospects who get exploited, are as much victims as any of them in my view.'

Annie wanted to point out that not all disadvantaged youths turn to crime, but she knew this wasn't the moment. And she recognised too that Francis had a point. Whatever his own flaws, Carl had simply been chewed up and spat out. He wasn't the real villain. 'You don't know anything else about who Carl might have been working for? This local outfit you mentioned?'

Jim Francis frowned. 'I'm trying to think. This was a few months back. He was sounding pleased with himself then, too, because they'd been taken on for this work. It was all supposed to be deeply hush-hush, so of course he couldn't stop himself blabbing about it. To be honest, it sounded a bit weird to me. A bit cultish. Some outfit that was supposed to be helping youngsters who were struggling or in trouble. Carl even reckoned they were prepared to provide him with accommodation.'

'Accommodation?' Annie glanced at Zoe.

'That was what sounded the alarm bells. I didn't really know what to say to him. If I'd tried to tell him not to get involved, that would have just made him do the opposite.

And for all I knew, it was genuine. So I just told him to be careful and not to let himself be taken advantage of.'

'He didn't say anything more about it subsequently?'

'Not really. When I asked him about it, he said it was all fine but he wouldn't say anything more. To be honest, I thought that just meant it hadn't worked out for whatever reason. Either they'd sacked him, or it hadn't been what he'd expected.'

Annie nodded. 'I'm sorry. We've pressed you far too much in the circumstances. You've been extremely helpful.'

'Have I?' Francis looked mildly surprised. 'Look, I may come across as a callous bugger, but I'm not really. I loved Carl and, like I say, this will hit me later, I'm sure. I just feel a bit numb at the moment. But I'll do anything I can to help you catch the bastards who killed him.'

'Thank you. We'll need to talk to you and Mrs Francis more formally later, but that can wait. You've given us plenty of useful information for that.' She turned to Kelly Francis. 'I'm sorry we've had to put you through this. And I'm so sorry about your loss.'

'We lost him years ago,' Kelly Francis said. 'That's the awful thing. That's the really awful thing.'

–

Annie waited till they were back in the car before saying to Zoe, 'Accommodation.'

'Which brings us back to Werneth Holdings,' Zoe said. 'Who seem to have been remarkably generous with our three victims.'

'I think a visit to this Robin Kennedy has just leapt to the top of our priority list. Werneth seems to be the only clear link we have between the three victims, and it sounds as if their involvement might have been something a bit more than bar work. Still, that's for tomorrow. I'd better get you back to Gary.'

'That reminds me. Someone texted while we were in there. Gary's about the only person who sends me texts these days. Hang on...' She pulled out the phone and thumbed through to the message. 'Bugger. He's got held up at work. Reckons we'll probably be back before he is. You think Sheena's going to be okay?'

'What could happen to her?' Annie said. 'Nobody else even knows she's there.'

Chapter Thirty-Eight

'I don't understand.'

'No, I don't imagine you do, Clive. You really don't seem to understand much of what I say to you.'

'But what does this MP have to do with me?'

Kennedy sighed. 'That's rather the point, Clive. It'll be a random killing by someone with severe but sadly undiagnosed mental health problems.'

'But I don't have—'

'You're really not terribly bright, are you, Clive?'

Clive looked around at the others in the room, hoping someone else here would be able to expose this for the madness it clearly was. But there was no sign that they were prepared to do anything except listen to Kennedy's ravings. Rowan and Charlie seemed like different people from those he'd encountered previously, to the point where he'd initially wondered whether they were under the influence of some drug. But after a while it had struck him that this was more the adoration offered to the leader of a cult.

Kennedy knew how to manipulate people and he had this group under his spell. Rowan had said he'd helped them through some kind of 'spiritual journey' during a difficult point in their life. Perhaps that kind of emotional leverage enabled Kennedy to behave as he did. It was the kind of controlling behaviour that, in other contexts, led to death cults and mass suicides.

In reality, he understood all too well what Kennedy was telling him. It sounded like utter madness, but the scheme itself was clear enough. He just couldn't begin to envisage how they might expect to get away with it. The whole thing sounded so absurd, he almost didn't even feel frightened.

Almost.

Except Rowan had mentioned people being bumped off, and the MP's near miss at the hands of a gunman had been all over the news. He might feel as if he'd slipped through into someone else's fantasy, but this was all too real. He hadn't yet made a serious effort to escape, but from the way he was being watched by Charlie and the others, he knew they would have no difficulty in preventing him.

His only hope was that, if they really were serious in their threats, they might prefer not to do anything here in Kennedy's own house. If they moved him, that might give him the only chance he was likely to have.

For the moment, Clive's only real option was to keep Kennedy talking. Kennedy clearly loved the sound of his own mellifluous voice, and was only too eager to respond to Clive's questions, however inane they might be. From the time that had passed since his arrival, Clive also had the sense that Kennedy himself was playing for time, waiting till whatever they were planning was all set up. 'But I don't understand what this MP's supposed to have done? This can't be just because you disagree with her politics?'

Kennedy laughed. 'As it happens, I do disagree with her politics. Pretty fundamentally. She's the type who'd tax us till we can't pay any more, who'd destroy business, who'd want to stop me making a decent profit as a land-lord. I wouldn't be sorry to see her go on those grounds alone. But that's not really what this is about. She's become a direct irritant.'

'In what way?'

'She's spent her time in Parliament campaigning against the ways in which we make most of our money. She believes we're exploiting the poor benighted communities up here.'

'Aren't you?'

'We provide services people need. Accommodation, quick cash, even drugs. If we didn't do it, someone else would.'

'I thought it was your route to enlightenment?'

'Perhaps you're finally beginning to understand, Clive. That's exactly it. It's not our job to change this world. Our role is to embrace it, extract what we can from it and find our own form of nirvana.'

'And this MP would stop you doing that?'

'She's gradually been building a dossier of cases from around her constituency. A lot of them relating to our network. She's not come close to connecting them with our businesses because of the way we've organised ourselves. We're at the centre of the web, and she's only teasing at the edges. But eventually she'll get to a point where she starts to join the dots. Her partner's a police officer, and at some point, if she continues, this could begin to feel uncomfortable for us. So, best she isn't allowed to continue.'

'But if she's killed, the police will be raking over every-thing. Isn't that more likely to put you in the spotlight?'

'This takes us back to where we started, Clive. Not if they think this was a random act by someone with mental health problems. Even if they decide it was politically motivated, they'll think the killer was just a fanatic.'

'You'll never make this work. It's ridiculous.'

'I think we will, Clive. This is also a test, an initiation process. I think I mentioned earlier how we initiate our neophytes. We've had a few of those recently, and we ask them to prove their worth by working with Eric. Eric, of course, would be only too happy to do this work by himself. He gets his pleasure that way. But we also ensure all our newcomers work alongside him to gain experience and show their full commitment to the movement.'

'So they're fully implicated, you mean?' Clive was finally beginning to get an inkling of what Kennedy was talking about, and he felt a cold finger running down his spine.

'You might say that. Of course, some of them succeed and some of them fail. If they fail, Eric deals with them. If they succeed – well, ask our friend Mo here.' He gestured towards the man Clive had recognised as the far-right activist. 'Mo's become an active member of our senior team. He helps recruit young people to our cause through his political activism. And he helps us deal with those who don't meet our high standards. Isn't that right, Mo?'

Henley nodded. 'Like little scumbags who start dipping their hands in the till.' His voice was soft, unexpectedly posh-sounding, and undoubtedly menacing.

'Mo and Eric have dealt with a few of that kind in recent weeks, as well as issuing a few warnings to those who might have crossed us in the past. As we grow the movement, we like to have the occasional clear-out. It helps to keep everyone honest.'

'I still don't understand.' Clive had decided he had no choice but to keep pushing this now. The more he knew about Kennedy's plans, the more he might have a chance to find a way to disrupt them. 'You're never going to persuade anyone that I'm some kind of fanatic.'

'You don't think so?' Kennedy sounded genuinely surprised. 'Your interests are a little – eccentric. Unexplained phenomena. Conspiracy theories.'

'That's still a long way from murderous fanatic.'

'Perhaps not when there's evidence in your house of an obsession with your victim. When the police find your house filled with suitably fanatical material. Far-right politics.' He laughed. 'Some of the more sensationalist material linked to the "left-hand path". The knives that were used in the recent apparently ritualistic murders. Not to mention the firearm used in the previous unsuccessful shootings. There'll be enough there to convince them. Along with your body, of course.'

Clive felt a new clutch of fear in his stomach. 'My body?'

'That's obviously how this all ends, Clive. You commit suicide in a way that appears suitably deranged. As a bonus for us, you die in a way that links you to other recent murders in the area. It all slots neatly into place, or at least neatly enough that no one's likely to be inclined to look much further.'

'You'll never make that work,' Clive said. 'Apart from anything else, how are you going to get all that stuff into my house?'

Kennedy's mobile phone buzzed on the table. He picked it up and glanced at the screen, then rose to his feet. 'I think we're ready to go. As for placing the evidence in your house, Clive, well, it's part of the initiation process.

We've already received a great deal of help in this. Tonight we hope to welcome another neophyte into the movement.'

Chapter Thirty-Nine

As soon as the light waned outside, Sheena Pearson had carefully closed all the curtains around the ground floor before turning on any lights. It felt more like a superstitious gesture to ward off the darkness than anything of practical value, but it somehow made her feel more secure.

There was nothing for her to worry about. If her life really was under threat – and, even now, despite everything that had happened, she still struggled to believe it – her security here was protected by her sheer anonymity. No one could know she was here. That simple fact offered more protection than any amount of security.

She switched on the television, searching through the channels until she found a news broadcast. There was a brief mention of the continuing investigation into the shootings, but no indication that any further progress had been made. There was a similar short report on the continuing murder investigations, but it seemed that only limited information had so far been released to the media. Sheena switched off the television and reached for her briefcase. She'd brought a range of paperwork with her in the hope she might at least make good use of this unexpected hiatus in her working life.

It was then that she heard the sound.

It took a moment to realise what she was hearing. The noise of a window being broken, somewhere in the rear of the house.

She reached for her mobile phone on the table, already preparing to dial 999. Even so, she was too slow. The living room door was thrown violently back to reveal the figure of a man framed in the doorway.

She'd instinctively placed the phone behind her back and now, still scarcely conscious of what she was doing, she slipped it into the waistband of her jeans, hoping it would stay in place. 'What the bloody hell is this?' She tried to sound angry but knew she simply sounded terrified.

The man walked forward and grabbed her by the arm. She was on the point of pulling away when he placed the point of a knife under her chin, the blade almost piercing her flesh. When he pulled her towards the front door, she made no effort to resist.

Outside, there was a car parked in the driveway, one of its rear doors already open. The man pushed her forward and thrust her into the rear seat. There was a moment, as he loosened his grip and lowered the knife, when she thought she might pull herself away, but it was already too late. The man climbed into the seat beside her, grabbed her head and pulled her down so that she was half lying on his lap. She was hidden from anyone outside the car, and the knife was once again pressed against her skin.

'Okay.' It was the first word she'd heard the man say, and it was addressed to a second man in the driver's seat. 'Drive. But slowly. Don't do anything to attract attention.'

Sheena was still trying to concentrate, trying to gather any clues she could about what was happening. She had to keep believing she could somehow get herself free, and the key to that, more than anything, was not allowing her fear to overwhelm her. She could still feel the mobile phone pressed against her back, but its presence was irrelevant for the moment.

She tried to gauge from the movement of the car which direction they might be taking, but even the first few turns out of the estate left her confused. She twisted her head to look up at the man holding her, wanting to be able to recognise him again, assuming she ever had the chance. He was holding a mobile phone in his free hand, apparently sending a text. But his attention remained on her and the knife was still steady against her throat. The man clearly had no concern about concealing his appearance. That thought alone sent a chill down her spine.

She could tell the car had picked up speed, suggesting that they had perhaps left the estate, but by now she had no idea which way they might be heading. There was nothing she could do but wait. Wait, and hope and pray.

–

'Where are they?'

'They'll be here. Relax.'

'I don't like this. There's too much that can go wrong.'

It was almost like the first time they'd visited Kennedy Farm, Clive thought. In a car with Rowan and Charlie. This time, though, there was no Greg Wardle, and it wasn't Rowan's car but one that had been waiting for them at the rear of the house. Charlie was in the back seat beside him.

It was Charlie who'd manhandled him into the car, with some assistance from Mo Henley. Neither had shown any compunction in using whatever force they felt was necessary, and Clive had been left with no doubt about what they would do if he made any effort to escape.

Henley was seated in the front beside Rowan, and he was the one expressing concern. 'How do we know it's going okay?'

'Because he texted to say they'd got her.'

'It all just feels too complicated to me.'

'Too complicated for you, maybe,' Rowan said. 'It's how Robin works. He's always been like this. He's done okay so far.'

Henley clearly wanted to say more, but was silenced by a glare from Charlie. It was the first time Clive had seen any evidence of dissent among Kennedy's followers. He wondered how long Henley had been part of this group. Was he one of the recent so-called neophytes? If so, Clive wondered quite what Henley's initiation had involved. For that matter, what had Rowan and Charlie done to become part of Kennedy's inner circle?

They were parked just off the road, somewhere on the moors west of Chesterfield. It was a bleak, windswept area that Clive knew only as somewhere he had driven through on his way to more conventionally picturesque parts of the Peak District. Kennedy had said something about the location closing the circle, but that had meant nothing to Clive. All he knew was that the area was sufficiently remote that any chance of finding assistance was likely to be small.

'They should be here by now,' Henley said.

'It's a good twenty-minute drive,' Rowan said. 'They'll be here in a few minutes. Just relax.'

Henley looked far from relaxed but said no more. In the event, it was another ten minutes or so before they saw a set of car headlights approaching along the single-track road. 'That'll be them,' Rowan said.

The car drew to a halt alongside them, immediately extinguishing its lights. Beside him, Charlie pushed open the door and dragged Clive out into the night. The rear door of the second car opened, and Clive saw Eric Nolan push a woman out in front of him. Clive had no interest in politics but he recognised the woman's face. It was the MP.

He decided to have one more shot at reasoning with them. 'Look, I don't know if this is some sort of protest or statement or what it is, but it's all gone far enough now—'

'Just shut up.' Charlie sounded bored rather than threatening, but there was no doubting he was serious. 'Let's get this done with.'

Rowan and Henley had left the car to join them. 'We need to do it properly, though.' She gestured towards the second car. 'How's he doing?'

'He's done okay so far. We planted all the stuff in our friend here's house. But, frankly, that was the easy bit. Now's the real test for him.' He turned and tapped on the car windscreen, gesturing for the driver to join them.

Clive assumed that this was one of the so-called neophytes. The one who was supposedly being initiated tonight. He had begun to feel a panic that made him sick to the stomach. This was finally beginning to seem real, rather than just some convoluted piece of psychological torture.

He watched the driver emerge from the car. At first, in the darkness, he thought he must be mistaken. But he knew he wasn't. And he knew, too, that he'd suspected this ever since Kennedy had mentioned the help they'd received. It was impossible, but it was also obvious.

'Greg.'

Chapter Forty

'Oh, Jesus Christ.'

They had seen the open front door as soon as Annie Delamere turned in to the drive. In the few moments it had taken her to stop the car and run into the house, she'd told herself that there could be countless explanations. But she couldn't really think of a single one. There was no reason that, given what had happened, Sheena would have left the door wide open or gone out by herself into the night.

'Sheena!'

She rushed through the house, peering into all the ground-floor rooms, calling out Sheena's name, but she could already tell that the house was empty. She had seen, with a sick feeling of dread, that the patio doors into the rear dining room had been smashed open.

Zoe had followed her into the house and had run up the stairs to check the upper floor. She returned to the head of the stairs, shaking her head. 'Nothing.'

'Shit. How the hell is it possible? Nobody even knew she was here.'

'I don't know. Christ…' Zoe was staring around in bafflement, as if she expected Sheena to emerge from hiding at any moment.

Annie had dialled Sheena's mobile number but, as she'd expected, the call simply rang out. 'She's hopeless at answering it anyway. Has it on silent all the time because she's usually in meetings.'

'You better call it in. I'll go and check with the neighbours. See if anyone saw anything.'

Annie took a breath, trying to force herself back into her professional mode. It was generally one of her strengths. When she was really up against it, she normally had the capacity to put all her personal preoccupations behind her and focus on the job at hand. But she'd never previously been in a position like this.

It took her a few moments to explain the situation to the enquiry desk, throwing in a few references to Stuart Jennings to persuade them to throw whatever resource they could at the operation. But the reality was that they had almost nothing to work with. They had no information on what might have happened to Sheena, no description of a vehicle or any assailants. Nothing.

She finished the call, having achieved as much as she could, and then called Stuart Jennings' mobile. He answered almost immediately, as he always seemed to, and she explained what had happened.

'Christ,' he said. She could almost hear him considering the implications of this happening on his watch. She knew he'd be silently thanking his lucky stars that Annie hadn't sought his permission before moving Sheena over here. At least he was off the hook for that. 'And you've really nothing to go on?'

'Not unless one of the neighbours saw something. Zoe's checking with the immediate ones.'

'I'd better get on to Andy Dwyer—'

A sudden thought struck her, a cold finger along her spine. 'Stuart. I'm probably not thinking straight. But it's just me that Andy Dwyer's the only other person I told about bringing Sheena here. I thought he ought to be aware of what we were doing.'

'You're not suggesting...'

'I'm not suggesting anything. I'm just stating a fact. Dwyer may have told some of his team, though I told him to be discreet. He knew that the whole point of this was to keep it under wraps.'

'I know Andy's got a bit of a reputation for wheeling and dealing when it suits him, but this would be a whole other thing.'

'I don't know, Stuart. I just know there's been something odd about this throughout. Like how someone knew that Sheena was leaving the hospital by that rear entrance.'

'You can't seriously—'

'I don't know, Stuart. This isn't the moment anyway. We need to be focusing on tracking down Sheena. It was just an idea that popped into my head. Something for later.'

There was a moment's silence at the other end of the line. 'Leave it with me. And I'll get on to Ops and get everything I can thrown at this. Keep me posted with anything from your end, and I'll do the same.'

He ended the call in his usual abrupt manner. Her main consolation was that she knew Jennings would be pulling out all the stops to prevent this turning into a monumental fuck-up. He might not care too much about Sheena, but he sure as hell cared about his own reputation.

Zoe reappeared at the front door, breathless. 'I'm sorry. I've got nothing. One of the neighbours saw a car in the drive, but didn't think anything of it. Couldn't even tell me what colour it was.'

'I suppose we can at least tell the dispatchers that we're looking for a car, but that's hardly a major breakthrough.'

'So what now?'

'Christ knows. All we can do is sit here and pray for a miracle. Or hope that Sheena's even more resilient than I've always thought she was.'

–

Greg Wardle was staring at the ground, clearly trying to avoid Clive's gaze.

'Greg's been with us for some time,' Rowan said. 'He was the one who first alerted us to your interest in our type of organisation, even before you started making indiscreet calls. He's the one who told us about your tabloid contacts.'

Greg finally looked up. He looked nervous and embarrassed, his expression suggesting he'd ben dreading this moment of revelation. 'I'm sorry, Clive. I'd have preferred it not to be like this. But there's nothing I can do.'

'I don't understand.' Clive was staring at Greg, trying to make sense of what he was hearing. 'Surely you can't be part of this.'

Greg shook his head. 'I don't have a choice, Clive. You've got to understand that. It's too late now. I got involved with them a while back. They paid me some backhanders for inside info on planning applications and the like. Just pin money, but every little helps when you're working in the public sector. Well, you know that. But it's a one-way street. Once you've done it, you can't go back. So I've got to go on. It's a step-by-step thing, the movement. Building trust with them. But tonight's the big step.'

'The initiation?'

'There's more than one initiation,' Rowan said. 'We ask people to do acts that are normally considered taboo. Greg's already progressed through several levels. Tonight is a chance for him to enter the inner circle.'

'Christ, you make it sound like a pyramid selling scheme.'

Rowan laughed. 'Very good. You know, I'm not sure Robin's entirely right about you. I think you could have worked with us. If you could ever have persuaded yourself to take that first step.' She gestured to Eric Nolan, 'Okay, let's get this done.'

She led the way along a footpath past a row of trees out on to the moorland. Once they were away from the trees, the stiff breeze hit them. The valley was stretched out in the darkness, the lights of the surrounding villages dotted across the landscape. Nolan was half pulling, half dragging Sheena Pearson. Charlie pushed Clive in front of him, and Henley and Greg Wardle brought up the rear.

They continued until they reached an open stretch of moor. The land was uneven, scattered with stone and cairns, but Rowan led them to a comparatively flat patch of ground. 'Here.'

Nolan pushed Sheena forward. 'Take off your clothes.'

'What?' It was the first word Sheena had spoken since leaving the car. Up to this point, she had seemed cowed, deferential.

'Take off your clothes.'

Sheena straightened up. 'I'm not taking off my fucking clothes. I'd rather you just fucking knifed me.'

'This needs to be done properly.' Rowan's voice was gentle. 'We don't want to make this any more difficult for you than it needs to be. But if you won't undress yourself, we'll do it forcibly.'

'You can fucking try.'

She looked like a different person now, Clive thought. Perhaps the initial shock of the kidnapping had worn off, but she looked determined, formidable. Her resistance might be short-lived, but it was impressive.

Rowan gestured to Greg Wardle. 'I think this is for you, Greg. The beginning of the act.'

He reached towards Sheena, who glared back at him. 'Just fuck off. Don't even fucking think about it.'

Wardle looked around confusedly, and Nolan handed him the knife. 'Make her do it.'

There was a long silence. Wardle was holding the knife as if it were some unfamiliar object. After a moment, it fell from his fingers. 'I can't do it. I just can't do it.'

'Oh, for Christ's sake—' Nolan leaned over to retrieve the knife. In that brief moment of confusion, Sheena pulled away.

Nolan made a grab for her, but Clive threw himself forward. His first instinct had been simply to run, seizing the moment as Sheena had done, but he knew that was likely to be futile. His second instinct, unconsidered, was to protect Sheena Pearson.

Sheena was already running, stumbling her way across the moorland into the darkness. Clive was rolling on the ground with Nolan, conscious that the other man was much larger and stronger than he was. Nolan was forcing him back on to the earth when Clive felt the chill of metal under his fingers.

His hand closed on the handle of the knife and, scarcely thinking what he was doing, he plunged the blade into the side of Nolan's stomach. Nolan gave an agonised cry, and began to writhe above him.

'Christ, stop the bastard. He's stabbed Eric.' The voice was Rowan's. 'Charlie!'

Charlie and Henley had already set off in pursuit of Sheena. Now both hesitated and turned back to see what was happening.

Clive was trying to withdraw the knife, but with Nolan's weight on him he was succeeding only in twisting it. He could already feel the warm blood pouring from Nolan's body.

'Shit.' The voice was Charlie's. He was standing above them, clearly trying to work out what was happening. 'What the fuck are we going to do?'

'Just get the knife off him,' Rowan said. 'We need to stop him before he does any more damage.' Her voice remained disconcertingly calm.

Clive had finally extracted the knife from Nolan's body. Nolan himself was still twisting on the ground, but Clive managed to extricate himself just as Charlie was bending over to intervene. He raised the knife and slashed it at Charlie's face, catching him across the cheek and nose, the blade slicing neatly through the flesh. 'Christ, he's cut me!' Charlie cried.

Clive was on his knees now, and he took one more lunge at Charlie, driving the knife into his chest. Charlie fell backwards, blood billowing on his T-shirt. Clive pushed himself to his feet, and turned. Henley was already backing away towards the footpath.

Rowan, though, stood, unmoving. 'Put the knife down, Clive.'

Clive stood with the knife held out in front of him. 'Just let me go and I won't hurt you.'

'We can't let you go, and you're not going to hurt me.' She began slowly to walk toward him, her eyes calmly fixed on his. 'Just give me the knife.'

As she drew close, he raised the knife, prepared to slash at her as he had at Charlie. But before he could move, she had grabbed his wrist and twisted it, agonisingly. She twisted more and he fell to his knees, the pain now even more intense. The knife fell from his fingers and, still holding him down, she reached for it.

The last words he heard were, 'If you want a job done properly...'

Chapter Forty-One

The decision to run had been little more than instinctive. Sheena Pearson assumed that they would catch up with her within a few yards. She was an accomplished runner, and had been a sprinter in her younger days. Now, she did relatively frequent marathons for various local charities, and she could still achieve a good balance of speed and stamina. Even so, she'd only had the shortest of head starts, and she didn't expect to elude the men for more than a few minutes.

She just kept her head down and ran, trying to navigate the rough terrain in the darkness. The last thing she wanted was to trip and damage an ankle.

There was some kind of commotion behind her. She could hear shouting but had no intention of looking back to see what had happened. All she knew was that the expected hand on her shoulder or rugby-tackle to the ground had not yet materialised.

She was running downhill across the moorland. As far as she could judge, her route would intersect with the road eventually, but she wanted to keep to the open country in case any of the group returned to the car with the intention of cutting off her escape. She altered her direction slightly, heading for a patch of woodland that she hoped might provide her with some shelter.

As she reached the edge of the trees, she finally slowed and glanced back. To her surprise, there was no one behind her. She slipped between the trees, trying to move as quietly as possible through the undergrowth. When she was certain that she would be invisible from outside the trees, she stopped.

She had almost forgotten the mobile phone, but by some miracle it had remained firmly lodged in the rear waistband of her jeans. By another miracle, given the remoteness of the location, there was even a signal.

Sheena whispered a prayer of thanks to any gods who might be listening and began to dial.

–

Rowan Wiseman stood for a moment, surveying the scene. She had always had her doubts about this, and had expressed them to Robin. But she'd never expected it to end quite like this.

The only option was to clean up as best she could. Nolan was dead, and for the moment Clive Bamford was lying unconscious at her feet. She'd been tempted simply to finish him off, but she knew she needed to think this through properly. Landing herself with a pile of dead bodies wasn't going to improve anything. As it was, they'd have to find a way of dealing with the bodies of Nolan and Charlie.

As for the other two, Wardle was little more than a mess, curled up on the ground without the will either to flee or fight. Mo Henley had backed away along the path, and she'd thought for a moment that he was simply intending to bugger off and leave her with this shambles. She suspected the thought had crossed his mind, but in the end he'd had second thoughts and had returned to help her.

The question was what next?

Their first priority was to catch up with Sheena Pearson. If she managed somehow to escape, they really would be screwed. She couldn't have got too far. Wiseman had made a point of scoping out the area in daylight and knew there was a patch of woodland further down the valley in the direction Pearson had been heading. The best guess was that she had hidden herself in that. Beyond the woods there was only the road, and further open moorland where she'd be much more exposed. She had assumed Nolan would have had the nous to check Pearson didn't have a mobile with her, but she was recognising now that competence was in shorter supply here than she'd realised.

She turned to Henley. 'We've got to get this sorted. First thing is to catch up with Pearson.' She pointed across the moorland. 'If we drive down there, we've more chance of heading her off.'

'What about these two?'

'I'll get Robin to come up with the van. We'll have to lock them in the back for the moment. They'll be secure enough till we work out what's best to do with them.'

'And what about Eric and Charlie?'

'They're going nowhere,' Rowan said bluntly. 'We can decide how to deal with them later. Speaking of which…' She pulled out her mobile and dialled Kennedy's number. The call was answered almost immediately.

'Success?' Kennedy said.

'In your dreams, Robin. It's all gone completely fucking tits-up here. Don't say I didn't warn you. I want you out here now to help us get it sorted.'

'I don't think—'

'I know you like to keep above the fray, Robin, and let your minions take the hit. But we're past all that now. If you come and help, we've a chance of salvaging it. If you don't, we're all screwed. And I swear to God, if I go down, I'm taking you with me.'

There was a long silence. 'What do you need me to do?'

'Get your arse out here now in the van. First thing is to get Pearson back.'

'Shit. You mean you've lost her.'

'It was your precious neophyte who lost her, Robin. Now get out here and help us get her back. She's somewhere in the woodland at the lower end of the moor. Bring the van up here first so we can secure Bamford and Wardle. Then if you take the van down to the road and I head her off in this direction, she's not going to get far.' She ended the call without giving Kennedy a chance to argue. 'Okay,' she said to Henley, 'let's deal with these two and then get after Pearson.'

–

Annie had answered on the first ring. 'Sheena? Thank Christ. Are you okay?'

Sheena had lowered herself to the ground and was sitting with her back to a tree, peering into the darkness for any sign of movement. 'Not exactly,' she whispered into the phone, 'but I'm still alive. And healthy for the moment.'

'Where are you?'

'Up on the moorland. Near where you found that first body. Wait…' She removed the phone from her ear and switched to a mapping application that showed her position in relation to the road. 'I'll use the "share location" thing on my phone. That'll tell you exactly where I am.' She fumbled awkwardly with the phone, conscious of the trembling in her hands. 'There.'

'Okay, got it,' Annie responded.

Sheena was staring into the darkness, trying to control her rising panic long enough to give Annie a coherent account. 'I've managed to get away from them for the moment. I'm hidden here but the woodland's not huge, and the landscape around is pretty exposed. I don't know what they'll do but, given I can identify them, they won't be too keen for me to get away. They don't know I've got the phone, so they probably think they've a window to track me down before they're likely to be disturbed by anyone.' She knew she was gabbling and tried to force herself to be calm.

'We're on our way, Shee,' Annie said. 'Just hang in there. Ops have already been alerted, so we should be able to get people up there quickly now we know where you are. Leave the line open, so we can keep in contact if you need to move.'

'Will do.'

'Keep strong, Shee. We'll be there.'

Sheena slipped the phone back into her pocket. The wind was still blowing strongly across the moorland, rattling the trees around her. In the darkness, it was easy to imagine movement, someone slipping silently towards her. She tensed, listening intently, staring into the blackness.

For what seemed like an eternity, she saw and heard nothing beyond the movement of the branches. Then, somewhere beyond the trees, she saw a flash of headlights. She pushed herself back into the undergrowth, on her knees now, watching for any further developments. A moment later, a second set of headlights flickered through the trees. Another vehicle, heading from the opposite direction. As she watched, the lights ceased moving as the vehicle drew to a halt. The lights grew brighter as the vehicle manoeuvred to shine the full beam into the trees.

She moved further back into the woodland, trying to ensure she wasn't visible. She could see a figure moving now, silhouetted against the headlights. Then she saw a second figure join the first. She could hear some kind of shouted verbal exchange but could discern none of the words.

She pulled out her phone. 'They're here,' she whispered. 'I'm going to try to stay in the wood, but there's at least two of them. I don't know if I can stay hidden for long.'

'We're about ten minutes away.' It was Zoe's voice. 'And we were told that there'd be uniforms arriving even sooner.'

'I'll try to keep my head down, but I don't know for how long.'

She could now see two figures moving through the trees in her direction. Both vehicles had been parked so that their lights were shining full into the woods. The two figures had diverged but were both heading steadily towards her, shining flashlights ahead of them. She moved back into the darkness, trying to see if there was any way she could outflank the two approaching figures.

Even if she could somehow slip past them, there was only the road and further open moorland beyond. Behind her, the boundary of the woods was rapidly approaching. She needed to evade capture just for a few more minutes, but it was already feeling hopeless.

She continued to move backwards, hoping to buy herself more time. Her ears were straining to hear the sound of approaching police sirens, in the hope that that would deter her pursuers, but she could hear nothing. The two figures were still approaching, now only fifty or so metres away from her.

She took another step back and then, too late, realised another figure was waiting behind her. As she half-turned, she again felt a cold steel blade pressed against her throat and heard a woman's voice whisper in her ear.

'Hello, again.'

Chapter Forty-Two

'Oh, Jesus Christ,' Annie said. 'We're nearly there, too. Where are the bloody uniforms?'

Moments before, they'd heard the unmistakeable sound of Sheena Pearson being apprehended. Sheena had made sufficient noise to give them no doubt about what was happening, and then the call had been cut. Annie didn't know whether Sheena had ended the call herself in the hope of keeping the phone undetected, or whether her captors had discovered the device.

She called back to the dispatcher and told them what had happened. 'I don't know where your guys are,' she said. 'But I want this area sealed off. There aren't that many roads around this stretch.'

Finally, she saw a pulse of blue lights across the open moorland. At least one car approaching from the opposite direction. Whether there'd be enough resource to do what she'd asked or whether they could get it organised to do it speedily enough, she doubted.

She turned right onto the road leading up to the stretch of moorland that Sheena had described. Her attention had been momentarily focused on spotting the turning, so the oncoming vehicle took her by surprise. It was a large van, travelling well in excess of the speed limit in the middle of the road.

For a moment she considered trying to block it, but, given the speed and size of the vehicle, she knew she and Zoe could easily be seriously injured or killed by the impact. As it was, the vehicle caught the front wing of her car, driving them almost off the road, before continuing onto the road behind them. Annie did a rapid U-turn, thankful that the car was still drivable, and set off in pursuit.

'You think that's them?' Zoe said.

'Must be, mustn't it? Going at that speed. They were hoping to get off the scene before we arrived. Which suggests they've discovered that Sheena made a call.'

In just the few seconds it had taken them to turn the car round, Annie had lost sight of the vehicle. They were still surrounded by open moorland, but the unevenness of the landscape meant their view was limited. The satnav showed that there was a crossroads a half-mile or so ahead. At that point, she'd need some clue as to which road to take.

'There.' Zoe pointed off to their left. As the road had risen again, a set of retreating red rear lights had become visible across the moor. The left turn, then.

'I just wish we had some inkling of where they might be heading,' Annie said. Then she stopped, struck by a sudden thought. 'Werneth Holdings. Their offices were somewhere round here, weren't they?'

'I can't remember exactly. Hang on. Let me check.' Zoe pulled out her phone and found the Companies House website. It took her a few seconds longer to search for the entry for Werneth Holdings. 'Looks like the offices are based at that guy Robin Kennedy's house. Kennedy Farm, would you believe?' She reached forward and keyed the postcode into the satnav. 'Yup. Just a few minutes away and in that direction. You think that's where they could be heading?'

'We've no other leads, have we?'

After the crossroads they lost sight of the rear lights once more as the road ahead dipped into a valley. Unless they had another sighting of the vehicle, they had no option but to trust Annie's hunch.

'If that's where they're going,' Zoe said, 'it's about a half-mile ahead. Somewhere on the right.'

There was no further sighting of the fleeing vehicle. The satnav directions were only approximate, and Annie initially missed the turning to Kennedy Farm. Cursing, she spun the car around and headed back, finally spotting the sign. She turned in to the entrance, feeling a mounting sense of panic and despair. Even if Robin Kennedy was involved in all this, they had no strong reason to believe that Sheena was being brought here.

On the other hand, she thought, if whoever had taken Sheena had been aware that the police were closing in, they'd have wanted somewhere nearby to lie low rather than being stopped on the surrounding roads. It was a long shot, but it was possible.

The uneven driveway led uphill, and somewhere ahead she could see a cluster of lights. As they reached the summit, the house appeared in front of them.

Annie slowed the car and took a breath.

The van was parked in front of the house, its rear doors still open.

–

'It's too late,' Kennedy said. 'You saw the blue lights back on the moors. There were half a dozen or more cars. They're closing in.'

He looked like a different person, Rowan thought. Older, hunched, no longer in control. He'd lost it. 'They don't know we're here,' she said. 'They don't know who we are. I checked it all out beforehand because I always do. There's no CCTV between that stretch of moorland and here. They've got no way of identifying us or the cars. We've always made damn sure that none of the vehicles can be traced back to you.'

'What about that car we passed?'

'They won't have had chance to get your number. They won't have known which way we were heading.'

'What about Nolan and Charlie? They'll find the bodies.'

'It won't take them long, no. But neither had a record. I checked all his clothing and there was nothing to identify them. They had no close relatives or friends other than us. It'll take them a while to work out who they are, if they ever do. But, then, so what? They've no reason to connect them to you.' She wasn't sure she even believed all of this herself but she could see that, without some kind of reassurance, Kennedy would just freeze.

'We've still got to deal with Pearson.'

'And with Bamford and Wardle. So we kill them. All three of them. It won't be the elegant outcome you'd envisaged, but I can't see an alternative.'

'And what do we do with the bodies?'

It was like dealing with a toddler, she thought. One of those spoilt kids who just tries to gainsay every argument. She sighed. 'We drop them in the septic tank,' she said. 'I'm told it's good for the system. And if they've no reason to suspect your involvement, no one will have a good reason to go searching in there.'

'You're a cold bitch, aren't you?'

'Luckily for you. Right, let's deal with this one first, shall we?' She gestured to Sheena Pearson, who was hunched on the sofa at the far end of the room. Sheena had already made one attempt to pull away as they were leaving the car, but Rowan had simply struck her hard across the face. For the moment, Bamford and Wardle had been locked in one of the bedrooms. Rowan expected little immediate trouble from them. Bamford had recovered consciousness but was still groggy. Wardle just seemed scared out of his wits. There'd be time to deal with those two later.

By this point, she was almost inclined to screw Kennedy over and simply disappear, leaving him to sort out the mess. After all, it was largely his creation. But she knew that if she left these loose ends dangling, she would always be vulnerable. Better to deal with them, and think about the future afterwards.

'We'll do it in the barn at the back. That way we can hose everything down afterwards. We won't be able to clean it perfectly, but that won't matter as long as the police have no reason to come snooping round here. I sent Mo out there to prepare it.'

'I don't know if I can do this.'

She stared at him for a moment. 'Christ, Robin, you've got some brass neck. We're all involved and we're all implicated, remember? I was even involved in the murder of my own fucking son. Not that the little bastard didn't deserve it. But that's how it works. Unless you just want me to leave you in the shit.'

He nodded. 'Okay. It's all just been a bit of a shock. I didn't expect it to turn out like this.'

'Really? You're telling me your smartarse plan turned out not to be foolproof? You're a piece of work, Robin. Come on. Let's get this done.'

She walked across the room, pulled Sheena Pearson up from the sofa and dragged her forcibly over to the door. 'Now, Robin, you lead the way and I'll make sure Ms Pearson follows.'

Chapter Forty-Three

Despite the strong wind, the night had remained clear, with only an occasional cloud scudding across the star-filled sky.

Annie had left their car in a shaded corner of the driveway. She'd called for backup and, given the police presence already in the area, she expected it to arrive imminently. But there was no time to waste. She and Zoe had approached the house, alert for an sign of an intruder alarm that might reveal their presence.

Although the rear doors of the van had been left open, as if the occupants had vacated it hurriedly, the front door of the house was closed and firmly locked. 'Let's have a look round the back,' Annie said. 'We need to get inside, but I'd like to get an idea of what we might be facing before we try.'

She led the way round the side of the house into a sizeable former farmyard, now largely converted to create an attractive-looking semi-walled garden, with views out over the moorland. This was a large and impressive place, Annie thought. However he might make his money, Kennedy was obviously doing very well for himself.

She took another few steps forward, Zoe close behind her. At the far end of the yard was a large open barn, which had presumably once been used for storing agricultural equipment but now appeared to be simply decorative, a renovated reminder of the house's former life.

The interior of the barn was lit by spotlights and she could see, assembled as if on a stage, a tableau of four individuals. Two men and a woman standing. Beside them, another woman kneeling. The kneeling woman, Annie saw at once, was Sheena.

At first, Annie couldn't work out what she was seeing. The second woman was standing behind Sheena, holding Sheena's head down, a knife glinting in her hand. It took Annie a moment to realise what the scene reminded her of. Then it came to her. It was a painting she'd seen somewhere, years before, of Abraham preparing to kill his son Isaac. The figures were very different, but the pose was identical.

Her fear was that, by revealing her presence, she might startle the woman into completing the act she had already started. But they had only seconds to spare, and she was too far away to reach the barn in time.

'Police! Don't move!' Her voice echoed around the yard. She could see the individuals in the barn look up in surprise, but the woman remained focused on her task and for a moment Annie thought she was too late. Then she realised that Zoe had already started running towards the barn.

The woman hesitated a moment too long, surprised by the sight of Zoe Everett pounding towards her. Then Zoe was on her, forcing her back, trying to wrestle the knife from the woman's hand.

Annie was running too and had reached the barn. She'd been wondering how best to deal with the two men so that she could focus on helping Zoe. But neither man appeared to be in a state to offer any resistance.

Both looked defeated, dispirited, as though everything had fallen apart for them. She was startled to realise that, now she was closer, she recognised the younger of the two men. That far-right bastard, Mo Henley. The other man, she assumed, was Robin Kennedy.

She had no time to consider the implications. Zoe was on top of the woman, forcing her back on to the ground, desperately trying to weaken her grip on the knife.

Then Annie realised the woman was saying something, a stream of venom directed apparently at Kennedy. 'This is your fault,' she was saying. 'You've led us to this. You've never had any real belief. You've just used us for your own fucking ends. God, I hope you really do end up burning in the fires of hell. I just want to see your flesh melt.'

The effect on Zoe was sudden and unexpected. She jerked back as if the woman had physically struck her, and Annie could see a look of absolute terror on her face. It was as if she was frozen, struck down by the woman's words as if by some kind of incantation.

The woman clearly realised that something had changed and pushed upward, forcing Zoe away from her. Zoe fell backwards, still apparently unable to move, as the woman raised the knife and began to swing it down.

Annie reacted instinctively, throwing herself forward and grabbing the woman's arm, pulling the knife away from Zoe, pushing the woman back on to the ground. She realised immediately that the woman was going to be too strong for her, and she knew she was in no position to gain any further leverage. The woman twisted away, the knife still clutched in her hand. But instead of moving towards Annie, she moved to the left and grabbed Kennedy, who had been watching the scene in horror.

Annie moved to stop her, but it was already too late. She had plunged the knife into Kennedy's chest and then, extracting it with unexpected skill, she drew it across her own throat. Annie closed her eyes as the blood spurted from the severed artery.

Beside her, on the ground, Zoe had begun to sob.

Chapter Forty-Four

'Christ, what a bloody mess.' Stuart Jennings was sitting behind his desk, slowly rubbing his temples as though to soothe a headache. Annie guessed that the headache was largely metaphorical.

'It could have been a lot worse,' she pointed out. 'You could have a dead MP on your watch.'

He nodded, wearily. 'Sorry. I realise how traumatic it must have been. How is she?'

'She's okay. Was in shock at first, I think, but she's getting through it. There'll be nightmares and flashbacks, I don't doubt, but we'll organise counselling. We need to think about what we do next. But she'll carry on. That's who she is.'

'I can see that. Speaking of nightmares and flashbacks, how's Zoe?'

'I spoke to her last night. She seems okay.'

'You think she'll be all right to continue?'

Annie looked up at him in surprise. 'In the job, you mean? I don't see why not.'

'What was it, anyway? I mean, what happened to her?'

'Seems to have been some kind of panic attack. But I've no idea what triggered it at that moment. She still doesn't really want to talk about it, but Gary's finally persuaded her to seek some help. Apparently she went through a phase of similar attacks when she was younger, but she thought she'd put it behind her. Gary reckons it's something to do with her upbringing, but says she won't talk about it. But I think it was probably at least partly work-related, maybe prompted by finding that first body on the moor. It was after that I first noticed a change.'

'If it's work-related, we have a duty of care. We can organise counselling for her.'

Annie had known that, whatever his other faults, Jennings was a stickler for following HR protocols, if only to ensure his own back was covered. One of her objectives in meeting him today was to secure support for Zoe. Much better if he thought it had been his idea. 'That would be good, as long as we can coordinate it with whatever she organises for herself.'

'And you think she's up to the job?'

'She always been a highly effective officer. I don't see why that should change.'

'Her panic attack could have resulted in more deaths. Including her own. Not to mention yours and Sheena Pearson's.'

Annie took a breath. 'Stuart, the only reason Sheena's still alive is because of Zoe's courage and quick thinking. If she needs some help now, we owe her the support.'

'I'm not disagreeing, Annie. But there's bound to be an enquiry into all this. We need to make sure we're squeaky clean. If you've any doubts about Zoe, I need to know.'

'I understand that, Stuart. I've every confidence in her. She just needs some time and support.'

He nodded. 'Okay. I'll trust your judgement. But keep an eye on her.'

'That's my job, Stuart. Or part of it.'

'And mine. Along with sorting out all this. The only small consolation is that with Kennedy and Wiseman out of the picture, we're not going to have the nightmare of trying to bring them to trial. It's going to take a hell of a lot of disentangling as it is.'

'Sounds like Kennedy had his finger in a lot of pies.'

'Hell of a lot. He had a huge empire, and I don't think we'll get near a lot of it. Seems to have been cleverly set up so a lot of the lower links don't directly connect to Kennedy or Werneth Holdings. The "left-hand" religious stuff seems to have been essentially a scam, a tool for recruitment and a front for some of their dubious activities. But there's enough material in Kennedy's house to suggest he was serious about it, and certainly his inner circle believed it. His technique seems to have been to persuade people to implicate themselves by committing relatively small misdemeanours for him, then gradually pull them in. With the kids it mainly started with drug dealing. But he operated at all levels, when it suited. This guy Gregory Wardle, for example, got suckered into taking backhanders for leaking planning information. It's not even clear that the information had much value, but it meant Wardle found himself pulled further and further in.'

'Until he was in too deep.'

'And Kennedy was generally ruthless with the ones who couldn't cope or who tried to double-cross him.'

'Like Garfield, Parkin and Francis.'

'That's scary. The lesson is never try to scam the scammers.'

'And we really do think that Wiseman was Parkin's mother?'

'Looks like it. She was the one who got him involved in the first place.'

'Christ. And she had no compunction about him and the others being killed.'

'Not once they'd tried to rip the operation off. But that's how it worked. Everyone involved. Everyone implicated. Henley's confessed to being directly involved in the killings, along with this guy Eric Nolan. But it was an "all for one" deal, he reckons.'

'Utterly merciless.'

'Exactly. Even that farmer, Tom Miller. He'd been drawn into Kennedy's orbit early on but had the sense to get out when he got a glimmer of what Kennedy was up to. No doubt Kennedy was less ruthless in those days. But he still took the opportunity to send Miller the occasional reminder in case he was ever tempted to expose Kennedy. Like dumping a body in his back garden. To encourage the others.'

'Kennedy had lost the plot somewhere, though, surely. I still can't believe his grand scheme would have worked,' Annie said. 'I mean, trying to pin theirs and Sheena's killings on this guy Bamford. We'd have seen through it, surely.'

'Would we?' Jennings asked. 'I reckon one of Kennedy's talents was to tell you what you wanted to hear, give you what you wanted to believe. That's how his whole scam worked, religion and everything. I mean, some of us would have had an uneasy feeling about it. But if you get the solution handed to you gift-wrapped, it's very tempting just to accept it. We've got more than enough on our plate without opening up cases that have apparently been resolved unless there's a good reason. No one was ever likely to stand up to plead Bamford's posthumous case. He doesn't seem to have anything much in the way of family or friends, and he does appear to be something of an obsessive, albeit a harmless one.' Jennings shook his head. 'So who knows? But I do feel as if, professionally, I might have just dodged a bullet.'

'You and Sheena both, then.'

It took Jennings a moment to realise she was joking. 'Yes, I suppose so. Sorry.'

She smiled. 'Stop apologising. I'm not that sensitive. Speaking of professionals, what's the position on Andy Dwyer?'

'Suspended pending the investigation. He's denying everything, and I don't know if we'll prove anything either way. But he's exactly the type Kennedy would have got his claws into, and my guess is there'll be enough skeletons in Dwyer's cupboards for something to emerge. We'll see.'

'Never neat, any of this, is it? Only straightforward bit of good news is Mo Henley heading for trial. I won't be sorry to see him behind bars.'

'Even that'll be a PR nightmare,' Jennings said, gloomily. 'I can just see his supporters trying to present him as a political prisoner.'

'He was involved in the kidnap and attempted murder of an MP.'

'Like I say, political. You just wait.'

She pushed herself to her feet. 'Chin up, Stuart. After all, there is one other piece of good news.'

'Go on.'

'My mother. At least with Bulldog Henley out of the picture, they've abandoned the idea of her big TV break.'

Jennings laughed. 'Small mercies, eh?'

'Exactly, Stuart. Small mercies. Let's make the most of them.'